Never a Duchess

Scandal Sheet Survivors
Book 3

ADELE CLEE

Never a Duchess
Copyright © 2023 Adele Clee
All rights reserved.
ISBN-13: 978-1-915354-28-0

Cover by Dar Albert at Wicked Smart Designs

Chapter One

Lord and Lady Kinver's Wedding Ball
New Cavendish Street, London

Like the calm before the storm, the first slow strains of a waltz breezed through the candlelit ballroom. It was Lillian Ware's cue to leave before the man who haunted her dreams came to claim his dance.

A lady dared not refuse the enigmatic Duke of Dounreay. The handsome Scotsman had pushed other suitors aside, snatched Lillian's dance card and scribbled his name boldly next to both waltzes. Though an hour had passed, she kept revisiting their conversation.

"Will ye disappoint me, Miss Ware?" His soft Scottish burr had stirred her senses. His sinful smile had sent her heart fluttering to her throat. "Will ye make me watch another man take ye in his arms tonight?"

Heat warmed her cheeks, but she had given her usual

dispassionate reply. "Please forgive me if I fail to keep our appointment. As you know, I'm quite forgetful, Your Grace."

His dark eyes challenged her to defy him, as she had done so many times of late. Thank heavens he only spent three months of the year in London. Thank heavens he was to return to the rugged wilds of Scotland within days.

"Why do ye avoid dancing with me?"

Because whenever he pressed his hot hand to her back, a strange sensation flooded her body. When Dounreay twirled her about the floor, she lost herself in his warm gaze and wicked grin, and she had sworn never to become any man's property.

"Perhaps because you have two left feet, Your Grace." She loved teasing him, enjoyed convincing herself he had flaws. "Why do you not seek another partner? Many ladies crave your attention."

Every woman wanted him.

She pictured him pulling Miss Pilkington against his hard chest, the sudden stab of jealousy stealing the air from her lungs. Oh, the man was a dreadful distraction. A menace to a lady's sanity.

Dounreay had stepped closer, his exotic cologne flooding her senses. "Because when we dance, Miss Ware, I forget about my deformities."

And therein lay the problem.

How did a lady distinguish falsehoods from the truth?

How did she avoid being duped by a rogue?

Many women believed in love only to find themselves ruined and—

Mina nudged Lillian's arm, dragging her from her reverie. "Ah, it's time for the waltz. I see the duke is heading this way."

Panic gripped her, urging her to run. "Tell him I've gone

to the retiring room." And before Mina could comment, Lillian bowed her head and slipped away through the crowd.

She entered the ladies' boudoir—her sanctuary from the only man who might tempt her to sin—and sagged in relief. Yet her reprieve was short-lived. The duke was the topic on everyone's lips.

"Oh, he's so handsome, Felicity. I might die."

"And he's as rich as Croesus, too."

"I heard he asked Miss Cartwright to ride out with him tomorrow. She has Scottish blood on her mother's side. A sturdy constitution is an attribute Dounreay seeks in a wife."

A sturdy constitution?

What poppycock!

During Lillian's research into men's wants and desires, none longed for a lady who could brave the bitter Highland winds. Large breasts and a biddable temperament were often top of the list.

Lillian grumbled to herself. Would she be forever haunted by the devilish Duke of Dounreay? Disgruntled, she snatched a clean bourdaloue from the maid and darted behind the screen.

One woman tittered. "I might invent a Scottish ancestor."

"Penelope, you complain when there's a wee draught tickling your toes," a lady replied, feigning Dounreay's educated burr. "Beneath those fine clothes, the duke is like his brethren, wild and untamed. How would you handle a man who's as sturdy as an ox?"

"For a night with Dounreay, I think I could manage."

Laughter rang through the room.

Lillian was in no mind to listen, let alone pee into the pot. She stormed out from behind the screen and thrust the empty bourdaloue into the maid's outstretched hand.

"Dounreay is like a wolf not an ox," she said aloud. When

it came to the duke, her body reacted before her brain engaged. "He's clever and cunning. He knows what he wants, and he stalks his prey." She should know. Dounreay watched her with an intensity that warmed her blood. "Miss Cartwright will need more than a sturdy constitution if she means to hold his attention."

And with that, Lillian left the women gawping and flounced out of the retiring room. Seeking a distraction, she waited until the coast was clear before darting along the corridor and up the staircase.

Having scouted the rooms during the wedding breakfast last week, she made for the spare bedchamber overlooking the garden.

Once safely inside, she locked the door and pulled off her gloves.

In her reticule, she carried a collapsible telescope, note-book and pencil. Should an amorous rogue attempt to accost her, she would whip out a vial of pepper and blow it in the miscreant's face.

"Now," she said, dragging a chair to the window and willing herself to forget the attractive Scotsman, "let's watch the deceivers at work, shall we?"

Pencil at the ready, she settled in the seat to observe the comings and goings in the garden. The moon was full in a cloudless sky—a perfect night for lecherous lords seeking bed sport.

Based on her studies, the moon's phase turned sensible fellows into mindless beasts. They prowled the paths at balls and soirees, searching for any witless female to seduce.

Hearing faint strains of laughter, Lillian reached for her telescope and studied the shady area near the high topiary hedges.

Someone was there.

A man in a dark coat.

She had become skilled at identifying silhouettes.

He was tall and broad, and her mind conjured an image of the dashing duke. Had Dounreay grown tired of looking for his dance partner? Bored with her antics, had he set his sights elsewhere? Had he escorted Miss Cartwright into the garden for a secret moonlight rendezvous?

Seeking confirmation, Lillian narrowed her gaze.

The devil had Dounreay's warm brown hair. He stood strong and firm, like an idol to a Greek god. Then she noticed pale pink skirts flapping about the fellow's legs, and her heartbeat thumped like a drum in her ears. The bruised organ thundered so hard in her chest it would likely crack a rib.

"I swear you'll be the death of me, Dounreay."

"I assumed ye'd nae heard me enter," her nemesis whispered from the shadows behind her.

As fast as a spooked hare, Lillian shot off the chair and whirled around to see the man who turned her blood molten.

Heaven help her!

In the gloom, the duke appeared compelling, formidable. His dark eyes were like obsidian pools, the wicked glint a dangerous component. On the scale of devilish grins, his had the power to slice through her defences, to send delicious shivers down her spine.

Panicked, she cried, "What are you doing here?"

"I came looking for ye."

"Have you lost your mind?"

"Dinnae shout unless ye want to draw undue attention." His playful tone said he found the situation amusing. He gestured to the door she had locked minutes earlier. "Lord Forrester and his mistress are having relations in the corridor. Ye wouldnae want them to find us alone here. Else ye may be forced to do more than dance with me, Miss Ware."

Was he threatening marriage?

She had no intention of being a wife, let alone a duchess.

"I'm accustomed to seeing my name in the *Scandal Sheet*, Your Grace. Nothing as petty as ruination would tempt me to wed."

He laughed, the sound so deep and seductive it would bring most women to their knees. "Rest assured, I have nae intention of marrying an Englishwoman. My clansmen would never forgive me."

So why did he keep asking her to dance?

Why had he bothered putting his name on her card?

He stepped closer—too close.

"Don't move. Stay where you are." Lillian raised her hand, hoping he would remain on his side of the invisible barrier. "How did you get in? I locked the door."

"I followed ye to the retiring room, watched ye cling to every dark recess before mounting the stairs. Then I paid a footman to show me the secret passage." He motioned to a section of the wall behind him, which he pushed open to reveal a narrow wooden staircase. "Kinver said every bedchamber in the house has one."

Lillian stared, unable to say anything but, "Why?"

"So the servants can move freely, I suppose."

"No. Why did you follow me?"

He shrugged, his coat stretching tight across his muscular shoulders. "Since we danced at the Pemberton ball three years ago, ye've let me claim every waltz but disappear when the orchestra strikes the first chord. I'm curious why ye feel the need to deceive me."

"Deceive you!"

He made her sound like the scoundrels who prowled the garden, making empty promises, collecting broken hearts. Still, she could not tell him the truth.

"Explain the problem, Miss Ware, and I shall leave ye alone."

Alone.

The word was like icy claws squeezing her heart.

She blinked, her mind whirling in confusion. Part of her wanted to touch him, kiss him wildly, be one of the foolish girls who threw away their virtue. Part of her wished he would prove himself false so she might remove him from her thoughts altogether.

"When we danced at the Pemberton ball, you mentioned taking a wife. I panicked, worried you had set your sights on me." And this man could tempt a nun to sin. "You know my feelings on love and marriage."

"Aye, ye refuse to marry, and crave a life of adventure." His tone carried a hint of mockery. "Whereas I have nae choice but to further my bloodline and sire an heir. We're opposites in every regard, Miss Ware."

She closed her eyes against his misconception.

She wasn't chasing her next thrill.

She sought freedom from pain, freedom from a crippling childhood memory. A betrayal by the person she'd trusted most.

The harrowing images lived with her. Waking to her mother's soft kiss on her forehead in the dead of night. Waking the next morning to news they had pulled her lifeless body from the lake.

Happiness was an illusion.

Humankind's greatest deception.

"Then let us make a pact," she said, keen to get rid of him and settle her pulse. "You will not ask me to dance again." The thought roused a profound sense of regret. "And I will have no need to deceive you."

"Agreed."

His blunt reply hit her like a blow to the stomach.

He had grown tired of her antics, understandably so.

Her hands shook, and she turned to the window, tears stinging her eyes. "You should go now so I can continue my work. Please don't reveal my whereabouts to my friends."

In a few days, he would head north.

And she would have months to grieve the loss.

"Spying isnae work," he said, moving closer.

She quickly sniffed away her tears. "It is if you're employed by the Crown. I have information to suggest someone is passing secrets to the French."

Dounreay came to lean against the wall near the window. He folded his arms across his broad chest and studied her intently. "The fact ye admit to working for the Crown says that's another lie."

"What I'm doing here is a private matter, Your Grace."

He glanced at the locked door. "Have ye planned to meet someone?"

"No!"

"Have ye played me for a fool, Miss Ware? In a desire for adventure, have ye taken a lover? Does that account for yer eagerness to get rid of me?"

A lover!

She should be shocked at the suggestion.

Yet she was intrigued.

A gentleman did not discuss lewd topics with a lady.

She gave an incredulous snort. "You think I'm foolish enough to trust the gentlemen here tonight? They wouldn't know honesty if it chased them around the garden and bit their behinds."

"Yet ye find honesty just as challenging."

She deserved that.

"Around you, I seem to find many things challenging."

He rubbed his jaw thoughtfully. "That explains why ye inhale sharply whenever I lay my hand on yer back. Why ye avoid my company and refuse to dance."

"I imagine most women inhale sharply in your presence." His potent masculinity oozed from his pores. He could wield it as a weapon to make timid damsels swoon. "You're an extremely handsome man, Your Grace."

Dounreay straightened. "Ye admire my countenance?"

Oh, he was so beautiful she could hardly breathe.

"Every lady gawps at your physical attributes. You're the topic on every woman's lips tonight." At twenty-seven, the wealthy duke was the most eligible bachelor in London.

"Yer lips are the only ones that interest me, Miss Ware."

Lillian laughed lest she melt into a puddle at his feet. "I thought we had agreed not to play these flirtatious games."

"I agreed nae to ask ye to dance," he said, quick to correct her. "But I want us to be friends. After lying to me all these years, ye owe me that, at least."

Guilt rose to the surface.

She *had* led him on a merry dance.

"I see no harm in us being friends, Your Grace." Until he married. Then she would avoid him like the plague. She would rather stick pins in her pupils than see those dark eyes devour any other woman.

"One should always be honest with a friend," he said, a slight air of warning in his tone. "Tell me what ye're doing with that telescope. Show me what ye've scribbled in that little notebook."

"It's private."

"Then, as a friend and someone interested in yer welfare, I must take the matter up with yer brother, Lord Roxburgh. I'm sure he would like to know I found ye alone in a locked bedchamber."

Oh, the devil!

"So, you have moved from coercion to blackmail."

"Having an adventurous spirit can be dangerous."

"It is not your concern."

"I am making it my concern."

"My brother knows about my hobby."

The duke frowned. "Needlecraft is a hobby." His gaze moved from the telescope to the window, and he made entirely the wrong assumption. "By all the saints! Ye write for the *Scandal Sheet*. Ye're here gathering evidence."

"What? No!" She would not take the blame for writing utter rubbish and ruining ladies' lives. "My name has appeared in that ridiculous rag more than once. Why would I damage my own reputation?"

"'Tis the perfect ruse." Dounreay dragged his hand through his thick brown hair and sighed. "Do ye know what the *ton* will do if they find out?"

"I do not write for the *Scandal Sheet*."

"Then why carry a telescope?"

Mother of all saints!

Why could he not simply find another dance partner instead of prying into her personal affairs?

"If I could trust you, I would tell you." She pointed to the secret door. "Instead, I beg you return to the ballroom before people realise we're both missing."

Dounreay stepped closer, lowering his voice to a husky whisper. "Ye can trust me, Miss Ware. I would never betray a confidence."

"You threatened to tell my brother."

"Perhaps I've decided to pledge my loyalty instead."

Something passed between them.

A crackle of energy.

A heightened tension she could not explain.

Dounreay was as dangerous as he was dashing.

"Promises are quickly made and easily broken." She blinked to dismiss bitter memories. "Nothing you could say would persuade me to trust you."

"Aye, because ye're a woman of action, nae words. What if I do something to prove my fealty?"

"Fealty? You're a duke, not a vassal."

"Yet ye make me forget I'm anything but a man." He reached down, hiked up his right trouser leg and pulled the small knife from a sheath strapped to his calf. "It's a *sgian dubh*. A Scotsman's survival tool. A weapon of many purposes."

Lillian swallowed hard. "And what do you mean to do with it?"

Fear and excitement coursed through her when Dounreay held up the blade and examined the steel beneath a shaft of moonlight. "I mean to draw blood."

Blood!

She should flee, but every instinct said he would not hurt her. And by God, she found this man utterly fascinating.

She met his gaze. "Your blood?"

"Our blood."

What in the devil's name!

"I'll not partake in some strange form of handfasting," she said, shaken. Everyone said the Scots were savage heathens, and this proved the point. "I'll not make a pledge I cannot keep."

She would not give herself to any man. Least of all, one capable of breaking her heart as quick as he might snap his fingers.

"I'm the one who makes the vow." Dounreay captured her hand, the mere sensation of him touching her bare skin setting her body aflame.

She had spent an age observing couples' interactions. Yet she had learnt more about lust's potency in the last few minutes than watching a hundred amorous clinches.

"Look into my eyes, Miss Ware."

For fear of crumpling beneath the duke's gaze, she focused on the finger he gripped tightly. "What are you going to do?"

"Prick the skin. Say now if ye want me to leave."

I want you to leave!

The words rebounded in her mind, but she lacked the strength to voice them aloud. Dounreay appealed to her adventurous spirit. He could seduce her with minimal effort, and that made him the perfect subject to study.

"I'm writing a book," she confessed.

He frowned. "A book about what?"

A book to help women learn how to avoid men like you.

"I'll tell you when you have made your oath."

Dounreay kept his eyes locked with hers but released her hand. Disappointment sank to the pit of her stomach. Had she said something to deter him?

Then he pricked his finger with the blade's tip, drawing a drop of crimson blood. He stabbed the sharp point into her skin and then pressed their fingers together, mixing their blood in a mating ritual.

Foreign words left his lips as he made his oath in Gaelic.

Mesmerised, Lillian watched while Dounreay's tongue slid over every strange syllable as if repeating an erotic incantation.

They were in a dark, dusty room, yet she imagined herself atop a Highland mountain, the wind whipping at her hair, lost in the smell of heather and rain and ancient pinewoods.

"I swear by Almighty God, I will be faithful and firm,"

Dounreay said in English. "Ye have my undying loyalty always, Miss Ware."

A lump formed in her throat.

The power of those words tugged at her heart. Once, she'd had her mother's love and devotion, and the woman had cast it aside in a moment of weakness.

This was all an illusion.

A trick the duke used to get his own way.

She was about to snatch her hand free when the scoundrel did the unthinkable.

Dounreay studied the blood coating her finger. Then he closed his wet mouth over the tip and sucked it clean.

Lillian stared at him, fighting against an inner tug—a desire to explore every inch of his wicked mouth. She had seen clothed couples copulate in corridors, against hedgerows and garden statues, never understanding what made them lose their minds until now.

"It's an old family tradition," Dounreay said, quickly releasing her hand. "As ye didnae take the oath, there's nae need to reciprocate."

His breath came as hard as hers. Time stilled before he returned the blade to the sheath and straightened his trousers.

"Now," he began while she struggled to overcome her erratic emotions, "as nae one has ever questioned my loyalty and lived to tell the tale, be assured yer secret is safe in my hands."

She remained silent—her thoughts in a quandary.

If he cut out his heart and presented it on a silver platter, it wouldn't be enough to sway her opinion. Not entirely. But this man possessed a hidden power. A way of bending people to his will. Hence why she avoided his company.

How did one learn such a skill?

Maybe he would answer her questions.

Could he offer insight into the workings of a man's mind?

"So many young ladies are duped into believing in love." Having fallen for a tale five years ago, she counted herself amongst them. "They marry based on a lie, or worse still, they give themselves to a man who abandons them shortly afterwards."

Thankfully, she had only held Mr Bloom's hand and kissed his cheek. But then her brother's secretary had been respectful, and she'd soon realised her feelings amounted to nothing more than a young girl's infatuation.

"Society is nothing but a hive of hypocrites." Dounreay arched a disapproving brow. "Hence why ladies should remain in the ballroom with their chaperones, nae venture alone along dark corridors."

"Why? For fear a devil will accost them in a bedchamber, stab them with a *sgian dubh* and suck blood from their finger?"

His mouth curled into a wicked grin. "At least I didnae lure ye away with the promise of something illicit. I came to save ye."

By turning her mind to mush?

By making her body burn?

"What has this to do with writing a book?" he said.

Lillian hesitated for a second or two. "I'm writing a manual to help ladies identify a rakehell."

"A manual?"

"I list real examples, the lies, the tales told, the promises made and broken. I'm hoping to prepare young ladies for the iniquitous den commonly called the marriage mart."

The duke jerked his head. "And ye gather this information by spying on the *ton*? Hellfire! Tell me ye've nae mentioned names."

"I'm not an idiot."

Frustrated, he dragged his hand through his hair. "I've never met a more intelligent woman, which is why I find this so surprising."

Lillian's breath caught in her throat.

But then she remembered wolves were cunning beasts, and compliments were like bait to lure victims into unknown territory.

"Mere moments ago, you implied I was foolish for leaving the ballroom."

"Aye, such recklessness makes ye a confounding package of contradictions, madam."

"A package? Is that how Scotsmen refer to ladies, Your Grace?" Would he call her a delightful creature as if she were anything but human?

Dounreay laughed. "Can ye forgive a man for his heathen ways?"

The comment drew her mind to the finger-sucking incident, and she spun back to the window. "Time is precious. Now I've been honest, you must leave. I need to conduct my investigations."

She closed her eyes, willing him to go.

"I fear yer studies lack one crucial element."

"And what is that, Your Grace?"

"The testimony of a scoundrel. Ask me questions, and I'll answer honestly. On condition ye dinnae name me."

She cast him a sidelong glance. "I hate to break this to you, but you're not a scoundrel." He was far more dangerous.

He smiled darkly. "Miss Ware, ye could tempt any man to sin. Believe me, I can be anything yer heart desires."

Chapter Two

Callan had over-stepped the mark.

The moment he decided to follow Miss Ware upstairs, he knew he would be unable to control his wild urges.

As a Highlander, he took what he wanted.

As a duke, he conformed to society's dictates.

As a man, he found himself wavering between the two.

This woman drove him to distraction. He spent nine months of the year trying to forget her, three months stalking her and following her about like a lovesick fool. Tonight, his patience had suffered a seizure, and he'd asked her to state her issue. But he had not stopped there.

His heart had thundered in his chest when he drew her blood.

His cock had hardened as he sucked her finger.

He wished he were a damn scoundrel. Then, he would hike up her skirts and drive home. With every hard thrust, he would rid her from his memory.

Except he was a duke.

And dukes did not ruin innocents.

"Are you offering to assist me in my research?" Miss

Ware sounded amused, but it was a facade. Nerves left her chin quivering.

A sliver of moonlight danced over her rosebud lips and dark auburn hair. Many times he had envisioned pulling her into an embrace, pressing his nose to her silky locks and inhaling her unique scent.

Callan cleared his throat. "Ye're in danger of sounding biased. Ye need to understand the workings of a man's mind before offering an objective opinion."

She laughed. "I'm not sure a man thinks with his mind."

No, like a disobedient scamp, a certain part of Callan's anatomy wept for her attention. "Which proves my point. Ye've made a hypothesis based on the actions of one party."

"Society women are notoriously naive."

It was his turn to laugh. "Are ye saying females dinnae have the same urges? Ye may lack experience—"

"I know what desire feels like, Your Grace."

Callan firmed his jaw. He did not want to hear a story of a young buck stealing a kiss from her luscious lips. He knew something of Miss Ware's past but refused to imagine her with any other man.

"What does desire feel like?" he challenged.

Her eyes widened, shock giving way to defiance. "What does it matter? People are not interested in my opinion."

"Ye're the one writing a book. Why would anyone buy a manual from someone who lacks experience?"

She gulped and resisted answering.

Callan folded his arms across his chest. "Ye'll need to define desire. Else, how will readers understand?"

"It's h-hard to explain."

"Try. I mean to help, nae judge."

Silence ensued, but he waited until she was forced to say, "Well, it's … it's like you're possessed."

"Possessed?" Lust *was* a demon dominating the mind and body. His need to feast on this woman would earn him a place at Lucifer's table. "Ye'll need to elaborate. Tell me, do ye feel certain sensations?"

Thank God he had followed her tonight. Now he might learn what drove her to avoid him. Had he imagined the spark of attraction? Might he find a way past her barricade?

"I'm not discussing it with you," she snapped.

"I'll tell ye what desire is like for a man." A flicker of intrigue in her eyes encouraged him to be bold. "I can explain the physical feelings and mental process. Tell ye why a man would risk everything to satisfy a craving."

Tell ye why I'm standing here when there's every chance we'll be caught, he added silently.

Suspicion danced across her delicate features. "And what do you want in return, Your Grace?"

"One thing. Honesty."

Miss Ware blinked rapidly. One would think he'd asked her to steal into the palace and murder the King.

"I'll show ye how to tell the difference between a false statement and one expressed with real sentiment," he said, attempting to gain her trust. "Such insight will prove invaluable in the efforts to save the next influx of debutantes."

"Yes," she mused, tapping her finger to her lips. "I might produce a pamphlet, have hundreds printed and distribute them secretly at Almack's."

"Ye're sure to save more than one naive lass," he said, but for the life of him, he couldn't understand why she would go to so much trouble.

"People talk. It won't be long before the knowledge spreads." Excitement flashed in eyes as blue as the Aegean Sea. "Then I might continue my archaeological studies and venture to Egypt."

Egypt!

What the devil went on in this woman's head?

"If I'm nae mistaken, Roxburgh has a brood of young children demanding his attention." The doting husband and father was rarely seen at balls these days. "I doubt he would accompany ye on a wild adventure."

The lady raised a determined chin. "I mean to travel with the Archeological Society, not my brother."

Venture into the unknown without a proper chaperone?

Like hell she would!

Still, it was not his place to comment.

"Push all thoughts of Egypt aside and focus on the current task," he said. Helping her with the ladies' manual would buy him some time. "Perhaps I might give a quick demonstration. Show ye how to tell if a man has lust or love on his mind."

Miss Ware clutched her chest. "What would you do?"

Relieved he had managed to distract her from talk of exotic travels, he said, "I'll start with something simple, like asking ye to dance."

"Oh!" She sounded a tad disappointed.

"It all begins with my approach, Miss Ware." He moved back to the door and kept his voice low. "If my gaze wanders, I'm bored and seek to dance as a mere distraction. Notice my stride lacks purpose."

He spoke from experience, showing her how he dealt with other women when she was the only one he wished to hold in his arms.

"Do ye see?" he said.

"Yes, there's an air of indifference about you."

"Aye. The real problem comes when telling if a man is consumed by lust or love." Callan belonged in the first group, but the spark of energy between them suggested potential for the latter. Why else would he persist in being patient?

"How might I know if a man is in love, Your Grace?"

"Because he will gaze into yer eyes like he's peering into yer soul." He walked towards her again, this time as if drawn by the earth's magnetic pull. "It willnae falter."

She swallowed hard when he breached her personal space.

"Watch how I take yer hand." Damn, he'd forgotten she wasn't wearing gloves. It took every effort to stem a lustful shiver. "I touch ye like ye're delicate, like my only motive is to protect ye."

Had she been wearing gloves, he might have kissed her knuckles. Instead, he kept his mouth a mere inch from her hand as he bowed low.

"Are ye able to distinguish the difference?" he said.

"Yes, you looked at me as if I were precious."

Oh, she was beyond precious.

He had never enjoyed a woman's company more.

"And you were breathing quite deeply," she added.

"I imagine love steals the breath from the soul, nae the lungs."

Her lips parted as she studied him. "Have you never been in love, Your Grace?"

How in blazes did he answer?

He professed to be a man of experience.

"I know infatuation and admiration, but I am yet to feel the all-consuming power of true love." He knew how obsession kept a man awake at night, how it had him hunting the ballrooms, searching for his prey.

"I know a little of that, too," she said, surprising him.

So, he had not imagined this inexplicable attraction.

"Mr Bloom was my brother's secretary," she began, the comment hitting him like a spray of barbed arrows. "I thought he loved me and became swept up in false emotions. That was five years ago. When I was but a slip of a girl."

Mr Bloom!

Mr Bloody Bloom!

"I pray the devil kept his hands to himself." Which was more than could be said for Callan. When he found Roxburgh's secretary, he would wring his damn neck.

She jerked as if insulted. "Of course."

"Is that why ye're writing a book about rogues?"

"Yes," she uttered, the word carrying a heavy sadness.

He realised two things then. Miss Ware had a secret. And her experience with Bloom was not the reason she wanted to identify deceivers.

As she wasn't ready to trust him, he returned to the topic at hand.

"And now to the final example." Callan arched a brow. "Are ye sure ye want me to play the rakehell? I'll need to touch ye without asking permission."

She bit her bottom lip, unaware the sight made his stomach flip. "You won't do anything scandalous?"

He snorted. "Madam, we're alone together in a dark room. If found, it will cause the scandal of the season. But be assured, I'll touch yer forearm and elbow, nowhere else."

Frown lines marred her brow, but Callan took his position by the door. He closed his eyes briefly, recalling how hard he had been in bed this morning at the mere thought of seeing her tonight.

Lust flowed hot and molten in his veins.

He opened his eyes, hoping the heat of his gaze scorched her as it slipped slowly down her body. Five years was a long time to ache for one woman.

The air crackled as Callan prowled closer.

Miss Ware brought a trembling hand to her throat.

Could she feel the powerful thrum of desire?

"Good evening, Miss Ware." He spoke in a seductive timbre, tilting his head, studying all the places he shouldn't— her luscious mouth, the soft swell of her breasts. "I've come to claim ye for the next dance."

He wrapped his fingers around her wrist, owning her, if only for a moment. The rapid beat of her pulse pounded against his thumb. With his eyes fixed on hers, he moved to cup her elbow, stroking the soft skin of her forearm.

She moistened her lips. "Your name is not on my card."

"Dance with me, and my name will be forever imprinted in yer memory." He could easily lose himself in this game. Be a rakehell who only bedded one woman. "Dance with me, and I promise to leave ye breathless."

Though she trembled beneath his touch, she tried to douse passion's flames. "Are you skilled in the cotillion, then?"

Callan leaned closer, his mouth brushing against her ear. "I'm skilled in the only dance that matters, madam. And I mean to show ye every wicked step."

Miss Ware sucked in a sharp breath. A little flustered, she snatched her elbow free and stepped back. "You have demonstrated your point quite well, Your Grace."

Callan straightened and forced a smile, although his body failed to make the same quick recovery. "Now, having witnessed three different approaches, ye have a better understanding of the subject."

"Yes," she said, looking everywhere but at him.

"As part of yer studies, I can continue in the same vein."

"But you're returning to Scotland soon."

Yes, he was due to leave in a few days. If only they'd had this conversation months ago. "Nae for another week or two." He could cancel appointments, delay his departure.

"I see." Nerves had her biting the inside of her cheek. "It would be unwise to partake in similar exercises."

Unwise? Had he aroused her with the mere suggestion of a dalliance? "Because ye're afraid?"

"I'm not afraid."

"In the interests of safety, use me to observe the male species. If ye would rather someone else be the subject, watch me at work with Miss Withers. It might—"

"No!"

"No?" he said, mimicking her.

She fell silent and turned to face the window.

He could almost hear her inner turmoil.

He was conflicted, too. Returning to the ballroom should be a priority. First thing tomorrow, he should visit Roxburgh and berate him for not taking proper care of his sister. But in all likelihood, he would never get to see Miss Ware alone again, and that made him want to lock her in the chamber and throw away the key.

Regret hung heavily in his chest.

He could have any woman, yet he wanted her.

His need was like a living thing growing inside of him. No medicine or tonic could cure him of his ailment. All he could do was suffer and try to ease the crippling symptoms.

But then fate handed him a boon.

"Very well. We shall continue our studies in the name of science," she said, staring at those strolling about the garden. "After all, human advancement is the topic of the moment."

"Will ye play, or do ye have someone else—"

"No one else need be involved. You will help me to understand men, Your Grace. It will be our secret. Heaven forbid the gossips learn about my hobby."

Such was the rush of euphoria, it took effort not to punch the air and cheer. "We must be discreet."

"Yes, we wouldn't want your clansmen to know you're seducing an Englishwoman." Mockery clung to her tone. "Even if it is for the purpose of education."

Callan smiled to himself. He was the Duke of Dounreay. His friends and family would not challenge his decision. "Which is what makes this experiment so perfect. Neither of us will be forced to wed."

"It's the only reason I agreed to your proposal."

"So, when do we meet again?"

Time was of the essence.

She thought for a moment. "Lord Templeton's ball is on Friday. His extensive gardens provide many places to conduct a secret liaison."

Her choice of words sent Callan's pulse soaring. "Which role would ye like me to play? The lovesick Romeo or the lustful rake?"

"Both. You will ask me to walk in the garden while my friends play chaperone. Later, you will attempt to lure me to a private location."

The plan seemed too straightforward.

"Verra well. But I won't mention the roles beforehand. Ye must identify the characters based on my manner." Perhaps he might play the lothario while in the presence of her chaperone.

"Excellent." Miss Ware glanced back at the secret door. "You should leave now. Before we're both missed and our friends send out a search party."

"I'll nae leave ye here alone."

She must have detected the determination in his tone.

"Then wait in the shadows and follow me back to the ballroom." The clang of the supper gong echoed in the distance, sending Miss Ware into a panic. "Good heavens!

We've been here far too long. Someone is bound to see me creeping about."

Callan silently cursed.

With the sudden flurry of activity, it would be almost impossible to return to the ballroom unnoticed. "I shall fetch yer friends, the Masters. They will escort ye to the supper room."

The sensible idea had her scrunching her nose. "No. I'll use the stairs and head through the servants' quarters."

"Servants are notorious gossips."

"I'll take the risk. I cannot disappoint my friends." Miss Ware snatched her white gloves from the bed and tugged them on firmly. "I'll not have them think we arranged an assignation. They'll have us married before we've stopped to catch our breaths."

Callan smiled to himself. "And ye refuse to marry anyone."

"Yes, and you won't marry an Englishwoman, so you see the dilemma." She began pacing while lost in thought and happened to glance outside. "Typical!" Grabbing her telescope, she peered into the night. "While the guests take supper, a scoundrel has come out to play."

The hairs on his nape prickled with unease. "Now that I've made a solemn promise, I expect ye to stop spying on other men until we conclude our studies."

It was only a matter of time before she ruffled the wrong rake's feathers.

"Yes. And I will. But this is a prime opportunity to watch a real devil at work." She beckoned Callan to the window and offered him the scope. "We have a duty of care to the lady in question. Our rogue may become aggressive in his eagerness to get his own way."

He suppressed his frustration and put the scope to his eye.

"Do you see the path to the right of the garden?" She moved closer, her arm brushing his, distracting him momentarily.

"The one leading to the wrought-iron tunnel?" he asked, scanning the area.

"Yes, look to the left of the tunnel's entrance."

Callan moved the scope a fraction. He spotted the gentleman stepping out of the darkness to stare at the house. The fellow wore a hat, which was odd in itself, the brim kept low to hide his features.

"With such keen eyesight, ye should be a constable, Miss Ware."

She snorted. "I would if society allowed women to do anything but sew and raise children. Might I take a peek?"

Callan handed her the scope. In her impatience to take the instrument and study the suspected villain, their fingers brushed. Desire rippled to his toes. When a man craved a woman's company, even the small things caused an intense reaction.

"He looks of average height and build," she mused.

"Aye, he resembles half the men here tonight." His mind returned to their own pressing problem. "His identity is of nae consequence. We cannae afford to hide here a moment longer."

Callan cupped her elbow and gave a gentle tug.

"Wait." Miss Ware gasped. "I see a woman stealing along the path. She's wearing a dark cloak with the hood raised. She doesn't want to be identified. Do you think she might be married?"

Though he hated to admit it, this was an intriguing game. "Maybe I might have one last look before we leave." He was surprised when she offered him the instrument without complaint.

Callum closed one eye and focused on the unfolding scene.

The couple met near the tunnel and had a brief conversation before the man seized her by the arms and shook her violently. "This isn't an assignation," he said, blood suddenly flowing too quickly in his veins.

"What do you mean?"

The woman drew a letter from the depths of her cloak and handed it to the angry gent. "He's reading something she's given him and has shoved it into his coat pocket. She seems desperate to escape him."

"Yes, I see her now. She's stepped into the moonlight." Miss Ware's voice was all a quiver. "She's gesturing to the house."

The raised hood prevented Callan from seeing the lady's face, though her outstretched hand suggested she wanted payment. The rogue cupped her cheek and pulled her into an embrace, but a struggle ensued.

"Your Grace, this encounter is unlike anything I have ever witnessed." Miss Ware gripped his coat sleeve, fear marring her tone. "You must do something. You must help her."

"Cursed saints! He's pulled a knife from his pocket."

"A knife! Quickly! You must go now."

But it was too late. The devil grabbed the woman, clasped his hand over her mouth, and dragged her away through the tunnel.

Callan's heart thundered in his chest. He thrust the scope at Miss Ware. "Wait here. I'll arrange for Devon Masters to collect ye. Open the door to nae one else. Do ye understand?"

Miss Ware swallowed hard. "Yes. What will you do?"

"I'll chase after the devil, but I'll likely be too late." He charged from the room and hurried down the narrow wooden stairs onto the first-floor landing.

He crashed into Devon Masters and his wife while descending the main staircase. "There ye are! Thank the Lord!"

Mrs Masters cast her suspicious gaze over him and whispered, "Have you seen Miss Ware, Your Grace?"

Masters was less than polite. "If you've laid a damn finger on her, you'll marry her," he said, his mood as black as his ebony locks. "Do you hear me?"

"There's nae time to explain now." Though struggling to catch his breath, Callan told them where to find Miss Ware. "She will tell ye everything." Although he hoped she kept their private interactions to herself. "I need to scour the garden, and then I shall come to the supper room."

Callan ignored Masters' demands for information and hurried outside to the suspected crime scene. He pulled the *sgian dubh* from the sheath, gripped the black handle, and crept through the tunnel.

All was quiet but for the faint clatter of horses' hooves on the cobblestones and the distant hum of music and conversation.

The tunnel led to an unlocked door in the boundary wall. Lord Kinver's abode was one of two houses in the row with a private entrance to the mews.

The yard was dark. One lit lantern hung from a nail on the post, providing the only light. The chill in the air nipped the cheeks and numbed the fingers. Still, a young lad dressed in a thin coat and cap was sweeping out a stall.

Callan narrowed his gaze and scoured the shadows.

Had the devil dragged his victim into a coach house?

He called to the lad, who looked up but did not stop working. "Did ye see a man drag a woman out here? She wore a dark cloak with the hood raised."

The lad gave a hapless shrug.

With the mews being the only exit from the garden, doubtless he had seen more than he ought. More than he cared to admit.

"Come find me when ye regain yer memory. A gold coin might make it worth the trouble."

"Let's see the blunt, gov'nor," came the canny lad's reply.

Callan stepped closer and flicked the lad a sovereign. "Tell me everything ye know, and I'll double the bounty."

Callan would be a fool to trust this scamp's word. A boy with a grumbling belly would sell his mother for a shilling.

The lad pocketed the coin and took up his broom. "He shoved her into a waiting carriage and climbed in behind her."

Cursed saints!

"Did either of them say anything? Did ye see his face?"

"It ain't my business to notice. But he told his coachman to head for the docks. Said he didn't want to keep O'Malley waiting."

Callan scrubbed his hand over his face. Miss Ware would not let the matter rest. She would insist on saving the woman from the murderous rogue. Demand they journey to the docks tonight and jostle with Irish sailors in a bid for answers.

"Did he speak to the woman? Refer to her by name?" They needed a clue else they'd have no hope of finding her.

The lad pursed his lips and held out his hand.

Callan pressed another sovereign into his grimy palm.

"She begged him to let her go. Told him she would keep her mouth shut. But he said they were partners and would see the business through till the end." The boy leaned forward. "Happen he said that so she'd stop blubbering."

"Do ye think he means to kill her?"

"Happen so. Fancy coves have cold hearts."

"He was well-spoken?"

The lad nodded. "Though he might have faked an accent."

"And the woman?"

"A voice as sweet as honey. A lady, I don't doubt." The lad glanced over his shoulder and lowered his voice. "She dropped something. On purpose, I reckon."

Was this where Callan paid a king's ransom for fool's gold? "I've nae more coins, but ye can have my sapphire stick pin if I deem the item worth trading."

"A sapphire ain't no good to me," the boy sneered. "They'll think I stole it and cart me off to gaol quick as a wink."

"What about my knife?" Callan flashed the blade.

The boy's eyes shone brighter than a new penny. "I've got her handkerchief with fancy letters sewn in the corner. Do you want to trade gov'nor?"

"Aye."

They swapped items—a *sgian dubh* for a white lace handkerchief bearing the initials A. G. and stained with blood.

Callan considered the evidence as he walked back through Lord Kinver's garden, picturing the excitement on Miss Ware's face as she studied the clue. Indeed, he suspected he would have a new role in the lady's life. As well as being her tutor in what he hoped would be the beginning of a glorious love affair, he feared he would be her partner in the hunt for a villain.

Chapter Three

"What did Dounreay say to you before you climbed into the carriage?" From the opposite seat, Devon Masters considered Lillian through narrowed eyes as the vehicle rumbled through the dim Mayfair streets. "It looked like a heated conversation."

The duke had been firm in his opinion.

"Just that I should put thoughts of the poor woman out of my mind. We had probably witnessed nothing more than a lovers' tiff."

That was not what Dounreay had said.

What he'd said had shocked Lillian to her core.

The duke had insisted she heed his warning. "Ye'll nae investigate this matter alone. Accept my help, else I'll put ye in my carriage and tell Dewart nae to stop until we reach Inverness."

She had tried to tell him she would enlist professional help yet was forced to agree to his demands, fearing he would make a scene.

But she could not tell Mina and Devon the truth. They

would stalk her night and day and insist on accompanying her to Little Chelsea tomorrow.

Devon cast Mina a sidelong glance. "Perhaps we should mention the matter to Roxburgh when we reach Hanover Square."

No!

That would ruin everything!

"If you must burden my brother with pointless problems, at least wait until he's had a good night's sleep," Lillian interjected.

Little Alexander's teeth were cutting his gums. Her nephew's distressed cries kept the household awake from dusk until dawn.

"Someone may have seen you entering the bedchamber," Devon challenged.

"It was dark, and I kept to the shadows."

"Did you meet Dounreay for a secret rendezvous?"

Mina jumped to Lillian's defence. "You know she avoids the duke at all costs. Since the mystic told her she would marry a man who bears his knees in public, she refuses to give the Scot the time of day."

Thankfully, Dounreay had worn trousers tonight.

"The duke followed me out of concern for my welfare." It was not a lie. It was undoubtedly why he had agreed to meet her at the home of an enquiry agent in Little Chelsea tomorrow.

Devon snorted. "We care about your welfare, Lillian. I know how a man looks at a woman when he wants her."

Don't tell me how Dounreay looks at me!

Else I shall torture myself in the lonely hours until dawn.

Still, her burning curiosity could not be tempered. "Pray enlighten me so I might take notes for my book."

"You're so worried about saving women from rogues, you're in danger of being ruined yourself," Devon countered.

Lillian gestured to the couple. "If ruination looks like this, perhaps I should write a different book." They had married for necessity but were so desperately in love it gave the most cynical hope.

"We are merely reminding you to be careful," Mina said.

"And I am blessed to have your friendship, but you do not need to worry about the Duke of Dounreay. In future, I shall insist on a chaperone."

Thankfully, the carriage slowed to a halt outside her brother's home in Hanover Square. The midnight hour had passed, and Lillian prayed Alexander slept soundly.

Not that it mattered tonight.

She would lie awake, thinking about Dounreay stroking her arm, about his compelling brown eyes and flirtatious banter, about the poor woman seen dragged to her doom.

Devon sat forward. "I shall speak to Kinver about the incident in his garden. Perhaps I'll mention it to Lucius Daventry, too."

Lillian nodded. "It might help if Lord Kinver shared the guest list. I'm visiting Mr and Mrs Sloane tomorrow and will explain everything to Evan. He might investigate the matter."

Evan Sloane worked as an enquiry agent for Mr Daventry and had befriended Lillian five years ago when her brother hired an agent.

Mention of the competent investigator banished Devon's frown. "Excellent. Let Daventry's man handle matters. You'll only place yourself at risk if you attempt to identify the blackguard."

She was capable of making a few discreet enquiries. Besides, she planned to keep her interactions with Dounreay to a minimum, and he would be her constant shadow if she dared venture to the docks.

"I shall follow Mr Daventry's advice to the letter."

Mina reached for Lillian's hand and gave it a gentle squeeze. "The duke is right. Doubtless, you witnessed a silly argument. Get some rest and I shall call on you tomorrow."

Devon alighted and handed Lillian down to the pavement. She bid him good night, but he said, "Did he touch you?"

"Who?"

"The duke."

The memory of Dounreay's hot breath against her ear, of his firm hand gripping her elbow, did strange things to her insides. "Only my wrist while insisting I wait in the bedchamber until you came to my rescue."

Mistrust flashed in Devon's eyes. "Rarely do men reveal what's on their minds."

She gave a knowing smile, for she was just as secretive. "I'm writing a book on that very subject. Rest assured, the duke is a friend, nothing more. I avoid him merely because of the mystic's silly prediction."

"Indeed," was all he said before inclining his head.

Like a protective brother, he waited until she entered the house. She had thought to tiptoe upstairs, but the butler appeared like a ghost in the gloom, tapping his finger to his lips.

"The young master is asleep, miss." He pointed to the drawing room door. "Lady Roxburgh is awake and keeping guard."

Lillian smiled. "Thank you, Greyson."

She crept to the drawing room and slipped quietly inside to find her sister-in-law Eliza settled in the wing chair, a plaid blanket draped around her shoulders.

Adam—or the arrogant Lord Roxburgh to most people—

lay stretched out on the sofa, fast asleep. He wore trousers, and his burgundy silk robe gaped open, drawing the eye to where his son slept soundly on his bare chest.

"It's the only way to settle him," Eliza whispered.

Eliza referred to the child, yet Lillian had never seen her brother looking so relaxed, so at peace.

Memories of the day they found their mother's body in Glendale's lake invaded her mind. The shock had Adam darting into the vast maze. For two whole days and nights, he had stayed hidden in the dark depths, refusing food and company, and Lillian had been scared she would lose him, too.

A stranger left the maze days later.

A cold, indifferent boy who had buried his grief in the verdant tunnel, the location nigh on impossible to find.

"The sight warms my heart." Emotion tightened Lillian's throat. "I never thought to see him so happy and content." It would take one tragedy to shatter the illusion. "He's an exceptional father. But what if he had not found you, Eliza? What if he'd struggled to love you? I dread to think where he would be now." Or how he might lapse into a depression if he suffered heartbreak again.

Was that Lillian's destiny?

To avoid intimacy for fear of being hurt?

To distrust every man's motives?

Eliza smiled through her obvious tiredness. "It is best not to question fate. If one listens to their heart and trusts their feelings, things work out for the best."

"It's plain to see you love him, truly love him." Every woman dancing the waltz tonight sought the same thing. To feel precious. To make someone feel precious in return—regardless of the consequences.

"I love him with every breath. With every beat of my heart."

And yet some people lived for the thrill only lust could bring.

How did one make that choice? How did one feed a man's voracious appetite for carnal pleasures? "How do you keep him happy when you're with child for nine months of the year?"

Eliza probably wished someone else would answer her blunt questions. "Adam is quite protective of me, especially when I'm carrying his child. Yet he has never lost sight of how much we need each other." She arched a coy brow. "Make of that what you will."

Eliza asked about the Kinvers' wedding ball, though Lillian did not mention her interlude with the Duke of Dounreay. Nor did she speak about the abduction. Eliza had once worked as an agent for Mr Daventry and would want to know every minute detail.

"I'm to visit the Sloanes in Little Chelsea tomorrow evening, so I won't be home for dinner. Might I have use of the carriage?"

Eliza gestured to the sleeping babe. "I cannot see either of us venturing far from the sofa for the next few days. Although Mrs Abbott dotes on the children, nothing but Adam's touch settles Alexander."

The need to do something for those she cared for most in the world had Lillian suggesting, "Once things have settled down, you should visit Brighton for a week. I shall remain here and help Mrs Abbott. It would be good for you both." That said, Eliza would likely claim to be with child within a few months, and the cycle would begin again.

Eliza's eyes held a glimmer of excitement. "That's

extremely kind, Lillian. But I'm not sure you'd want the burden."

"Nonsense. I would be glad to help."

Eliza frowned. "You seem different tonight. Happier than I've seen you in a long time."

"Do I? I cannot think why."

The wind had shifted course.

Change was a tangible thing in the air.

Nothing would be the same again. And it had all started with a scandalous offer from the Duke of Dounreay.

Keel Hall,
Little Chelsea
The home of Evan Sloane

Much like a lone ship on the sea at night, Keel Hall was a monstrous shadow amongst the sprawling fields of Little Chelsea. Candlelight fluttered in the lamps beneath the portico, guiding weary travellers safely to the door. Those ignorant of Mr Sloane's pirate heritage might wonder why he had statues of mermaids in his garden. Those who knew him understood a love of the sea was in the blood.

Lillian loved being away from the bustling metropolis. Keel Hall had been her sanctuary in the months after her brother married, when the newlyweds had needed privacy. The Sloanes were excellent hosts and knew how to make a person feel anything but lonely.

After receiving her note earlier today and understanding her desire for secrecy, Evan Sloane had suggested sending his coachman to ferry her to his country abode instead.

Turton brought the carriage to a halt outside the impressive entrance, and Mr Sloane's steward, a Scotsman named Buchanan, was there to escort her into the mansion house.

There was but one question on Lillian's lips.

Has the Duke of Dounreay arrived?

Instead, she said, "It's terribly cold out tonight." She glanced up at the sprinkling of stars in the night sky. "But I would gladly suffer frozen toes to witness such a breathtaking spectacle."

Buchanan took a moment to appreciate the sight, too. "Aye, when ye gaze upon the heavens in all their glory, it steals the air from yer lungs. Some nights, from the coast of West Kintyre, the sky sparkles like polished amethyst. Now that's a wonder to behold."

"I'm afraid I lack the sturdy constitution needed to brave the wild Highland weather." It was far from the truth, but she refused to let her heart yearn for the impossible.

The middle-aged Scot cast her a sidelong glance. "Aye, yer nose is as red as a berry. The mistress has a glass of punch waiting, with just a wee drop of rum to heat the blood."

They mounted the sweeping staircase and approached the front door, but the thunder of horse's hooves pounding the ground stole their attention.

A figure on horseback charged out of the darkness, the muscular black mount galloping along the gravel drive like the devil chased its tail. The wind whipped at the gentleman's brown hair and tartan kilt. Breathing heavily, both man and beast left a trail of white mist in the chill night air.

Lillian's mouth dropped open.

The Duke of Dounreay cut an elegant figure in gentlemen's attire. In the garb of a Highlander, he appeared a specimen of rugged male perfection.

Agreeing to meet here was a mistake. There should be a law against virile men riding whilst in a state of dishabille.

"Ah, Dounreay has arrived," Buchanan said cheerfully.

Yes, with his bare knees visible beneath the hem of his kilt. Knees weren't the only part of his anatomy on show. Solid thighs gripped the horse's flank, though Lillian daren't let her gaze or imagination roam higher.

"You know the duke?" she said as a distraction.

"Every man born north of the border knows Dounreay."

Every woman south of the border wished to know him better, too.

"I'll let the duke escort ye into the house while I take his horse to the stable." Buchanan descended the steps before she could object.

Like old friends, the men conversed in their mother tongue. The words and gestures were foreign, but mutual respect was a universal language, and their esteem was as tangible as the stars.

Dounreay dismounted and brushed creases from his kilt. As Buchanan took hold of the horse's reins, the duke thanked him and slapped him playfully on the back. Then his gaze found hers, and her heart almost stopped beating when he smiled.

Mother Mary!

Nerves swirled in her stomach.

A wise woman would feign illness.

She would make an excuse to keep the man at bay.

But her feet were rooted to the spot as Dounreay mounted the steps, closing the gap between them. His approach was that of a man in lust, his gaze ravaging her body like wildfire.

Lillian swallowed hard. "I thought you always wear

trousers when south of the border." He'd worn a kilt the first night she danced with him, but that had been at a ball full of Scots.

Dounreay brushed road dust off his coat sleeves. "I wear trousers when I'm in London playing the duke. Tonight, I'm here as a Highlander, keen to keep a lady out of trouble."

Trouble?

She was in more danger of being ravished by a duke than being attacked by the mystery abductor.

You'll marry a man who bears his knees in public.

The fortune-teller's words invaded her mind.

Lillian quickly dismissed the notion as folly.

Firstly, mystics were frauds. It was mere coincidence that two of the seer's premonitions had come true. And Lillian had no intention of marrying, so what did it matter what the duke wore?

"Are you not cold?"

Dounreay laughed. "The temperatures in England are almost tropical." He gestured to the sable muff that hid her trembling hands. "Are ye off on an Arctic adventure?"

"I feel the cold terribly." It was a slight exaggeration, but she had to make herself sound unappealing. "I would hate to live in a draughty castle in the Highlands."

Dounreay leaned closer, a rakish lock falling over his brow. "We keep the fires burning. It's so hot in my chamber I sleep without clothes."

She quickly banished a vision of him strutting about naked.

This blackguard enjoyed teasing her to distraction.

"Your habits are the topic of conversation in every ladies' retiring room, Your Grace. Still, you consider a hardy constitution an asset in a wife."

Mischief twinkled in his eyes. "Aye, so I might chase her over brook and glen and tumble her amid the heather."

Lillian's breath caught in her throat.

The picture he painted touched a secret place deep in her chest.

"You have too many responsibilities to spend your time frolicking."

"On my oath, if I loved a woman, I would spend my life making her happy." His intense dark eyes held hers for a heartbeat too long.

Coherent thoughts scattered like leaves in the wind.

Until a velvet voice she knew broke the spell. "Should we bring chairs and sit beneath the portico?" Mr Sloane said, amused. "Or will you come inside and discuss the case?"

Dounreay stepped back and inclined his head. "We were examining the night sky. 'Tis beautiful out tonight."

Being anything but pretentious, the duke did not draw attention to Mr Sloane's lack of reference to his title.

Mr Sloane laughed. "The heavens are more beautiful when reflected in a woman's eyes, eh, Dounreay?" He gestured to the candlelit hall behind him. "Come, we've warm punch waiting. My wife has made a special concoction to chase away the cold."

Dounreay guided her forward and whispered, "Why do I get the impression we'll struggle to stand after a few sips?"

Lillian laughed. "Mr Sloane can take his liquor. You would be wise to limit your consumption. But you must be accustomed to downing a dram or two yourself."

"To cope with the bitter Scottish weather?"

"Aye," she teased.

Dounreay waited for her while she handed the footman her outdoor apparel. They followed Mr Sloane into the drawing room, an inviting space with burnt sienna walls, gilt-framed paintings and a vibrant Persian rug.

Mr Daventry occupied a seat next to the hearth, though he stood when he saw them. "Your Grace. Miss Ware."

"Mr Daventry? I did not expect you to attend the meeting." Mr Sloane must have thought the matter grave enough to seek his employer's counsel. "I'm sure we witnessed nothing more than a lovers' quarrel. I hate to trouble you when you're so busy solving crimes."

Mr Daventry's gaze shifted to the duke. "Dounreay visited the Hart Street office this morning to express his concern over the incident. He said you sought professional help."

"That is what we agreed, Miss Ware," the duke added.

"Yes. I'm merely surprised you acted so quickly. I didn't know you were acquainted." That said, Mr Daventry made it his business to know everyone in the *ton*.

Mr Daventry laughed. "I introduced myself to Dounreay many years ago, soon after he inherited."

It made sense. Mr Daventry was a duke's son, too, albeit illegitimate. Still, disappointment lodged like a brick in her chest. He would take charge, putting paid to her hopes of tackling the investigation herself.

"Doubtless, you have already made enquiries at the docks," she said, keen to learn whether they had found the poor woman.

"There are twenty dockworkers with the surname O'Malley. We need to focus on other lines of enquiry. Hence why I want to hear the story from the beginning."

Mr Sloane tugged the bell pull. "Let's discuss the matter over a glass of hot punch. Vivienne will be down soon."

The one-eyed butler entered, carrying a tray of porcelain tankards, each painted with a seafaring scene. Steam rose from the vessels, the potent scent of citrus and cinnamon wafting into the air.

They all took a tankard and found a seat.

Dounreay waited for her to sit on the sofa before settling into the chair opposite. He made himself comfortable, his muscular legs falling open in a sign of masculine dominance.

Lillian kept her gaze fixed on her tankard, blowing the punch while pretending she didn't care to know what he wore beneath that darn kilt.

Vivienne Sloane entered, and they spent a few minutes conversing before Mr Daventry cleared his throat. "I've heard Dounreay's account of the event. Might I hear yours, Miss Ware?"

"Certainly."

"Begin by explaining how you became locked in a bedchamber with the duke," Mr Daventry said, sounding more intrigued than concerned.

Heat flooded her cheeks. "Is it relevant to the case, sir?"

"Your emotional state will have significantly affected your perception."

"I assure you, I had a full grasp of my faculties." She glanced at Dounreay, her traitorous gaze slipping to his bare knees. The man was a damnable distraction. A fallen angel sent to corrupt the weak. "My reason for being there is a private matter."

Mr Daventry did not press her further but asked that she begin her recount. "Let's hope you're less evasive when it comes to the facts."

The previous night's events were fresh in her mind. Her heart had raced while being seduced by the duke's smooth repartee. It had pounded upon watching the violent tussle outside.

"The woman looked terrified," Lillian added after giving

a detailed account, "and then the rogue dragged her into the tunnel at knifepoint."

"In your experience, do men usually become violent during a lovers' quarrel?" Mr Daventry mocked. "Is it commonplace to press a knife to a woman's throat and remove her with force?"

A past encounter burst into her mind, a scuffle with a rogue who'd made vile threats. "No. Instinct says we're right to air concern. I fear the woman will survive for as long as she's useful."

"Indeed." Mr Daventry reached into his coat pocket and handed her a white handkerchief. "What do you make of this, Miss Ware? Dounreay found it in the mews while searching for the victim."

Lillian blinked in surprise as she took the silk square. Not because burgundy blood stained the lace trim. The duke had failed to mention finding any evidence.

As if party to her thoughts, Dounreay added, "A young groom saw the woman drop it before she was bundled into an unmarked carriage. I traded the handkerchief for my *sgian dubh*. We might have discussed it last night, but the Masters were keen to ferry ye home."

The Masters feared her suffering any slight to her reputation.

"You can gain much from a simple piece of evidence," Mr Daventry said, and had probably made a list a mile long. "Tell me what you determine from the handkerchief."

Lillian sensed it was a test.

Perhaps Mr Daventry wanted to make her look foolish. To belittle her before warning against the dangers of creeping along dark corridors and sneaking into strange bedchambers.

Despite being the object of everyone's attention, she studied the item in her hand. The delicate Chantilly lace was expensive, but she could not afford to make assumptions.

"It belongs to a lady, but not necessarily the one thrown into the carriage. Either way, the initials in the corner provide a vital clue."

"For a reason other than the obvious?" Mr Daventry asked.

"Items bearing monograms are often sentimental. We might presume she dropped it because she wanted someone to find her." Though that was an impossible feat with what little they knew. "It's a cry for help. The bloodstains reinforce the point she is in danger."

Dounreay watched her keenly as he sipped his punch. "Doubtless the villain nicked her with the knife."

"I would wipe blood on a dark cloak before ruining a white handkerchief, Your Grace. I would suck blood off my finger before mopping it up with expensive lace."

A slow smile formed on Dounreay's lips. "Evidence suggests she is a reluctant participant and knows her life hangs in the balance."

Lillian turned to Mr Daventry. "You should question Lord Kinver, sir. Someone in his household must know the owner? Why drop a handkerchief no one can identify?"

"Excellent, Miss Ware. We might make an enquiry agent of you yet."

Pride filled her chest, and she inhaled deeply. The faint whiff of something familiar teased her nostrils. Perfume. An uncommon scent.

Lillian brought the lace to her nose, closed her eyes, and sniffed to locate the source. She gave a broad smile when realising the significance of her finding.

"Sir, we have another clue." She handed Mr Daventry the handkerchief, prompting him to smell the fragrance. "*Conval-*

laria majalis, otherwise known as lily of the valley. In perfume, the extraction process means the flower loses much of its potency. I know of only two perfumers in London capable of producing a blend accurate enough to mimic the original flower."

"Valmary's in Old Bond Street," Vivienne Sloane said.

"Yes, and Baudelaire's in Ludgate Hill." Perfumers often kept a list of clients, particularly those willing to spend over the odds. "They might have a record of the ladies who purchased the fragrance."

Mr Daventry returned the handkerchief. "Visit them tomorrow with Dounreay and search their records. Kinver is on honeymoon but see what his staff say about the handkerchief."

"Me?" Lillian feared she had misheard. "I beg your pardon? We've come to hire an agent, sir. A professional who can deal with the intricacies of this case. Someone with experience."

At best, she had hoped to assist Mr Sloane in an investigation, not spend endless hours with the handsome duke.

Mr Daventry shrugged. "I have no agents available, and I'll not trust this matter to the local police office. They pulled three women from the Thames last night alone. One might be our mystery lady, but we must know for sure."

"I'm to return to Scotland soon," Dounreay said, reminding her they had limited time together, though he did not sound remotely panicked. "But I'll help in any way I can."

"Good." Mr Daventry clapped his hands together. "I shall arrange for a chaperone to accompany you tomorrow."

Lillian scoured her mind for an alternative.

"We can investigate the matter separately and meet at

your Hart Street office." Spending time alone with Dounreay at balls and soirees was as much as she could cope with.

"Together, you will make more informed decisions, and I'll not risk your safety, Miss Ware. If you refuse, I'll have no choice but to refer the matter to the magistrate. Lord knows what will happen to the poor woman then."

Lillian looked at Dounreay, willing him to offer an objection.

The devil sat there, a gleam of satisfaction in his dark eyes. He raised his porcelain tankard in salute. "Here's to our new adventure, Miss Ware."

Chapter Four

Callan instructed his coachman to park on Fleet Street.

The decision had nothing to do with navigating the bustling crowds on Ludgate Hill. Lord MacTavish and his daughter Ailsa were acting as chaperones, and the fellow wagged his bushy red brows at Callan, desperate for a private audience.

Moreover, after spending the journey squashed next to Miss Ware, their thighs touching as the vehicle rattled over the cobblestones, Callan needed air. Needed the breeze to cool his heated blood.

MacTavish gestured for the ladies to walk ahead. Being firm friends, the women linked arms and kept their heads together while sharing secrets.

"Tell me ye're suffering from a malady," MacTavish whispered as they walked along Fleet Street towards the obelisk. "Tell me all this hot air hasnae frazzled yer brain."

Callan shot his friend an amused grin. "Lucius Daventry is short of agents. There's nae one else to investigate the crime, and he can be mighty persuasive." He didn't care about helping Daventry. The desire to spend time with Miss Ware had motivated Callan to accept the case.

"Aye, Daventry could convince the King to dance through the streets naked." MacTavish stroked his long red beard. "But I'm referring to yer interest in Miss Ware. She's nae intention of ever marrying. She'll be off on a wild adventure when her brother's bairn is settled. Where will that leave ye then?"

"Are ye trying to protect my poor heart, MacTavish?"

It was too late.

Miss Ware had claimed a sizeable piece long ago.

"Surely ye see, it's pointless investing time in a woman who doesnae want ye. 'Twill end in nothing but a lifetime of regret. Mark my words."

Oh, Lillian Ware wanted him.

His touch left her breathless. He was in no doubt.

But she fought this mutual attraction with the strength of a Norse shield maiden. If Callan had any hope of breaking through the barricade, he needed to know why.

"Then I shall use my Scottish charm and convince her to stay. Were my forebears nae famous for their strength and courage in battle?"

"Yer forebears were murdering heathens," MacTavish teased. "Dinnae brag about that."

Their ancestors were once sworn enemies, fighting over land centuries ago. Now, this Scot was Callan's closest friend and ally. A father figure who had helped him through the toughest times.

"Ye could have any woman of yer choosing."

Did MacTavish fear Callan might follow in his parents' footsteps and spend years in a loveless marriage?

"Aye, and I choose her."

Miss Lillian Ware. The woman who haunted his dreams.

MacTavish sighed. "Ye dinnae make things easy for yerself, lad. The lass has a Scot's stubbornness. She'll fight ye to the bitter end. It will be a clashing of swords, make nae mistake."

"Maybe that's why I like her."

Good things never came easy.

And unlike other women, she wasn't interested in his fortune or title.

MacTavish chuckled. "If ye can work a miracle, Lady MacTavish will be thrilled. She thinks of the lass as a daughter."

"Still, my clansmen willnae want me marrying an Englishwoman."

MacTavish frowned. "Now I know the mild air has turned yer brain to mush. Yer own grandmother was from Northumberland."

"Hush." Callan tapped his finger to his lips. "Do ye mean to ruin my chances of snaring Miss Ware? I'll nae scare the woman away. She'll take to the hills if she thinks I might marry her."

MacTavish gave a sly wink. "Canny devil. How do ye plan to make yerself seem more appealing?"

Callan pushed all doubts aside and slapped his friend affectionately on the back. "By giving the lady what she desperately desires. The adventure of a lifetime."

Society's elite used scent to flaunt their wealth. Lazy devils used it to mask the stench of stale sweat and days' old grime.

Nothing turned a man's stomach more than the cloying smell of heavy perfume. Hence why Callan stood at Baudelaire's marble counter, fearing he might cast up his accounts.

"While I often catch a hint of roses on yer skin, Miss Ware, I cannae recall ye ever wearing heavy perfume."

The lady kept her gaze trained on the busy assistant, keen to get his attention. "I bathe in nothing but rosewater. A friend recently told me perfume is just an artifice employed to attract a gentleman."

Callan fought to banish a vision of her lounging naked in a tub of rose petals. "A male friend?"

"No. Miss MacTavish." Miss Ware looked to the adjacent counter, where Ailsa stood, forcing her father to sniff a host of sample perfumes. "She is extremely practical, as you know."

"Aye, yet she's spoken in error."

Miss Ware faced him, gazing into his eyes for the first time since agreeing to take the case. "Then why do courtesans drench themselves until they smell sickly sweet?"

"Because they believe the same misconception, and nae man cares enough to tell them the truth."

"Which is?"

Callan leaned closer and whispered, "That there is nothing more alluring to a man than a woman's natural aroma."

Miss Ware swallowed, and her cheeks turned cherry red.

He could spend hours inhaling every inch of her bare skin. He could close his eyes and still find her in a crowded room.

"This establishment is built on a lie." Callan motioned to the shelves of elegant glass bottles, to the ladies pulling stoppers and dabbing scent on their wrists. "Should the secret become public knowledge, Monsieur Baudelaire would be bankrupt within a week."

She narrowed her gaze. "You're teasing me."

"I shall prove the point the next time we're alone. I guarantee ye will prefer my natural scent to the whiff of bergamot cologne."

"Why wear it, then?"

"To keep the horde of admirers at bay."

Miss Ware laughed. The contagious sound made him want to enrol in jester school. "You adore female attention. Did you not ride out with Miss Cartwright yesterday?"

Ah, did he detect a hint of jealousy in her tone?

"Why would I do that when I've made an oath to help with yer research? I'm nae the sort of man who pays attention to more than one woman."

Since meeting her, other women blurred into the background, paled into insignificance. He gave them as much notice as he did marble statues and potted ferns.

"I doubt we will have time to consider my book now."

"We'll make time." How else was he meant to seduce her?

She averted her gaze and beckoned the assistant.

A pompous fellow wearing a white periwig, pale blue breeches and tailcoat tottered over. "Welcome to Baudelaire's," he said, his poor French accent lacking any genuine inflection. He eyed Callan with some interest. "You wish to purchase an exotic scent for your wife, monsieur?"

"Oh, he is not my husband," Miss Ware quickly added.

"But I would buy her every bottle in this shop if I thought she might waltz with me just once."

"We agreed you wouldn't ask me to dance."

"The words didnae leave my lips. I merely expressed my deepest desire to—" He gestured to the assistant. "What's yer name?"

"Christian, monsieur."

"I merely expressed my thoughts to Christian."

Miss Ware grinned. "Why would you purchase perfume when you prefer my natural scent?"

"Because I might spend an entire evening comparing each fragrance to the intoxicating smell of yer skin."

Her brows knitted together in suspicion. "This is a test, an education of sorts." She tapped her finger to her lips. "Let me see. I am definitely not speaking to a man in love."

No, she was speaking to a man who needed to rid his body of this infernal ache. Needed Divine intervention to accomplish his task.

"What makes ye so sure?" he said, enjoying this game.

"You were looking at my mouth when you spoke."

Was he? He could not recall.

MacTavish moved past them. He leaned closer and whispered, "Ailsa likes the rosewater. The rest stinks like a horse's sweaty ballocks."

Callan laughed aloud, much to the assistant's horror.

"We require yer help and undivided attention," he said when a persistent lady at the end of the counter complained about the slow service. Callan removed a calling card from his silver case and handed it to the assistant.

Christian's eyes widened as he read the elegant script. He looked ready to have the gilt chairs carried in, serve the finest canapés and aperitifs to honour the esteemed duke's patronage.

But Callan leaned over the counter. "Ye'll nae mention my name or make any grand gestures. Ye'll tell us what we need to know, and we shall be on our way. Do ye understand?"

Christian blinked and nodded rapidly.

"We are investigating a matter of grave importance," Miss Ware said quietly. "We need the names of those who purchased your lily of the valley perfume during the past twelve months."

The man gawped like she had asked him to dance naked on the counter. "But the information is confidential, madame."

"Would you rather we fetch the magistrate?" she said firmly. "One whisper of trouble and your clients will go elsewhere."

"But we do not keep records."

"Ye expect me to believe that?" Callan growled. "Know, my friend is clumsy and prone to accidents. I would hate for him to break anything."

The fellow started shaking when MacTavish balanced a bottle on one finger. "Lily of the valley, you say? The scent, it was taken off the shelf a month ago. Monsieur Baudelaire, he is a perfectionist. Customers complained it was not as authentic as the one sold at Valmary's."

Callan slapped his hand on the counter. "Aye, but ye keep a list of patrons' names and addresses."

The sudden sound of shattering glass on the tiled floor had all the customers gasping. Aghast, poor Christian looked like he'd seen the ghost of Bronny Moor.

"Och, the thing just slipped from my hand." MacTavish picked up another delicate glass bottle, ready to demonstrate how easily it was done.

People hurried from the shop as if a horde of marauding pirates had taken occupancy. Shrieks accompanied the tinkling of the bell and the constant slamming of the door.

"Wait! Madame! Monsieur!" Christian called to those racing away down the street—while his colleague arrived with a brush and cloth and knelt to clean up the mess before they choked on the fumes.

"Give us the names," Callan said, taking advantage of the

chaos, "and I'll get rid of the Scotsman before he breaks yer wee neck."

"Monsieur Baudelaire keeps all documents locked in his office." Christian's French accent slipped to reveal something of a coarse East London twang. "But I can recall a few off the top of me head."

Miss Ware reached into her reticule and withdrew her notebook and pencil, the thrill of excitement dancing in her intelligent blue eyes. "I'm listening."

"Mrs Gregory, Captain Gregory's widow," Christian began, his gaze flitting from them to MacTavish as the lord examined another bottle. "Lady Sheridan. Erm, Miss Hudspith, daughter of Sir Gerald. Please. Tell him to put the bottle down, or I'll be forced to shine shoes on Piccadilly."

Miss Ware looked up from her notebook. "An authentic lily of the valley fragrance is considered the height of luxury. More than three ladies must have ordered the perfume."

Christian gulped a breath. "Mrs Jarvis. Last I heard, she was Major Rowlands' mistress. Oh, and the opera singer Madame Delafont. I can't remember the others."

They had enough information to begin their investigation. The obvious place to start was with Mrs Gregory as one of her initials matched those on the handkerchief.

"Have ye recorded the names, Miss Ware?"

"Yes, Your Grace." She finished scribbling and closed her notebook. "For obvious reasons, we should begin with Mrs Gregory."

"An excellent idea."

MacTavish coughed a few times. The pungent stench of aromatic oils wafting through the shop had irritated his nostrils. "We'll wait outside." He captured Ailsa's arm, propelling her towards the door. "I need some air before I choke."

Callan turned to the fake French assistant. "Ye have my direction. If ye recall anyone with the initials A. G. who purchased lily of the valley, send word, and I'll reward ye for yer efforts."

"For Lily," the assistant said, nodding profusely.

"I beg yer pardon?" Confused, Callan looked at Miss Ware, wondering how the assistant knew her given name or why he had spoken so intimately.

"It's the name of the perfume," Miss Ware explained. "At Baudelaire's, it is called For Lily. At Valmary's, it is May Bell."

"But May Bell, it is of inferior quality," the assistant interjected, loud enough for the few patrons left in the shop to hear. "At Baudelaire's, we pride ourselves on our superior notes."

The two perfumers were evidently rivals.

And desperate for clientele.

Upon hearing MacTavish coughing, Callan thanked the assistant and suggested to Miss Ware they visit the competitor and check the patrons' names against those on their list.

"My nostrils are on fire, I tell ye," MacTavish complained as they continued along Ludgate Hill. "I can barely catch my breath."

Ailsa hugged her father's arm and chuckled. "There's nothing like the sweet scent of freshly picked heather. Is there, Papa?"

"With that thick beard, I'm surprised ye can smell anything but last night's dinner," Callan joked.

MacTavish winked. "Aye, I'm storing a few crumbs for later."

Though Miss Ware smiled, she seemed lost in her thoughts. If a man could read a woman's mind, it would save a whole lot of bother. On the bright side, she spoke to him with ease now, when she had spent years avoiding his gaze.

During the twenty-minute carriage ride to Valmary's shop in Old Bond Street, MacTavish did nothing but complain, twitch and fidget.

"My legs ache like I've downed a quart of whisky and run up Ben More. It cannae be the weather affecting my bones." A muscle in his cheek spasmed, causing his mouth to contort into a pained grimace.

A bolt of alarm forced Callan to straighten. "Are ye unwell?"

MacTavish tugged at his cravat and craned his neck. "I've nae felt well since sniffing those vile French concoctions."

Miss Ware sat forward. "You look quite pale, my lord."

"I cannae think straight. My head is as fuzzy as a rabbit-fur sporran." MacTavish gasped a breath and his left arm jerked violently.

Alarm turned to raging panic.

Callan had seen similar convulsions once before. Many years ago. Yet the memory was as clear as Loch Eck's crystal waters.

"Ye've consumed or inhaled something toxic." With his clenched fist, he banged on the carriage roof and shouted for Dewart to return to MacTavish's home on Pall Mall. "Open the window, Miss Ware. Quickly."

Callan yanked down the window nearest to him, the chill air swooshing through the carriage when Miss Ware did the same.

Blood pumped fast in his veins. "Can ye breathe?"

MacTavish began swaying in the seat like a drunkard.

"Perhaps we should loosen his clothing." A worried Ailsa turned to her father. "At least remove his cravat so he might breathe easily."

"Dinnae touch him," Callan snapped. "We're almost home." Memories fought their way into his mind. A mother writhing in his arms. Foam bubbling from her mouth. Eyes wide in panic. "Merciful Lord! We'll need to strip off our clothes and toss them on the bonfire. We'll need to wash while a servant races to fetch a physician."

A whimper escaped Ailsa's lips.

Callan pinched the bridge of his nose in a bid to keep a tight rein on his emotions. Then Miss Ware placed her gloved hand on his arm, and the feelings he kept at bay threatened to burst forth in a torrent and drown them all.

"Your Grace, maybe he's having an adverse reaction to the scent. Ailsa, does your father suffer from allergies?"

"Nae, he has a hardy constitution."

An agonised groan escaped MacTavish. The tall man slipped from the seat, his back arching, leaving him twisted like an otherworldly creature.

"Good Lord!" Miss Ware gripped Callan's arm now. "We must get him into the house and give him space before he injures himself."

The carriage came to a crashing halt outside MacTavish's home on Pall Mall. Callan kicked open the door, clambered over his friend, and vaulted to the pavement.

"Fetch a footman, Miss Ware. Hurry. Take Ailsa. Have them draw a bath and light the fire as there's nae time to heat the water."

Both ladies climbed out and raced into the house.

Callan grabbed MacTavish around the waist and hauled him over his shoulder, his stomach churning at the thought of losing someone else he loved. "Saints and demons! Can I nae take my eyes off ye for a second?" he said, breaking into a thick Scottish drawl.

It took all Callan's strength to hold MacTavish tightly.

Passersby hurried away as if the man's weird jerks and moans were contagious. Still, Callan managed to get the writhing fellow into the house.

Lady MacTavish raced to the door, patting down her wild red curls. "Upon my oath, what the devil has happened? Angus? Are ye drunk?"

"It might be poison." Callan strived to mount the stairs with the hefty fellow on his back. "We need a doctor!"

He could almost hear the lady's thoughts as she hurried behind.

Yer mother's death was an accident.

Dinnae let suspicion cloud yer judgement, lad.

Callan burst into MacTavish's bedchamber and threw him down onto the mattress, the four-poster bed creaking under the strain. That's when the lady's composure faltered, and she saw her husband's movements were wild and unnatural. Feral.

"What wickedness is this?"

"I'm convinced it's poison." By God, if MacTavish had ingested something foul, he might not live to tell the tale. "Sit with him. Keep him propped on his side. Stop him rolling onto his back and choking on his tongue."

Mother, dinnae die!

Please, dinnae die!

The words echoed in Callan's mind.

Two footmen barged into the room, hauling a copper tub, their timely arrival banishing the ghosts of the past.

"We need water. Quickly." Callan was already shrugging out of his coat. "Has someone sent for the physician?"

"The maids are filling buckets, Your Grace. And your coachman went to fetch Dr Mackenzie. The master will see no one else."

Callan nodded. "One of ye light the fire." A Scotsman

could suffer the cold, but not while sick and bathing in cool water. He yanked off MacTavish's boot and threw it to the floor. "We need to get Angus out of these damn clothes."

A maid arrived, lugging a heavy bucket. She emptied the water into the tub before hurrying from the room. Like an army of ants, the other servants followed suit.

Amid the chaos, Miss Ware appeared like an apparition. Her complexion pale, her bearing sad and mournful, hesitance in every step. She looked defeated, ready to instruct her maid to air her black crepe mourning gown.

Seeing her always caused an inner conflict—a battle between pleasure and pain, hope and sorrow.

He'd tried hard to forget her.

But she lived under his skin.

He could scratch, draw blood, and it wouldn't ease the ache.

She met his gaze, and Callan saw his own panic reflected there. Without saying a word, she knelt before the fire.

Callan didn't ask if she knew how to use the tinderbox. A woman who wished to travel the world would need to be resourceful. For the same reason, he did not demand a maid resume the task.

Amidst the servants' comings and goings, and him removing MacTavish's neckcloth and coat, he sensed Miss Ware watching him.

"Ailsa is bathing," she eventually said, her timid tone mirroring her despair. "Must we burn her clothes?"

"It's unlikely we're contaminated. We would have shown similar signs of illness," he said, restraining MacTavish to stop him injuring himself as he writhed on the bed. "But best we all wash and change. Make sure ye clean yer hair."

Although frantic thoughts plagued Callan's mind, he imagined playing maid to Miss Ware, pulling every pin, letting the silky strands slip through his fingers. Touching her in all the ways he shouldn't.

"I pray he recovers," was all she said before leaving the room.

Dr Mackenzie arrived promptly. He questioned Lorna MacTavish about her husband's morning meal and asked where he might find the rat poison.

Callan explained what had occurred in Baudelaire's perfumery.

Dr Mackenzie kept his gaze on the patient, though MacTavish had stopped flailing since the doctor had shoved three spoonfuls of activated charcoal down his throat. "How long after inhaling the scent did he become ill?"

"Within twenty minutes."

"It's likely he had a reaction to the perfume. But I'll stay until after supper. We cannot have him lapsing into a fit."

"But ye think the worst is over?" Lorna said, teary-eyed.

"Whatever he inhaled probably entered his bloodstream through the nasal membranes. I'm certain it's not potent enough to kill him, but we should alert the local police office and have them remove the bottles for inspection."

A knock on the door brought Ailsa, who hurried to her father's bedside. The woman went to great efforts to make herself look plain. Yet with her wild red hair flowing, she looked like a Scottish temptress.

Still, Ailsa was like kin, and Callan's heartbeat remained constant until Miss Ware entered the room.

"How is Lord MacTavish?" she said, oblivious to her effect on him.

It should have been easy to answer the simple question, but he could not stop staring at her loose auburn hair, the shade darker being so damp. He tried to regain his composure, but seeing her dressed in Ailsa's red tartan gown sent his desire spiralling.

Miss Ware looked every bit a Scot. She belonged in the Highlands. He'd known it the first time he'd taken her in his arms and waltzed her around the floor. When he'd seen a beautiful future flash before his eyes. A vision he could not erase.

Wicked thoughts entered his head.

How he might use his mouth and tongue and cock to brand her.

"Dr Mackenzie thinks the worst is over," Callan said.

"Thank heavens."

They locked gazes, though she was the first to break the spell.

"Ye should wash, Dounreay." Lorna looked up from mopping Angus' brow. "Have a footman fill the tub in the spare room, as there's nae hope of me leaving Angus. I'll have Miss Ware bring ye some clothes, though I cannae promise they'll fit."

Callan nodded, keen to wash the stress from his tired limbs. While waiting for the staff to fill the bathtub, he wrote a note informing Daventry of recent events and arranged for his coachman to deliver it to the Hart Street office.

Miss Ware appeared, a red tartan kilt and white lawn shirt draped over her arm. "Lady MacTavish asked me to bring these."

He took the garments and placed them on the bed. "How are ye faring? Ye seemed shaken earlier." So shaken he'd wanted to kiss every worry away. "Understandably so, I might add."

She gave a half-shrug. "I may appear confident most of the time, but I'm not so good when tragedy strikes."

Her honesty proved refreshing.

It only made him want her all the more.

"We all have our weaknesses." She was his. Yet he could not help but prolong the seconds he spent in her presence. He remembered she had lost both parents, too. "The thought of losing someone close never gets easier."

"No." She glanced at the bathtub. "I should leave you. I promised to keep Ailsa company and agreed to stay the night. Once we know Lord MacTavish is well, we can continue with our investigation."

"Daventry may be forced to deal with the matter, but we shall see what he advises and take heed."

Miss Ware nodded and left him to his ablutions.

Only when he dragged his shirt over his head, and the lady's soft gasp reached his ears, did he realise she had left the door ajar.

Callan couldn't see her yet knew she stood in the shadows.

He felt her gaze roaming over his bare chest like a forbidden caress. The whispers of a secret only they shared.

Every muscle clenched in response.

For a heartbeat or two, he stared at the narrow gap.

Then he did something so opposed to his current needs.

He strode to the door and closed it gently, shutting her out.

If he had any hope of furthering his relationship with Miss Ware, she had to learn to want him. To ache for him. To toss and turn in bed and crave the feel of his naked body.

Chapter Five

The sound of measured footsteps on the stairs confirmed Lord MacTavish's health had not taken a drastic turn for the worse. Still, whenever Lillian closed her eyes and tried to sleep, she pictured the lord thrashing about like a trapped animal in his four-poster bed.

Except it wasn't MacTavish's face she saw.

Her mind conjured a story of her mother's missing hours. A horrible middle to a peaceful beginning and end. The mystifying part that came after the warm kiss on her daughter's forehead and before the cold stillness of death.

Being too painful to contemplate, she forced the images from her mind, leaving her with another disturbing vision. The Duke of Dounreay's impressive chest.

The sight had stolen her breath and hardened her nipples.

Left her aching in forbidden places.

Even now, her palms grew hot, the need to touch him as compelling as an opium craving. Not that she had ever craved opium. But a strange need lived inside her, pestering her to take the plunge and feed.

Hence the reason she kept Dounreay at arm's length.

Dangerous men did not need to boast of their sexual prowess.

Dounreay was irresistible even when silent.

Thankfully, a light knock on the door drew her from thoughts of Satan's servant. Lorna MacTavish opened the door a fraction and peered through the narrow gap. Noticing Lillian was awake, she sighed and slipped into the room.

"Are ye nae exhausted? Ailsa is sleeping like a bairn."

Lillian sat up and tried to find the words to describe this inner restlessness. "I keep revisiting the day's events in my head and cannot settle."

"Aye. I've been downstairs and taken a dram of brandy. I suggest ye do the same. It cannae hurt and might calm yer thoughts for a wee while." Lorna snatched the dressing gown from the chair and held it open. "Come. There's nae point lying here thinking and worrying yerself half to death."

Despite the cold nip in the air, Lillian threw back the blankets and climbed out of bed. "What time is it?"

"Almost midnight."

Lorna helped Lillian into the white gown. Like a doting mother, she tied the belt and straightened the frilly collar.

Aware of the growing emptiness in her chest, Lillian sought a distraction. "The duke cares for his lordship very much. He is usually so calm and composed, yet I saw wild panic in his eyes today."

Lorna tightened the bow securing Lillian's braid and brushed a stray tendril behind her ear. "Dounreay lost his mother to poison. I imagine he feared losing his closest friend in much the same manner."

"Poison?" Never knowing the woman, Lillian had no reason to cry. Still, she suddenly felt the duke's pain as keenly as her own, and tears welled in her eyes. "How old was he?" For some reason, it mattered.

"Twelve or thirteen, but I cannae be certain."

"Still a boy, then?"

"Aye."

The lump in her throat made it hard to breathe.

"'Twas a foolish mistake. A silly accident in the forest." Lorna cupped Lillian's cheek as if she were a porcelain doll that might easily shatter, not a woman who had buried her troubles beneath a thick skin. "But that's how these things happen. Now I've come to understand what Dounreay dealt with that day."

"He was there?"

Lorna released a mournful sigh. "Aye."

A single tear trickled down Lillian's cheek.

Poor Dounreay.

To have everything one minute and nothing the next.

Lorna dashed the droplet away with her thumb. "Go now and take a good swig of brandy. 'Twill chase away the cold and the memories. There's sherry if ye prefer. But I'll have nae more tears today. We've much to be thankful for."

Lillian inhaled a calming breath. She clutched Lady MacTavish's hands and gave them a gentle squeeze. A means of thanking her for her kindness and motherly affection. To say the words aloud would invariably rouse unwelcome emotions.

Barefoot, she crept downstairs.

All was quiet. The servants were abed. Despite the daunting thought of sitting alone in the darkness, she entered the drawing room.

She could still feel Dounreay's presence in the house, hear the soft whisper of his breath, as if he had left some remnant of his spirit behind to torment her.

Only when she neared the drinks table did she notice him sitting in the shadows, one arm stretched over the back of the sofa, those godforsaken knees visible beneath the hem of the borrowed kilt.

Her heart almost stopped. "Your Grace. I thought you'd left hours ago."

"Miss Ware?" Sounding surprised, he pushed to his feet. "I didnae mean to startle ye. I'm waiting for Dewart to return to take me home. I'd walk, but MacTavish's kilt is on the large side, and I'll nae be arrested for indecency."

She might have laughed, but the temptation for wickedness hung heavily in the air, and she daren't lower her guard for a second.

"I couldn't sleep and hoped a nip of brandy might do the trick."

His gaze slid slowly over her white dressing gown, leaving a hot trail in its wake. "I doubt I shall sleep either. Daventry arrived an hour ago and has only just left. I'd have sent for ye if I'd known ye were awake."

She swallowed down her nerves. The way he looked at her, as if she were a naked nymph walking the wild moorlands, left her at a loss as to what to say.

"Daventry agrees we must involve the magistrate." Turning to the drinks tray, Dounreay pulled the stopper from a decanter and splashed brandy into two glasses. "Baudelaire's perfumery will close until they can locate the source of the poison."

"Oh, I see." There would be no need to spend time with him. No excuse to force her hand. "Does Mr Daventry plan to oversee the entire case?"

A familiar feeling came over her.

Half relief. Half regret.

"Nae." He faced her and thrust a goblet into her hand. "We're to continue with our investigation as planned. We're to interview Lord Kinver's staff after breakfast in the morning. Daventry will arrange for Mr and Mrs Masters to act as chaperones."

Good Lord!

Devon Masters would watch them like a hawk.

"Then we have much to do tomorrow." The brandy warmed her throat but did little to relax her muscles. "We must visit Valmary's perfumery, and interview Mrs Gregory."

With unnerving intensity, Dounreay watched her over the rim of the glass as he drank. "Daventry sent an agent to the mortuary. None of the women pulled from the Thames that night wore a dark cloak."

She quickly banished an image of bloated bodies. "Then there is every chance our mystery woman is alive."

"In this instance, 'tis best to be pessimistic."

She nodded, and they both sipped their brandy in silence.

Compassionate words filled her head, ones she might convey after learning how his mother had died. But it would mean giving her emotions free rein, which was a dangerous thing in itself, let alone in the presence of this man.

"We'll be busy with the case tomorrow," he said, returning his empty glass to the tray, "which leaves little time for me to assist with yer research."

It was a blessing in disguise.

So why was her chest so tight?

Why did she feel sick to the pit of her stomach?

"Do not trouble yourself. You've been a great help already. I have far more insight into the workings of a man's mind than I did some days ago. Let that be the end of the matter."

"The end? I am more inclined to believe it is just the beginning." Dounreay held up his finger, though she could see little in the gloom. "I bear the mark of an oath made, madam."

"It will heal."

"The vow cannae be broken."

Nerves shivered down her spine. "What are you saying?"

Dounreay prised the brandy goblet from her fingers and placed it on the table. "That we have a window of opportunity. One we shouldnae waste." His gaze slipped from her eyes to her mouth, to her concealed breasts and bare feet. "What role shall I play first, Miss Ware?"

"You mean to instruct me now?"

"We might nae have another chance."

Dare to be bold!

That was her motto.

So why was she trembling like a chit fresh from the schoolroom?

Lillian raised her chin. "Be the fellow whose Mama forces him to approach marriageable ladies."

It would give her time to catch her breath. Rebuild her defences.

Dounreay inclined his head respectfully before slipping into the role with ease. "Ye shouldnae be here, madam," he said coldly, his gaze distant, his demeanour aloof. "Be assured, I'm nae one to fall for such a trap."

Her pulse settled. "Then leave, Your Grace. Before we're forced to wed."

"Gladly." He made for the door but turned quickly and spoke in his usual warm tone. "Such men are ruled by suspicion. They're the most dangerous of all."

"Because their mamas often orchestrate a lady's ruination?"

"Aye." He stared at her, rubbing his sculpted jaw, contemplating which part to play. "Now for my next role."

"Wait. Is that your carriage I hear outside?"

Or was it her nerves clattering, her resolve shaking?

"Dewart will wait." He put his hand on his heart like she owned the beating organ. "Ye shouldnae be here, madam." Dark eyes held hers, engulfing her in a warm embrace. Tender. Terrifying. "Be assured, I'm nae one to fall for such a trap. But say the word, and I am yers forever."

"Then leave, Your Grace, for I have no desire to wed."

No desire to have my illusions shattered.

No desire to lose someone so dear again.

A pained look passed over his handsome features. So convincing, she quickly urged him to play the rakehell. To show her the mannerisms of a man ruled by lust.

Forcing a smile, she readied her defences. "I suppose you will say the same lines but in that velvet voice you use." The one that stirred the hairs on her nape and sent her temperature soaring. "Don't forget, you must pretend to have an obsession with my mouth."

"I'll nae forget."

The atmosphere changed with his expression. Who knew that an arrogant smirk could steal all the oxygen from the air, could leave her gasping for breath, floundering?

Dounreay prowled towards her, his gaze devouring every inch of her form like she was his next meal.

Lillian stepped back until her bottom hit the console table.

He did not say the rehearsed line until his body was mere inches from hers, his nearness like kindling to her fire's flames.

"Ye shouldnae be here, madam." A deep hum rumbled in his throat. He braced his hands on the wall above her head, trapping her in a masculine prison. "Be assured, I'm nae one to fall for such a trap."

"Yet here you are, taking advantage of the situation."

Dounreay pressed his mouth to her ear, his lips tracing the

shell. "I mean to take advantage of more than the situation." He inhaled deeply. "Ye smell so good, love."

Lust was a wicked thing, a powerful thing.

The mere thrill of it left her sex throbbing.

She would squeeze her thighs together, but he was wedging his knee between her legs, pressing against the intimate place.

"Tell me to leave," he whispered huskily.

"Leave," she panted, the word lacking conviction.

Dounreay laughed against her neck. "Ye want me to stay."

She closed her eyes against the potent sensations.

Kiss me, Dounreay!

Kiss me now!

Kiss me forever and a day!

The compelling song played over and over in her mind.

An addictive tune one could not forget.

He looked at her, his mouth so close to hers they were sharing the same breath. Mating in the ether.

She was going to kiss him. She couldn't stop herself.

Logical thought took flight. He was the only thing filling her head. Hence why she came up on her tiptoes and brushed her mouth over his brandy-coated lips.

Dounreay inhaled sharply.

The world stopped for a second or two. A beautiful moment where nothing else mattered. No one else existed. Just two souls merging into one.

He closed his eyes as he captured her mouth, their lips moving together in a dance more dangerous than any ballroom waltz.

Heat pooled between her thighs.

Every inch of her skin tingled.

She knew what to expect next: his tongue slipping into

her mouth, his hands on her body, desire spiralling until she was drunk, intoxicated.

But Dounreay dragged his lips free, leaving them both gasping.

He stared at her, but she could not read his expression.

What role are you playing now?

Tell me, so I might prepare!

He stepped back, biting his bottom lip like he wanted to finish what she'd started. "I think ye have the measure of the situation, Miss Ware."

"I have a better understanding of how one might lose oneself in the moment," she admitted, though did not say this rampant hunger for him still consumed her. A barrel of brandy would not help her sleep tonight.

"Be warned." He adjusted the front of his kilt, touching himself. "The next time ye succumb to the scoundrel, the kiss willnae be as tame." He inclined his head. "Good night, madam."

Don't go!

"Good night," the farewell was but a whisper as she watched him leave. The front door opened and closed despite her willing him to return.

Lillian stared into the darkness, her eyelids fluttering closed. She touched her fingers to her lips, bathed in the erotic feelings until they disappeared like the sound of Dounreay's carriage into the night.

The man had put a spell on her.

With minimal effort, he had left her wanting.

How was it possible?

She had known what to expect yet lacked the restraint to keep him at bay. Lust's potency was a powerful thing. He had quite literally stolen her breath.

The experience gave rise to an interesting thought. As a

woman desperate to avoid the worries that came with loving a man, with Dounreay, she might indulge her wild desires.

Unlike the painful ache that accompanied love, lust's ripples had subsided quite quickly. Indeed, a plan formed in her mind. A daring plan. A dangerous plan. The answer to her prayers. Who safer to experience life's pleasures with than a Scot who refused to marry an Englishwoman?

Chapter Six

Callan had barely slept a wink. When he wasn't taking himself in hand amid visions of kissing an auburn-haired temptress, he had spent the night worrying about MacTavish and reliving the harrowing moment he lost his mother to poison.

Life was precarious—a constant pivot between pleasure and pain. Darkness and light. Sunshine and rain. There were good days and bad days and mediocre ones in between.

He might have spent miserable years wallowing in the past, but MacTavish said if one changed one's mindset, one changed one's life. No one wanted to live beneath a permanent cloud of sadness.

Still, when Callan called at MacTavish's house on Pall Mall, he struggled to rouse his usual optimism. He waited in the hall, his gaze shifting between the gloomy staircase and the drawing room.

What if MacTavish failed to recover?

What if Miss Ware regretted sharing one chaste kiss?

God, the woman fired his blood like no one else. Now he had sampled the forbidden fruit, he was desperate to scoff the whole darn apple. To sin and sin and sin until sated.

"Dounreay?" Lorna called, descending the stairs slowly. Through tired eyes, she scanned his face. "Do ye nae have an appointment at Lord Kinver's home this morning?"

Callan studied her intently, anticipating bad news. "Aye, at ten, but I wanted to check on Angus and thought to offer Miss Ware the option of riding with me in my carriage."

"The lass left ten minutes ago with her friend Mrs Masters."

Disappointment stabbed at Callan's chest.

He'd hoped to have a private word with the lady before they conducted the interviews under Devon Masters' watchful gaze.

"Angus is sleeping, but didnae have a seizure during the night. Dr Mackenzie called with a tincture this morning. He said Angus will need time to fully recover. Whatever he inhaled was nae strong enough to kill him."

Callan stroked Lorna's upper arm, saying a silent prayer of thanks. "'Tis a relief. I'll call tonight, if I may. Is there anything ye need in the meantime?"

"There is something I need," Lorna said, patting his cheek as if he were a wee boy.

"Aye." He would do anything.

"For ye to stop worrying."

He managed a smile. "Ye know what Angus means to me, what ye all mean to me. On my honour, I shall find the person who did this and make the devil pay."

Angus had picked up the perfume bottles at random.

Had he been in the wrong place at the wrong time?

Or was there something sinister afoot?

Lorna smiled despite tears welling. "Well, he's nae leaving us today. That's a blessing. Reassure poor Miss Ware.

At breakfast, she spent more time nibbling her bottom lip than her toast."

The comment sent his mind racing to their passionate clinch. Blood had pumped so fast through his veins he had never felt so alive. The promise of another encounter lingered in every muscle, every cell.

What if he had misread the signs?

What if the kiss left her so troubled she would end their research?

"What happened to Angus shocked us all," he said.

"Aye, near tragedies have a way of raking up the past. She seemed lost in her memories this morning. Dinnae let the lass fool ye. There's a deep sadness hiding beneath that bravado."

Yet he sensed nothing but a burning passion he longed to explore. "Then I shall find a way to make her smile today."

"Och, ye're a good man, Callan Maclean." She knew better than to remind him his mother would be proud.

He grabbed Lorna and kissed her cheek. "Because I keep the best company, even if yer forebears were savage heathens." He was halfway out of the door when he glanced back. "I'll sit with Angus tonight so ye can rest."

"He'll take comfort knowing yer close."

Callan left Pall Mall and made his way to Lord Kinver's abode in New Cavendish Street. The Kinvers were visiting the Cotswolds while on honeymoon. Being Lady Kinver's brother, Devon Masters had taken charge and had arranged the servants' interviews.

The ageing butler escorted Callan into the drawing room, where the Masters and Miss Ware sat drinking tea. "His Grace, The Duke of Dounreay."

Miss Ware gasped upon hearing his name.

"Please, there's nae need to stand." Callan's gaze settled on her, his heart rebounding in his chest. The lass had kissed him first last night. "Sorry I'm late. I went to Pall Mall to visit MacTavish."

"We must have just missed you," she said in the casual tone she might use with an acquaintance, not the man who had come close to slipping his tongue into her mouth.

"We were sorry to learn about the incident at Baudelaire's," Masters said, gesturing to his wife, "and wish MacTavish a speedy recovery."

"The man has the constitution of an ox."

"Hence why we're relieved Miss Ware didn't sniff the poisoned perfume. Being slight of frame, the consequences may have been dire. I confess, I cannot fathom why Daventry sent you there."

Miss Ware was quick to defend their position. "I have already explained. We were to gather names, nothing more. And I agreed to follow Mr Daventry's advice to the letter."

Masters motioned for Callan to sit in the empty chair, not next to Miss Ware on the sofa. "Still, you must inform Roxburgh of recent events, else I will."

Miss Ware's eyes widened in horror. "I'll not trouble my brother. He has a lot to contend with at present. Give me a few days. Once things are settled at home, I shall explain everything."

Devon Masters gave a curt nod.

"Your Grace," Mrs Masters began, "I cannot help but wonder why a Scottish duke would act as an enquiry agent. Surely you have pressing business at home."

The lady was as shrewd as her husband, just not as direct.

"A woman was dragged from the garden at knifepoint. I must know if she is alive. In following a lead, my closest friend almost died. Forgive me, but I cannae rest until both villains are in custody."

Mrs Masters glanced at the blue-eyed temptress seated on

her left. "How commendable, but why do you need Miss Ware's assistance?"

Callan thought the lady deserved the truth. "Because Miss Ware has an adventurous spirit. I'd rather her solve a crime with the aid of professionals than scramble on her hands and knees through ancient Egyptian tombs."

Though the last image raised something other than alarm.

"Why should it concern you, Your Grace?"

"Because we both witnessed the crimes," Miss Ware interjected. "And we have a common interest. We both care about Lord MacTavish." She slapped her hands on her thighs. "Now, can we begin the interviews? Might I remind you that you're leaving for Whitstable tomorrow?"

Masters stood abruptly. "Very well. I shall summon Hastings."

"We're to conduct the interviews in the drawing room?" Callan expected to be shown into the servants' dining room.

"Miss Ware thought they would be too comfortable below stairs."

Mrs Masters stood, a twinkle of mischief in her brown eyes. "We should leave you alone for a few minutes, so you might compose questions and devise a strategy."

"We do need to decide how best to proceed." Callan wasn't referring to the questions, though he made a mental note to repay the lady's kindness.

"We shall send the butler to the drawing room in five minutes." Mrs Masters closed the door, leaving Callan alone with Miss Ware, though he could hear a mumbled conversation in the hall as the lady tried to placate her husband.

Miss Ware placed her teacup on the side table. "I'm glad we have a moment alone. I—I need to talk to you about our *research*."

Dread left him momentarily numb.

"Oh?" He stood when she did, anticipating the worst when he watched her bite her bottom lip and wring her hands like a maid might sodden washing.

She struggled to look at him. "I'm not sure how to say this."

"I'll thank ye for being honest."

"Yes, hence why it is so difficult."

"Lies only add to the confusion." He was already inventing stories in his mind. Preparing himself for the worst.

"It's just this is the last thing I ever expected to say."

Based on all that had occurred during the last few days, she should be used to the unexpected. "Ye've decided against writing a book?"

"Good heavens, no! The information will be invaluable." She looked at the closed door for a third time. "What I have to say is specific to our research."

If the lady wanted others to understand her theories, she had to learn to be more succinct. "Are ye unsatisfied with my teaching methods?" She'd kissed him with a passion that had exceeded his expectations.

A soft blush touched her cheeks. "I find I like your methods a great deal."

Mother of all saints!

This was a promising development.

Glancing at his trousers seemed to give her the strength to continue. "Having never felt the warm rush of desire, it was difficult for me to understand a woman's motives."

Last night, her sharp blue gaze had turned soft and dreamy. He could have pressed for more than a simple kiss. It was the reason he had pulled away. With this woman, he lacked restraint.

"Ye never felt it with Mr Bloom?"

"No."

"But ye understand now?" He wished he had worn a kilt this morning so the breeze might cool the rush of heat to his loins.

"Yes, which is why I think we should research the matter in a little more depth."

"In more depth?" Callan coughed into his fist before the shock choked him. "Ye mean we should kiss again?"

Hell, he would be on her in a heartbeat, pushing her against the wall, plundering her mouth, filling her in every possible way.

"Well, yes." She waved her hand to suggest only an imbecile would fail to grasp her meaning. "I—I want you to arouse me to the point I almost lose my mind."

Callan bit the inside of his cheek hard, hoping the pain might wake him from slumber, for this was undoubtedly a dream. But the tangy, metallic taste of blood proved sobering.

"You were right," she said with some excitement. "How can I advise other ladies to avoid the pitfalls when I am a complete novice?"

"Aye, but I must advise against the dangers of such an endeavour." Yet every cell in his body was already anticipating the event.

Miss Ware frowned. "You don't want to kiss me?"

On the list of what he might do with her, kissing would fall under the heading *Tame*. "Lust renders one incapable of logical thought."

She snorted. "Is that not the point of the exercise?"

It was time to follow his own advice and hit her with the truth. "We may find ourselves doing more than kissing, Miss Ware."

"We've made a blood oath." She gave a half-shrug, and he sensed she had spent restless hours considering the risks.

"Whatever happens between us will be our secret. You're the only man I trust to assist me."

The last comment was like an axe to his resolve.

Well, the lady said she wanted an adventure. It wasn't quite what he had in mind. But had he not played the game to explore the possibility of them marrying?

"Then I shall stress my earlier point." The angel on his shoulder prodded him, warning of how hard he might fall, how the pain of rejection might cause lasting damage. The devil urged him to fill his cup and drink from the fountain of pleasure. "We must be honest with each other at all times."

"It seems like a perfect partnership," she said, not understanding that intimacy and trust were two key ingredients in a long and lasting union. "I'm not Scottish and have no desire to be a duchess."

Damnation!

He would be a hypocrite if he held his tongue.

"My grandmother hailed from Alnwick, Northumberland. I'm nae a pure Scotsman and have a wee drop of English blood."

She blinked rapidly, processing the information. "I'm sure the same might be said for us all. Was she welcomed into the family?"

"My great-grandfather opposed the marriage." Though the old devil had warmed to the idea eventually.

"Because she was English?"

"Aye."

"There we are then. That should be enough to deter you from playing the honourable card." Miss Ware clapped her hands together, keen to make the facts suit her purpose. "Besides, I'm approaching spinsterhood and would make a terrible bride, let alone a duchess. And it's impossible for me to fall in love with a man."

He might have ripped her argument apart, made her see sense, explain that one did not always choose who they loved, but a knock on the door stole their attention.

"We shall continue our lessons at Lord Templeton's ball tomorrow night," she quickly said before calling, "Enter!"

It was Hastings, not Masters. The doddery fellow bowed and, in a shaky voice, asked how he might be of service.

Callan instructed the butler to pull up a chair, and they resumed their seats. "We have a few questions about the night of the wedding ball and hope a servant can identify a woman of particular interest."

Hastings' eyes narrowed. His hollow cheeks made his face look almost skeletal. "Might you have a description of the woman, Your Grace?"

"We've nought but her handkerchief."

Miss Ware took the item from her reticule and gave it to the butler. "You will see a monogram in the corner. Do you know who it belongs to?"

Hastings gaped at the bloodstains, not the fancy stitches. "Erm, no, no. I've never seen it before." He was quick to hand it back.

"Did ye see anyone sneaking about the house?" Callan said.

"Guests are always sneaking about the house, Your Grace." Hastings' gaze flicked briefly to Miss Ware. "I'm trained to turn a blind eye."

Miss Ware sat forward. "Did anyone attend the party without an invitation?" When the butler shook his head, she added firmly, "Hastings, a woman was abducted from the garden at knifepoint. We're attempting to find her and save your master the shame of being questioned by the magistrate. You will tell us what you know."

Callan smiled to himself.

Miss Ware would make an excellent duchess.

"You'll have to give me a moment to think, miss."

They sat as silent seconds passed. Miss Ware tapped her lips with a little pencil while examining her notebook. Callan's mind ran riot as he watched her, not Hastings, absorbed in every movement of her mouth. Such a passionate woman would make an excellent bride.

"Someone called at the basement door," Hastings said, jolting Callan from his musings. "A lady bearing a wedding gift."

Miss Ware made a note in her book. "You saw her face?"

"It was the lady his lordship hired to sing for them on their wedding day, at their private supper. A famed opera singer, I believe. She did not want to disturb the party and wished to leave a porcelain figurine."

"Did ye fetch Lord Kinver?" Callan said.

Hastings nodded. "Lord and Lady Kinver spent ten minutes with her in the study and invited her to stay."

"Did you see her again that night?" Miss Ware asked.

"Only once. Not wanting to intrude, she declined their kind offer, though Lady Kinver permitted the singer to use an upstairs room to see to her toilette."

Or to steal a document of some importance, perhaps.

"There was a perfectly serviceable retiring room downstairs."

"The lady wished to remain incognito, miss. Indeed, moments after the clang of the supper gong, she left via the garden."

Miss Ware locked gazes with Callan, excitement dancing wildly in her eyes before she faced the butler. "Might the lady have been Madame Delafont? Might she have worn a dark cloak?"

Hastings' head lolled forward as he thought. "Yes, it was Madame Delafont. She wore a cloak of forest green."

While Miss Ware's smile broadened, Callan pressed the butler for more information. "Did she seem sincere? Did ye suspect she had another motive for coming here?"

"She was embarrassed to have disturbed his lordship. She seemed nervous and jittery, and was quite eager to leave. I found it odd considering she performs in front of an audience."

Interesting. "How long was she here?"

"Half an hour, Your Grace."

"And do ye recall anything else that might be seen as suspicious behaviour that night?" *Other than a duke sneaking up the servants' staircase,* he added silently.

Hastings' pale cheeks flushed. "Your Grace, if I might be so bold, half the *ton* are conducting clandestine affairs. There would be too many to mention."

Callan pictured the bare-arsed Lord Forrester servicing his mistress in the dark corridor. "Did ye see anything out of the ordinary?"

"Perhaps if I mention a few names, you might tell me if they were on the guest list?" Miss Ware interjected. "Mrs Gregory. Lady Sheridan. Sir Gerald Hudspith. Major Rowlands."

Again, it took an age for Hastings to search the dark, dusty recesses of his memory. "From my recollection, all those named were in attendance. There was an argument between Major Rowlands and one of the servants, Anne. She was reprimanded for her rudeness, but Lady Kinver refused to dismiss the girl."

"Might we speak to Anne next?"

"She packed her meagre belongings and left that night, miss."

Miss Ware gasped. "What is her surname?"

"Grimes, miss. She came from the Servants' Registry on Goswell Street and had been with us for two weeks. I believe she worked in the major's household for a time."

"What was the argument about?" Suspecting the major had lecherous intentions, Callan presumed to know the answer.

"The girl refused to say. Lady Kinver said she would address the matter on her return from the Cotswolds, but Anne was gone before the cockcrow."

How odd!

Perhaps she was running from Major Rowlands.

Or was Anne the woman abducted from the garden?

"I'm inclined to believe the girl is a thief, and that was the cause of the argument." Hastings sounded somewhat annoyed with himself for hiring a criminal. "We've been unable to locate the porcelain figurine presented as a wedding gift."

Miss Ware looked at Callan and frowned. "Madame Delafont might have had another reason to call that night. Perhaps she took the figurine with her when she left."

"Aye, but the Kinvers would know it was missing," Callan grumbled. They were supposed to find clues, not add to the list of unanswered questions. He turned his attention to the butler. "Was anything else taken, money, jewels?"

"Not that we can tell."

They sat silently debating the information before Miss Ware said, "Who did you wish to question next, Your Grace?"

"Tompkins. I believe that's the name of the footman in charge of the men's retiring room that evening."

The servant entered the second Hastings left, giving Callan no time to play the lustful rake with Miss Ware.

Standing six feet tall and with handsome looks, Tompkins

probably had many a wife and widow offering to pay for his services. They asked him the same questions about Madame Delafont and Anne Grimes, though he merely corroborated Hastings' story.

"Did you hear any retiring room gossip?" Miss Ware asked.

"Nothing suitable for a lady's ears, miss." Tompkins' gaze slipped over Miss Ware's body when he thought she wasn't looking.

Get yer beady eyes off her, Callan growled silently.

"I'm not easily embarrassed," she said, though Callan had lost count of the times she had blushed in his company.

Tompkins looked at Callan. "Perhaps I might tell His Grace."

She huffed impatiently. "For heaven's sake, Tompkins, I'm aware of what goes on in dark corridors. Did you notice a gentleman in a hat sneaking off to meet a lady in the garden?"

He shook his head. "All hats are left in the cloakroom."

Perhaps the mystery gentleman entered via the mews.

"Did you see a lady wearing a dark cloak?"

"Only the opera singer, but I'm told she was crying upstairs."

As eager as a hound for blood, Miss Ware scribbled that snippet of information in her book. "Do you know why?"

"No, but some say she keeps company with Lord Sheridan, and he was keeping company with Mrs Gregory that night."

They needed to speak to the opera singer as a matter of urgency. Establish the real reason she had come to the Kinver residence.

"Ye caught Sheridan in a compromising position?" Callan asked.

"He was in the men's retiring room while the perfumer

stocked the soaps and cologne. The assistant was supposed to deliver the items earlier that day, but he was sick, and Mr Valmary had to bring them himself."

This titbit left Miss Ware struggling to sit still. "Why would his lordship discuss personal matters with a perfumer?"

"They're related, miss. Second cousins, I think."

Chapter Seven

"If I write to my sister to mention the theft and the missing maid, she will return from the Cotswolds posthaste." Devon's frustration was evident as he paced the pavement outside the Kinvers' impressive townhouse. "After all she's suffered, I'll not ruin her honeymoon."

Lillian had no desire to spoil Lady Kinver's plans, either. "In all probability, we will have solved the case by the time the letter arrives. And if Anne stole the figurine, she will have sold it and likely left town."

Unless Anne Grimes was the woman abducted from the garden, and someone else stole the figurine and thought to blame the maid. But how could she afford such an expensive handkerchief?

"We'll question the opera singer after we've visited the perfumer," Dounreay said, sounding like an enquiry agent, not a devilish duke skilled in seduction. "Major Rowlands will be at the Templeton ball tomorrow night. We'll ask him why he argued with Anne."

"That reminds me, I received a note from Roxburgh while you were conducting the interviews." Devon reached into his coat pocket and withdrew the missive. He handed it to Dounreay. "He demands you visit him in Hanover Square within the hour."

Hell's bells!

Lillian's heart thundered faster than the muscled beasts on Rotten Row. "What does he want?" Oh, her brother would ruin everything.

Panic flared. No one had seen them kiss in Lord MacTavish's dark drawing room. No one had seen Dounreay enter the bedchamber via the secret staircase.

The duke studied the note. "Daventry called to tell him we witnessed an abduction and that he's asked for our assistance in the case."

"What?" Lillian gulped past the large lump in her throat. "Why on earth would he do that? Now my brother will insist on accompanying us during our investigation." Or he would refuse to let her leave the house, let alone question suspects.

Worse still, there would be no time for secret kisses. She would never know what it felt like to lose herself in Dounreay's arms. And that proved more troubling than it should have.

Dounreay's full lips curled into a confident smile. "Roxburgh will want certain assurances, that is all."

"What sort of assurances?" Lillian snapped, but knew exactly what her brother would demand. He'd wanted her to marry the duke five years ago. Feeling like a rabbit in a snare, she said, "I am almost five and twenty, past the age of majority, and will not be held to ransom."

Dounreay pushed the note into his pocket and cupped her elbow gently. "Come. Valmary's is a stone's throw from Hanover Square. Let us call there and continue our enquiries."

Lillian looked at him, half impressed, half annoyed. He

was so calm in a crisis. Did he not care to kiss her again? Was he not the least bit concerned this could mark the end of their research?

Before she could tidy her thoughts into neat little boxes, she was trundling along in Devon Masters' carriage with Dounreay squashed beside her.

No one spoke during the mile journey.

Devon held Mina's hand, a sensual energy radiating from the besotted couple, which only made Lillian acutely aware of the hot-blooded Scot whose thigh touched hers.

"We need to concoct a story," she whispered to Dounreay once they'd alighted outside Valmary's. Thankfully, the Masters had decided to wait in the carriage. "We must decide what to say to my brother."

"Dinnae fret. I shall deal with Roxburgh."

"How?"

"By offering the assurances he requires. Although we'll need to proceed with care if we're to continue our research."

Relief came like a lifesaving burst of oxygen in her crushed chest. Thank heavens! He did want to kiss her again. So much so, he would pretend to offer marriage if caught.

They might have continued the conversation, but Mr Valmary yanked open the shop door and ushered customers out like a shepherd did lazy sheep from a pen.

"We're closing for the day," the perfumer said in a flustered yet eloquent English accent. "We will be open as usual tomorrow."

The cloying smell of heavy perfume wafted into the air as women groaned and complained and tried to place their orders from the doorstep.

"But I need Queen Violette for my pomander."

A young woman waved frantically. "I need a bottle of

White Rose. My mistress will have my guts for garters if I return home empty-handed."

"Come back tomorrow. Good day."

Dounreay grasped Lillian's hand. He pushed through the group and wedged his booted foot between the door and the jamb. "I must speak to the owner as a matter of urgency."

Clearly, he did not know that the handsome olive-skinned gentleman was Mr Valmary. The perfumer's swathe of sable hair had just a light peppering of grey, but ladies came in droves when they knew Mr Valmary was serving behind the counter.

"I am Valmary, Your Grace!" Mr Valmary's dark eyes widened as the crowd grew more volatile. "Please, I must shut the door before there's a stampede."

A frown marred Dounreay's brow. "Have we met?"

Ladies started pushing and jabbing Lillian in the back, trying to barge their way into the exclusive perfumery.

"I was here first," one moaned.

"I beg to differ," another replied. "You were behind me in the queue."

Mr Valmary told them all to be quiet or he would ban them from his shop permanently. He turned to Dounreay and lowered his voice. "I assure you, regardless of what that devil said, it was not my doing."

Dounreay drew on his aristocratic breeding to take command of the situation. "Ye'll let me inside so we can discuss this matter, or there will be the devil to pay."

"Then hurry."

Dounreay wrapped his arm around Lillian's waist and hauled her into the shop when Mr Valmary opened the door. There was a mad scramble to close it quickly and keep the horde of irate patrons at bay.

"That beggar Baudelaire closed his shop this morning,"

Mr Valmary panted, tugging the cuffs of his coat sleeves and ignoring the women knocking on the window. "We've been unable to cope with the demand."

Dounreay wasn't interested in the perfumer's problems. He towered over the fellow. "How do ye know me? And what wasnae yer doing? The incident in Ludgate Hill?"

"The magistrate visited Baudelaire's. I was told Lord MacTavish suffered some sort of poisoning after smelling the samples. A constable came to warn of a potential problem with supplies." He gestured to the extravagant display of glass and porcelain bottles. "I will have to destroy half my stock unless we can locate the contaminated batch."

"That doesnae answer my questions," Dounreay growled, looking nothing short of magnificent in his temper.

Despite being confident and charismatic, Mr Valmary struggled under the weight of the duke's stare. "I—I supplied the perfume for the ladies' retiring room at the ball Lord MacTavish held in your honour. Lady MacTavish shops here. Your name is on many ladies' lips."

"And ye think I'm here because Baudelaire blamed ye for the poisoning?"

It was a logical assumption.

The perfumers were clearly in competition.

"The Frenchman is fit for Bedlam. It won't surprise me if he is poisoning his own clientele. He means to blame me and have me shut down. Means to see his profits soar so he can settle his mounting debts."

"Do you have any basis for your accusations?" Lillian asked, wondering why his rival would remove a popular perfume from sale if he cared about money.

Mr Valmary glanced at the two men packing away perfume bottles, then lowered his voice. "Someone took ill here two weeks ago. A customer suffered a seizure after smelling the samples. Baudelaire has threatened to put me out of business for years. He had to be responsible. Now he'll think I acted out of vengeance."

Lillian suspected both were guilty of spreading mistruths. This was not a case of vengeance, but of bitter rivals scrambling to get the upper hand.

"Where do ye manufacture the perfume?" Dounreay said.

"In our distillery at St Saviour's Docks in Bermondsey."

"At the docks?" Dounreay cast her a sidelong glance. "Does anyone named O'Malley work there?"

Was this a vital clue that connected both cases or a mere coincidence? Importers of exotic plants and oils would want a warehouse close to the Thames.

Mr Valmary drew his brows together in thought. "Not that I'm aware, but Mr Barbour is in charge and employs many men to assist in the process." A sudden realisation had the man gasping. "You think Baudelaire paid someone to poison my perfumes?"

"'Tis possible." Dounreay gave a casual shrug. "But we will leave the enquiries to the magistrate. I come merely to ensure nae one else suffers as MacTavish has."

A crash behind them had the assistants shuffling back and covering their mouths and noses with their arms.

Glaring at the shards of broken glass, Mr Valmary muttered a curse. "Do you mean to kill us all? Baudelaire would like to see me flailing on the floor and frothing at the mouth."

The duke flinched and recoiled. He gripped Lillian's arm, pulling her back two feet or more. "We've nae more questions. Let's pray the matter is resolved soon."

"Let's hope they send that blackguard Baudelaire back to France." Mr Valmary brushed a lock of sable hair from his brow, his gaze softening as he perused her figure. "Give

MacTavish my best. I would send a gift for his wife, but Lord knows, I wouldn't want to make matters worse."

Dounreay did not linger or offer a reply, but quickly ushered her out onto Old Bond Street as if they were escaping the Great Fire. He must have been holding his breath. So desperate to fill his lungs that he sucked in a mouthful of London's noxious air.

Just like she couldn't think about lifeless bodies pulled from the Thames, doubtless he did not want to consider the effects of poison.

Instead, she turned the conversation to something less personal. "I presume you didn't want Mr Valmary to know we are investigating the incident."

"There's a turncoat in every camp. The assistant was too busy studying us, hence why he dropped the bottle." He met her gaze, fear rippling in those dark pools. "I'll nae place ye in danger."

Lillian waited for him to look at her mouth. He did not. Evidently, the last comment was not part of the script.

Devon lowered the carriage window and reminded the duke he had an appointment with Roxburgh in Hanover Square.

Lillian was still trying to understand why Mr Daventry had persuaded them to act as enquiry agents, only to ruin everything by telling her brother.

"I'll take my own carriage." Dounreay pointed to the elegant equipage parked behind Devon Masters' vehicle.

"What will you say to him?" Disappointment sat like a heavy weight in her chest. She had assumed they would ride together.

How had it come to this? How had a woman who avoided intimacy become emotionally entangled with this man?

"I'll tell Roxburgh the truth," Dounreay said, sending

panic slicing through her as he handed her into Devon's carriage. "Protecting ye will always be my priority."

And then he closed the door, abandoning her to her friends.

Lillian pressed her nose to the window and watched him stride towards his conveyance. There were two ways he could protect her. Offer marriage or leave London and agree never to see her again.

Both options proved frightening.

Whenever he left for Scotland, she threw herself into a new project. Her love of Ancient Egypt stemmed from a desire to banish Dounreay from her mind. That was before they'd shared a heated kiss in Lady MacTavish's drawing room. Lord knows what she would do now!

"Will you take me home, Mina?" An unwelcome emotion tightened her throat. "I can walk if not."

Mina came to sit beside her. "Of course we will take you home."

"Perhaps it's best to let Roxburgh and Dounreay thrash the matter out privately," Devon cautioned.

"I'll not have them make decisions about my life while I'm absent." She sounded annoyed, though she was scared, scared she might feel pain when she wanted to feel numb, feel nothing.

The journey to Hanover Square took forever.

She met Dounreay on her brother's doorstep. "Wait!"

He made no comment and merely knocked on the door.

"I—I'll not let my brother force you to marry me."

His eyes flashed with steely determination. "Miss Ware, I'd rather die than marry a woman who doesnae want me. Rest assured, we'll nae walk down the aisle or have our hands joined over the anvil."

"Oh!" Her stomach twisted into knots. "That is a relief."

"I told ye I would handle the matter." His tone lacked his earlier avidity. "It will have nae bearing on our plans."

Greyson opened the door, his bushy brows rising in surprise to find her waiting like a visitor on the doorstep. Alexander's shrill cries echoed through the house, making her wince.

Dounreay appeared unaffected by the din. He thrust his card at the butler. "I'm here to see Lord Roxburgh."

Panic flashed in Greyson's eyes. With some reluctance, he stepped aside and welcomed the duke into the hall. "Please wait here a moment, Your Grace."

Lillian heard Adam and Eliza trying to placate the child. "I shall see if everything is all right."

She meant for the duke to wait in the hall, but he followed her to the family's private sitting room overlooking the garden.

Adam was in his shirtsleeves, pacing back and forth, cradling a wailing Alexander in his arms. The poor mite's cheeks were red, and he dribbled spittle on her brother's fine waistcoat.

"I'll not give him morphine or those terrible teething powders," Eliza said, rubbing her tired eyes.

Adam rocked the child. "I'm not suggesting we do. And though Mrs Abbott advises brandy on the gums, I fear it's just a method to help adults sleep."

Greyson hovered on the threshold and cleared his throat. "His Grace, The Duke of Dounreay, my lord."

"Damnation."

Lillian edged past the butler before her brother made a scathing comment about the duke. "We heard Alexander's cries and wish to offer our assistance."

Seeing Dounreay, Adam merely huffed. "Welcome, Your

Grace. As you may have surmised, we will have to postpone our planned meeting for a few hours."

Dounreay stepped into the room and bowed when Eliza curtsied. "With all due respect, we had nae such plans. Ye summoned me as if I were an errand boy."

Rather than appear annoyed, Adam seemed impressed by the duke's retort. "I was informed you're playing the role of enquiry agent not errand boy. That you've dragged my sister into this sorry mess. Though allow me to express my sincere regret over MacTavish's sudden illness."

"Angus isn't ill. Some beggar poisoned him."

It was hard to converse over Alexander's cries. Eliza took the child and rocked him back and forth to settle him.

"I can see an argument is the last thing ye need." Dounreay crossed the room and slipped his finger into the babe's clenched fist. "Let me make this easier. Nothing will prevent me from discovering who hurt MacTavish. Nothing will prevent me from striving to keep Miss Ware safe."

"By placing her in compromising positions?" Adam countered.

"Do ye honestly think she willnae try to solve this case without me? Ye know her character better than anyone. She's in mortal danger if she attempts to deal with the matter alone."

Lillian should object, but the duke had a point.

"And if she finds herself ruined?" Adam goaded amid the babe's piercing wails. "What then?"

"Ruined is preferable to dead."

Adam inhaled sharply. "Then let me be frank. Do you agree to marry her if she finds herself in an unfortunate predicament?"

Merciful Mary!

Lillian was about to throw her hands up in protest, but

Dounreay said, "I'll nae marry a woman who doesnae love me. And Miss Ware has nae desire to marry or live in the Highlands. It would be impossible for me to live anywhere else." The duke surprised everyone when he changed the subject and said to Eliza, "Might I take the bairn?"

Eliza stood dumbstruck.

Yet the kind gesture had heat coiling low in Lillian's belly.

Dounreay shrugged out of his coat and handed it to her. The warm garment carried his potent male scent, coupled with a hint of bergamot. It took every effort not to bury her nose in the material, hug it tightly and sigh.

He grabbed the plaid blanket off the chair and took Alexander into his muscular arms. "Have nae fear," he said in his soft Scottish burr. "I'm taking the bairn outside."

They watched him open the terrace doors and slip out into the garden. He held Alexander against his shoulder, the blanket draped around the boy like he was a child of the Highlands. Heir to a clan.

Lillian found herself drawn to the double doors where she merely watched Dounreay, her palm pressed to the glass pane, as he held the child up so the breeze cooled his cheeks. He broke into a Scottish ballad, a gentle tune that might lull the fraught babe to sleep.

For some inexplicable reason, tears welled.

Her chest grew tight, her limbs heavy.

The intense inner ache became unbearable.

What sort of witchcraft was this?

Sensing a presence behind her, she turned to see Adam standing at her shoulder, equally mesmerised by the unfolding scene.

"I've always liked Dounreay," he said almost to himself.

She had always liked Dounreay, too. Hence why she had fought the attraction with every fibre of her being.

"He's more dangerous than I imagined," she admitted aloud for the first time. "He makes me feel things, emotions I would rather keep buried."

"Emotions relating to Mother?"

"To Mother, to Mr Bloom, to all those who pretended to have an affection for me which proved false. To those who abandoned me when I needed them most."

"I'm sorry if you count me amongst those who neglected you, Lillian. But I struggled for a time too. Know I care for you deeply, as did Mother." Adam's hand came to rest on her shoulder, strong, reassuring. "And regardless of what you thought you felt at the time, you did not love Mr Bloom."

"No, but his attention filled the hole for a while."

"Nothing fills the hole left by Mother's passing. But love helps you navigate the void. Love helps the blood flood the heart's chambers, urging you to live again."

Though reluctant to tear her gaze from Dounreay, she faced her brother. "You suffered terribly and survived. Perhaps there is hope for me."

"Of course there's hope for you." He brushed a strand of hair from her cheek and kissed her forehead. "You should have told me about the abduction, about the investigation, about Dounreay's involvement."

"I know." For the first time in forever, she had felt excited, useful, desired. "I don't want to disappoint you. I don't want to lose your respect. I don't want to lose you, Adam, yet I fear rebelliousness is in my blood."

He smiled, though his watery brown eyes reflected something of their shared pain. "You could never lose my love or respect, Lillian. Tell me, tell me what you need. Tell me how I can help you. I shall do anything you ask."

He couldn't help her. This was something she needed to work through on her own. "I need you to trust me. To give me the freedom to deal with my problems." The insecurities she had never worked through. "You know I need never marry. My inheritance will support me well into my dotage. And though I shall do my utmost to avoid the gossipmongers' nets, I must learn to listen to my heart, Adam."

His gaze moved to the garden, to where his son slept in Dounreay's arms. "Then I ask one thing of you."

"Yes?"

"Live, Lillian! With every breath in your lungs, live."

Chapter Eight

The Templeton Ball
South Audley Street

Today's investigations had reaped little to no reward. Mrs Gregory was out of town. Madame Delafont was not at the theatre preparing for tonight's performance of Rossini's *La Cenerentola*, nor was she at her rented house in Long Acre.

Either might be the lady abducted from the garden.

Still, the day hadn't been a complete waste.

Callan loved every minute he spent in Miss Ware's company. Since asking him to arouse her for research purposes, he had caught her staring at his mouth and assessing his physique. A twinkle of fascination now sparkled in eyes as blue as a cerulean sky, eyes that used to reflect a cold, grey indifference.

Leaning back against the ballroom wall, he brought the champagne flute to his lips, his gaze searching the crowd before settling on the woman who plagued his thoughts. He watched Miss Ware converse with Viscount Denton, jealousy weaving through him like a malevolent spirit.

The first strains of a waltz cut through the hum of conversation. Being a man of his word, Callan had not marked his name on her dance card. Still, possessive words filled his head. Words he hoped to communicate through thought alone.

Dinnae dance with him!

Ye're mine!

Mine is the only mouth ye'll feel on yer luscious lips!

The lady's ears pricked upon hearing the music, though she did not need to narrow her eyes and scan the room. Her gaze met his instantly, hitting him like a bolt from the heavens, stealing his breath.

God, the lass stirred his blood like no one else.

Sporting a grin, he raised his glass in salute when he wanted to march across the dance floor, haul her into his arms and plunder her smart mouth.

But Callan spotted Major Rowlands leaving through the terrace doors and remembered he had business to settle before seeing to his pleasure.

He had waited five years to kiss Miss Ware.

He could wait another five minutes to kiss her again.

He found the major at the bottom of the stone staircase, puffing on a cheroot, barely a wisp of smoke leaving his mouth and hitting the crisp night air.

Callan cleared his throat and joined the man who, beneath the unflattering signs of age and gluttony, had a youthful glint in his eye.

"Rowlands, I've need of yer counsel. Might ye satisfy a curiosity?" Callan didn't wait for an answer and proceeded to lie. "My housekeeper interviewed a woman this morning for the position of maid. She claims she worked in yer household and left of her own accord, but couldnae provide a reference."

Being a stickler for respecting rank, the major nodded. "Tell me her name, Your Grace, and I shall attempt to confirm her claim." Suspicion danced behind his affable countenance.

If the major needed a name, perhaps he was a tyrant who chased servants away by the dozen. Maybe he summoned them with the mere click of his fingers.

"Anne Grimes."

The major's left eye twitched.

Was Anne missing?

Had this devil taken her?

"I know ye argued with her at Lord Kinver's ball." Callan gazed at the stars to avoid appearing accusatory, but found himself praying it stayed dry so he might lure Miss Ware into the garden. "Kinver gave her an excellent reference, yet I suspect she's trouble."

Major Rowlands' snort sent a puff of smoke into the air. "If you want a sentimental, opinionated harpy in your household, by all means, employ her. My advice is send her on her way."

"Sentimental? Did she become too *attached*?" It was a covert way of asking if Anne Grimes had been more than the major's maid. "I find it odd she left Kinver's house once he married."

The major's vigorous wave said Callan had misunderstood the situation. "No. No. Anne was my late wife's maid. She accosted me at the Kinver ball and accused me of betraying my wife's memory."

"Because ye didnae observe a sufficient mourning period?" Mrs Rowlands' obituary appeared in the broadsheets less than a month ago, and the major was already courting his mistress.

"Because she caught me with Mrs Jarvis in the study." The major's salacious grin turned Callan's stomach. "The wretched girl stood there like a wraith in the darkness, her gaze fixed on my bare buttocks, watching every damn thrust. It was terribly unnerving, terribly unnerving."

Callan feigned amusement. Yet the comment roused a bitter memory, one that brought bile to his throat. That of a father—who should have been grieving—driving long and deep into a woman sprawled naked on his desk. Not just any woman. The friend of his dead wife.

It was perhaps the reason for Callan's constancy.

For his patience in securing the only woman he wanted.

Why he had to know if Miss Ware felt this abiding attraction, too.

Why he looked to MacTavish as a father figure.

The accusations he'd wanted to scream as he watched his father rutting and grunting like a pig—ones he'd anchored so deep in his chest Poseidon couldn't reach them—suddenly burst to the surface.

Ye killed her!

Ye poisoned her!

Dinnae deny it!

The major's loud tut dragged Callan from his reverie. "Then the crazed lune grabbed books from the shelf and hurled them at me." He took a long draw of his smoke. "Accused me of killing my wife with my wickedness. Damn cheek of the gal. Damn cheek. In my day, she'd have been whipped with a birch."

Anne Grimes rose a notch in Callan's estimation.

He assessed the former military man. Might the major be the villain in the garden that night? Had he sought to silence the maid for good?

No. The major lacked the strength to breathe, let alone

kill his former maid. And surely the stable boy would have recognised Anne.

"I'll nae have a mischief-maker in my house," Callan said, drawing the conversation to a swift conclusion, for he needed to distance himself from this degenerate.

"One might make an exception were she pleasing on the eye," the major grumbled. "Besides, I'm told she stole something belonging to my wife, though found no evidence of a crime."

Interesting.

Kinver's butler spoke of Anne's light fingers, too.

Callan inclined his head while imagining throttling the major with his bare hands. "I thank ye for discussing personal matters. I shall leave ye to finish yer smoke."

Callan was about to mount the steps to the upper terrace to seek Lord Sheridan, but unwelcome visions of his father had him turning on his heel and striding away into the garden.

When the nightmares came, he walked the castle grounds, wandered over hill and glen. Breathing clean air had a way of dispelling the ghosts, yet he couldn't fill his lungs when in London.

Miss Ware made the visits bearable. And while his mother loved the metropolis, Callan always felt restless in town.

Bitter memories came and went as he marched past the topiary hedges and paced the gloomy path farthest from the house. It was colder out tonight, hence why the gardens were practically deserted. Once guests were merry on champagne, there would be movement in the shadows, every secret nook and cranny occupied by lustful libertines.

"Is something wrong, Your Grace?" Miss Ware said from somewhere in the darkness. "Are you unwell?"

Callan closed his eyes against the sultry voice, a siren

song that called to him in his dreams. The lady was not safe with him. While in this devil of a mood, he might succumb to every temptation.

"Ye shouldnae be out here, Miss Ware." He refused to look at her, couldn't trust himself to behave. "I shall come to the supper room in ten minutes."

A gentleman would escort her safely inside.

Yet they could not be seen strolling alone together.

Still, he'd rather suffer the consequences than place her at risk.

But then Lord Roxburgh's deep voice penetrated the gloom. "Lillian saw Major Rowlands return to the ballroom and was worried when you did not. The major said you disappeared into the garden, looking somewhat agitated."

The peer had no real interest in Callan's welfare and merely wished to prevent his sister's name from appearing in tomorrow's *Scandal Sheet*.

Callan faced the lord. "I needed a moment alone."

Roxburgh stood with his wife and Miss Ware, his suspicious gaze moving to the small topiary maze tucked away at the bottom of the garden. "Are we interrupting something?"

Hell! Did he think Callan had arranged an assignation?

Being a woman who studied scoundrels, Miss Ware understood her brother's implicit meaning. "We're sorry to have troubled you, Your Grace. Please, go about your business." Her voice broke on the last word, but she regained her composure.

"Rowlands said something to remind me why I hated my father," he reluctantly confessed. "I didnae wish to burden ye, Miss Ware. I came here for nae reason other than to walk and get some air."

Her posture remained rigid. "You don't need to explain."

She didn't believe him.

On most women, jealousy was an ugly mask that distorted their delicate features. On Miss Ware, the change held him spellbound.

Trust was an issue for her, but he quickly reminded her of his fealty. "We made a blood oath. Shall I explain why ye should have faith in my word?"

She swallowed. "That won't be necessary."

God, she looked so beautiful tonight. Her exquisite blue gown made her eyes sparkle brighter than the stars. The gold trim drew his gaze to the sweeping neckline that showed the soft swell of her breasts to perfection.

His cock hardened as he imagined kissing her there, taking a rosy nipple into his mouth, his tongue circling the peak. "Then let me tell ye what I learned from Major Rowlands. We can find somewhere private to discuss the case and examine the evidence." Examine the depths of each other's mouths.

Roxburgh glanced at the maze. "Wait here a moment."

He marched past Callan and entered the labyrinth. Miss Ware stared at the entrance through pensive eyes, as if fearing he might be swallowed by the blackness, never to return.

"I trust Alexander is sleeping tonight," Callan said, keen to fill the awkward silence.

Lady Roxburgh smiled. "I took him out into the garden for half an hour. The cool air seems to settle him. Indeed, it's a relief to spend a few precious hours alone with my husband."

"Perhaps the bairn has a Scot's temperament."

They spoke about Scotland's rugged landscape, the mere mention of seeing the morning mist creeping over Loch Awe rousing a deep need to return home.

"Ye're welcome to visit me in the Highlands." He glanced at Miss Ware, picturing her paddling her bare feet in the brook and gazing up at him from a bed of heather. "It will do the children good to roam wild and free."

Not just the children.

He longed to see Miss Ware's hair blowing loosely in the breeze.

Roxburgh reappeared. "The maze is empty. You have ten minutes to discuss the case. We'll remain at the entrance and ensure no one passes."

Shock had Callan's heart pounding in his chest.

Surely Roxburgh knew they planned to do more than talk.

Still, one did not look a gift horse in the mouth.

"Would ye care to stroll through the maze, Miss Ware?" He offered his arm. Tried not to look at her like she was a sumptuous dish he longed to devour.

A smile tugged at her lips. "I would be delighted to walk with you, Your Grace."

They met at the entrance, her dainty hand slipping through his arm as he led her into the darkness. The topiary walls were eight feet high, shielding them from anyone strolling about the garden, keen to snoop and tell tales.

They rounded the first bend, moving deeper into the labyrinth, the redolence of the boxwood filling his nostrils, a sensual undercurrent flowing between them.

Neither spoke.

Words weren't needed.

Miss Ware's fingers caressed his bicep, measuring the size and firmness, a gentle exploration that had every muscle clenching. Their rapid breathing said they longed to do something forbidden.

A few more turns led them to a dead end. They stopped abruptly, neither moving or attempting to retrace their steps.

Callan faced her, an uncontrollable lust coursing through his veins.

The pale moonlight touched her delicate face, bathing her in a silvery glow, drawing him closer. "Shall I tell ye what I learnt from Major Rowlands?" He stared at her mouth, at her heaving breasts, his cock already thick and pulsing in his trousers.

"Tell me later."

Clasping her arms, he forced her back against the foliage. "Shall we use the time to conduct research for yer book?"

Miss Ware was panting. "Yes."

"Which role shall I play?"

She gripped his coat lapel. "I don't care. Just kiss me, Dounreay."

Hellfire! In his current state, he'd not stop until he was balls deep inside her. "It willnae be tame like the last time," he warned.

"Good. I want more than a chaste kiss."

He pressed his finger to her lips, revelling in their softness. "Ye cannae make a sound. We cannae risk yer brother charging in here."

"Talking is the farthest thing from my mind." She looked up at him, her expectant eyes bright, her parted lips revealing the erotic nature of her thoughts.

Callan brushed imagined hair from her cheek, angled his head, and slowly closed his mouth over hers.

Lillian!

The spark was instantaneous, igniting a fire in his body that ravaged his restraint. She tasted of everything he loved. Earthy like a spring promise. Hot like the summer sun. Wet like the autumn air. Sweet like winter wine.

She was the woman he wanted for all seasons. The woman who'd turned a respectable duke into a randy rakehell.

Now she had to decide if she wanted him, too, because he would settle for nothing less than everything.

Aye, she wanted him.

Her fingers crept up his coat to toy with the hair at his nape, a sign he might press his advances and plunder her senseless.

Callan teased the seam of her plump lips, seeking entrance, coaxing them apart. Their tongues touched for the first time, one tentative taste before their passion exploded.

The kiss turned as wild as the Highland weather. So intense she shivered in his arms, whimpered into his mouth. She thrust her tongue over his with maddening urgency, their lips locked firmly as she probed deeper—drugging him.

Desire shot through him in fast, furious waves.

He was losing control.

He gripped her soft buttocks, crushing her to his body, pressing his erection into her belly, grinding against her to ease the infernal ache.

Gasping, he broke contact. "We should stop before I hike up yer skirts and touch ye intimately."

She looked up at him, eyes glazed, just as lost in the moment. "Don't stop yet. I want you to touch me. I was wrong. You're every bit a scoundrel when you kiss me, Dounreay."

Time was against them.

Roxburgh could stride into the maze at any moment.

He claimed her again, the kiss deep and passionate, his tongue mating with hers like he had not seen her for nine years, let alone nine months.

An internal war raged as he decided whether to touch her. But the temptress' hand slid to his abdomen, to the hard ridge bulging in his trousers, to stroke his solid length.

They both inhaled sharply.

Before he knew what he was about, his hands were coasting up her satin thighs to cup her bare buttocks.

"Oh, God!" she moaned.

He moved his hand, slipping his fingers along the soft folds of her sex, touching her, pleasuring her in a way he'd never thought possible.

"Ye're so wet, love."

"Is that a good thing?"

"Aye." He stroked the little bud, teasing in gentle circles.

She gripped his coat for balance. "Don't stop. I need you. I need more."

"I ken what ye need, but cannae give it to ye here. Nae with yer brother lingering in the darkness."

Her eyelids fluttered. "Where then? When?"

He daren't push his fingers inside her, though the thought of pumping hard into her wetness almost made him spill in his trousers.

"Tonight. We'll see if we can find an opportunity when we visit Madame Delafont at the theatre."

A loud cough rent the air.

They jumped apart, scanning the darkness.

There was no sign of her brother.

"We must leave before Roxburgh forces ye to marry me." It would be no hardship. He would never tire of bedding her. After such a thrilling encounter, Callan considered holding his hands high and confessing his sins.

She was still straightening her skirts as they navigated the narrow walkways. He was still trying to regulate his breathing and temper lust's flames. God, he was ramrod stiff and wouldn't sleep a wink tonight.

Before they rounded the last bend, she whispered, "Your Grace?"

"Aye." He stopped and faced her.

"I wouldn't want any other tutor but you."

His heart lurched. He'd asked for one thing in exchange for helping her with her research. The one thing she had denied him all these years. Honesty.

He smiled. "And ye're the only woman I'd agree to teach, Miss Ware."

Chapter Nine

Covent Garden Theatre
Bow Street

"We'll wait here for you," Adam said from the dim confines of his carriage. "You're to keep to the shadows. Under no circumstances are you to venture into the main auditorium."

Hearing every word, Lillian nodded. Yet her mind and body were in the verdant boxwood maze, reliving the moment Dounreay's tongue danced with hers. How he'd touched her so intimately she thought she might die from the pleasure.

No wonder ladies lost their heads.

Kissing Dounreay was beyond divine.

"Keep the hood of your cloak raised," Eliza warned. "You're bound to encounter a rakehell or two in the corridors. They'll likely be sotted. Let them think you're an actress or Dounreay's mistress."

The last role had immense appeal.

A groan left Adam's lips. "Perhaps we should come with you."

"Dounreay will protect me." It was time Adam got used to hearing gossip about his wayward sister. A woman determined to *live* would feature regularly in the *Scandal Sheet*. Still, she had to be somewhat mindful of her reputation for her family's sake. "Do you have the letter?"

Adam reached into his coat pocket and handed her the letter Mr Daventry had procured from Viscount Melbourne. The peer served as Prime Minister and Home Secretary and had given written consent for Mr Daventry's agents to investigate the poisoning of a Scotsman on English soil.

Adam withdrew his watch and observed the time beneath the lamplight. "It's almost eleven. The performance will end soon. Best get inside before the audience emerges."

As if he had read her brother's mind, Dounreay appeared from his vehicle and entered the alley off Bow Street. As arranged, he waited for her in the gloomy passageway. A masterful figure in the darkness.

It was Lillian's cue to join him. "I shall be thirty minutes at most unless Madame Delafont is disobliging." She raised the hood of her blue travelling cloak and climbed down from the carriage.

Scanning left and right, she hurried into the alley.

The thrill of this dangerous encounter had her pulse galloping faster than a Derby winner. Or did it stem from being in Dounreay's presence so soon after they had kissed and touched each other intimately.

He seemed unaffected.

"Do ye have the letter?" he said, his shoulders tense, his voice devoid of the sensual undertone that melted her insides.

She gave him Lord Melbourne's letter, which he read

briefly before taking her hand and leading further along the grimy passage.

"Is everything all right?" He seemed preoccupied. Did he regret kissing her so deeply, touching her so scandalously?

He sighed. "I shall feel better once ye're safely inside."

"Oh, you're worried someone might see me?"

"What else?"

"You might wish you'd not kissed me tonight."

He cast her a sidelong glance, the familiar glint returning to eyes as warm as a winter fire. "I like kissing ye. I thought I had made that clear."

"Good. Because I like kissing you." She hid a smile. Satisfied in the knowledge she would feel his mouth on hers again soon.

Dounreay stopped at a paint-chipped door and hammered hard with his clenched fist. The stench of urine and other unpleasant smells hung in the air, invading her nostrils, making her want to retch.

A minute or two later—after the third attempt to rouse someone's attention—the door flew open, and a thin, bespectacled man glared at them.

"You'll find the main entrance on Bow Street."

"We want to see Madame Delafont." Dounreay handed over the letter before the man could curse and slam the door in their faces. "We're here on official business. We come on behalf of the Crown."

Dounreay did not present his card or give his name.

The fellow read the letter and observed the official seal stamp.

"If ye'd rather, we can enter the auditorium and have a constable remove Madame Delafont from the stage. We would hate to have a reason to send the singer back to France."

As if pricked with a pin, the attendant jumped to attention. He thrust the letter back at Dounreay, stepped aside, and beckoned them over the threshold.

"Follow me. You can wait in Madame Delafont's room until the curtain falls. Mr Warren won't want you wandering about, ruining the performance."

He led them down the dim candlelit corridor while those watching the performance of Rossini's *La Cenerentola* had the privilege of gaslight.

The fellow opened the dressing room door and made them wait while he lit the lamps. "Don't go rummaging around. Madame Delafont don't like people touching her things."

Upon entering, one got an instant picture of Madame Delafont's life. Pretty hothouse flowers filled four vases, some wilting, some freshly cut this morning. Yet the heavy scent of perfume obliterated nature's sweet bouquet.

"We're here on the King's business," Dounreay reminded the attendant. "Ensure Madame Delafont meets us in this room, or we'll arrest ye for hindering an investigation."

Lillian waited until the man closed the door behind him, then wandered about the room, searching for clues. The best one would be the opera singer's reaction when she found them snooping about in her private domain.

Madame Delafont shared Lillian's trait of tidiness. Clothes were stored neatly away in the armoire. All hats were in boxes and organised by size. Hair pins lived in a china pot in a drawer of perfectly folded ribbons. Did the opera singer suffer from the same inner turmoil? Were her outward habits a means of maintaining control of a life gone awry?

"Your Grace," Lillian whispered, noting the orderly row of perfume bottles on the dressing table. "I see a bottle of For Lily and a bottle of May Bell perfume. You might want to compare fragrances."

But the duke did not have perfume on his mind.

Dounreay crossed the room, his hot hand resting on her waist as he pulled her around to face him. "Call me Callan or Dounreay. I think we've passed the need for formalities. We should take advantage of this time alone to continue our research."

"To finish what we started in the maze?"

"Nae finish exactly, but a means to help ease the ache."

"Then you should kiss me."

They didn't wait a second longer. Their lips met, crashing together as if compelled by a magnetic force. Their need was so tangible it crackled in the air, sparked as quick as wildfire.

The kiss was passionate, all tangling tongues and frantic touches, the rampant mating of mouths.

Oh, this man could tempt a woman to wickedness.

Heat spread through her body. She went limp in his arms, though she could feel the solid length of his manhood pressing against her abdomen.

He moaned into her mouth, made her weak-kneed and wet between her thighs. Her sex clenched—a persistent pumping playing havoc with her control. All she could think of was hiking up her skirts and spreading her legs wide to accommodate him.

A rugged Highlander lived beneath his fine title and expensive tailoring, one who would make love to her outdoors amongst the heather if she begged. And she was so close to begging him to fill the emptiness, to make her forget the pain of heartbreak.

Indeed, he pushed her arousal to new heights when he kissed her neck, sucked her earlobe and whispered, "I mean to give ye what ye need. Say now if ye've had a change of heart."

A sensual moan escaped her. "What will you do?"

"Pleasure ye."

She had heard the term and knew he meant to slip his fingers between her legs and massage her until she shuddered and cried his name. "Here? Madame Delafont will be back momentarily."

"We've time if ye're willing."

He waited for her to nod before pulling away suddenly, leaving her feeling cold and exposed. Dragging a red velvet chair to the door, he wedged the top rail under the doorknob and checked no one could enter.

Dounreay held his hand out to her. "Hurry."

She went to him without reservation. Lust roused an almost irresistible compulsion to sin. Yet she could not imagine feeling the same way with any other man.

She might have examined that thought and picked it apart, but Dounreay guided her into the chair and dropped to his knees. Time was of the essence, but when he raised her skirts and hooked her legs over his broad shoulders, a host of questions tumbled from her lips.

"What do you mean to do? Should we not stand?" Then she might not feel so vulnerable because he was moistening his lips, gazing hungrily at the place no man had ever looked upon before. "Good heavens. Are you going to put your—"

His mouth settled on her sex.

The quickening of her blood had her closing her eyes against an instant wave of pleasure. The slow licks over her soft flesh were an exquisite form of torture.

"God, ye taste so good, Lillian," he whispered in a velvet-edged voice. "Ye'll be my entrée, my main course, my dessert. Ye'll be my sustenance every day of the week."

Her mind whirled from his use of her given name. Like a wanton, her hips rose to meet the gentle flicks of his tongue. Yet she would never forget the possessive way he gripped her bare thighs. The way he devoured her as if she were a gourmet supper.

"Dounreay!" She thrust her hands into his hair, her cries mingling with the distant sound of the soprano delivering the last lines of the libretto. The steady rhythm of the duke's skilled tongue lured her closer to the edge of something just as extraordinary. "Oh, it feels so good." He was so good. So mesmerising and masterful.

He pulled away, his tongue skimming his lips. "I've imagined watching ye come so many damn times."

Then he pushed two fingers inside her and started pumping slowly, his thumb stroking her tight bud in the same tantalising tempo, shattering her world.

She wanted to join in with the thunderous applause reverberating above them, to celebrate his skill, plead for an encore.

"Dounreay!" She arched her back, her climax tearing through her. The spectacular shudders left her panting, moaning. She reached for him, grabbing his cravat, kissing him, tasting her own arousal on his tongue and lips.

The need to feel his full weight crushing down on top of her might have made her lose her head, but she heard a woman's raised voice echoing along the corridor.

"You let them wait in my private room?" The lady muttered something foul in French. "I shall speak to Mr Warren about this."

Dounreay stood abruptly, brushing Lillian's skirts, straightening his cravat and repositioning the iron rod in his trousers before quietly moving the chair from the door.

Lillian's legs shook. She felt sated to her bones. So connected to the man who stood watching her intently, it was like they were joined by an invisible thread.

Dounreay's smile turned sinful as his thumb grazed his

bottom lip. "Make nae mistake. Ye drive me wild, Miss Ware. I mean to relive this memory long after we've parted tonight."

She would store the memory in a secret place, in the only box bearing a man's name—Dounreay. When the loneliness became unbearable, she would dare to peer inside, savour every second.

Until now, she had not considered what this meant to him. How he might get lost in playing roles, might forget the rules of the game. Indeed, she feared every moment spent with Dounreay felt far too real.

There was no time to consider it further. The door burst open, and Madame Delafont swept into the room, her stern expression softening upon recognising the duke.

"Oh, Your Grace. Good evening." Madame Delafont's green gaze journeyed over Dounreay's fine physique before she curtsied. "Pike led me to believe you were a constable from the new Metropolitan Police Force."

The singer's gold silk gown contrasted perfectly with her silky black locks. In her thick cloak, Lillian felt like the poor relation. Jealousy might have reared its ugly head. But when the lady moved to place her gloves in the drawer, Dounreay's beguiling eyes skimmed every inch of *her* body, not the opera singer's.

Lord have mercy!

Heaviness pooled low again—the stirrings of a need she couldn't shake despite recently finding her release.

"We're here to ask you a few questions about the night you visited the Kinver residence," Lillian said, her voice shaky.

Madame Delafont turned sharply, as if surprised to find someone else in the room. "Forgive my rudeness. I did not give you the opportunity to introduce yourself."

The lady made it her business to know all prominent men, but as she scanned Lillian's face, she stared blankly.

"We're acting on behalf of Lucius Daventry and the new Police Force," Dounreay interjected, preventing Lillian from revealing her name. "As ye may have heard, Lord MacTavish took ill after inhaling perfume at Baudelaire's in Ludgate Hill. The Home Secretary wants the matter dealt with swiftly."

Madame Delafont gave an indolent shrug. "What has it to do with me and my visit to Lord and Lady Kinver?"

Lillian moved to the dressing table. "Your name was on a list of patrons who bought Baudelaire's lily of the valley perfume. We were making enquiries there when Lord MacTavish took ill."

"How dreadful. But it is a popular fragrance, *non*?"

"A woman was abducted from Lord Kinver's garden while the guests ate supper." Dounreay pulled the blood-stained handkerchief from his pocket. "She dropped this." He brought it to his nose and inhaled. "It bears yer perfume, and witnesses place ye at the scene at the time of the abduction."

The opera singer's eyes widened when she noted the dried blood. "It could be anyone's perfume. Had I witnessed a crime, I would have reported it to the authorities."

"We need to know why you were there," Lillian began, "and if you had a tussle with a gentleman in the garden. Be advised, this is a police matter, and we expect your assistance."

The Frenchwoman's long lashes fluttered like insect wings against her porcelain cheeks. "I—I called to present them with a wedding gift, a figurine. Theirs, it is a true love story, and I wished to offer a small gesture of support."

"And yet no one can locate the figurine."

Madame Delafont frowned. "It was in the study when I left."

"Ye went upstairs," Dounreay said in an accusatory tone.

"I did not think it appropriate to use the ladies' retiring room."

"Yet, in truth, ye were looking for Lord Sheridan."

"You found him in Mrs Gregory's arms," Lillian added, coming to the logical conclusion based on the footman's testimony. "Perhaps you were unaware the lord keeps more than one mistress."

The lady's resolve faltered. Tears sprang to her eyes. She gripped the arm of the chair and fell into the velvet seat. "I—I heard him in the corridor, spouting the same nonsense, making the same promises he made to me. Telling Mrs Gregory she had won his heart."

"You thought he loved you?" Lillian had lost count of those duped into believing a man's false protestations.

Looking like a shadow of her earlier self, Madame Delafont's sigh was almost painful. "Sometimes, it is hard to know if a man's heart is false." She gestured to the duke as if he were a walking monument to deceitful males.

He is different, Lillian wanted to shout from the rooftops.

And yet Dounreay knew how to play roles. He knew what to say to gain the advantage. Indeed, the desire to stop the games and get to know the real man pushed to the fore.

"Even with all my experience, I made a mistake." Madame Delafont dabbed tears from her eyes. "But yes, you are right. I went to deliver the gift so I might confirm my suspicions about Lord Sheridan."

"Did ye see Lady Sheridan?" Dounreay folded his arms across his broad chest in an obvious sign of contempt. "She also wears lily of the valley perfume. Did Sheridan encourage ye to make the purchase to throw his wife off the scent? Pardon the pun."

Madame Delafont jerked, for she must have felt a sharp jab to her conscience. "Lady Sheridan has a string of lovers. And I did not purchase the perfume. Monsieur Baudelaire, he likes to give me gifts."

Lillian glanced back at the perfume bottles. "Does Mr Valmary do the same? You have his May Bell fragrance. Most ladies have a preference, whereas you seem to favour both."

Madame Delafont gave a mocking snort. "Mr Valmary, he thinks he is London's greatest lothario. He heard I wore Baudelaire's scent and insisted his was superior."

"The men are in fierce competition." Lillian had witnessed the venom in Mr Valmary's gaze whenever he mentioned his rival. "Both want theirs to be known as the ultimate fragrance."

Madame Delafont's bitter laugh proved unnerving. "You think this is about perfume? How naive of you to suppose they would fight over something so trivial."

Lillian's cheeks flushed hot.

She scoured her mind, searching for another explanation, finding one when she recalled the licentious glint in Mr Valmary's gaze.

"The men compete for women," Lillian said.

Madame Delafont clapped her hands as if praising a child. "Bravo! Like skilled card sharps, they keep score and look for ways to undermine their opponent. Mr Valmary is handsome, but Monsieur Baudelaire possesses a charisma only found in Frenchmen. They serve in their perfumeries when in need of a new victim. A new muse to squabble over and inspire new scents."

Then what Mr Valmary said might be true. His rival might

contaminate the perfumes out of spite to place the blame elsewhere.

"Are their victims aware of their games?" Lillian said.

Madame Delafont shrugged. "That, I cannot say. Matters only become complicated if one develops an obsession. I would not like to think what would happen if the men ever fell in love."

It all sounded ridiculous, so implausible, but jealousy had caused many a war. Jealousy had brought down empires.

A thought sprang to mind.

If Lord Sheridan was related to Mr Valmary, perhaps he played the game, too. If both perfumers fought for Madame Delafont's affections, had Lord Sheridan swept in to claim the prize?

It would explain why the lord had moved to pastures new. Why he would discuss his conquests in the retiring room with Mr Valmary.

"Did ye leave the Kinver residence via the garden?" Dounreay asked, returning to the facts.

He could be quite commanding when the need arose. Oftentimes, Lillian forgot he was a duke. She had begun to see Callan Maclean as a virile man. One who rarely left her thoughts. One whose hands she imagined caressing every inch of her needy body.

"I planned to leave via the mews," Madame Delafont said, coughing a little. She moved to pour a glass of sherry from the crystal decanter on her dressing table, wincing as she drank, as if she'd swallowed nails, not fortified wine. "But I saw Lady Sheridan in the garden, no doubt off to meet a lover, and so I left through the servants' door in the basement."

Lady Sheridan?

Might she be their mystery abductee?

Lillian exchanged glances with Dounreay, his brown eyes flashing cool with intrigue, not burning hot and hypnotic like they had fifteen minutes earlier.

"Can anyone verify yer account?" Dounreay said.

"The maid. The one arguing with that lecherous fool Major Rowlands. Though she was so distraught, I doubt she will remember me."

Dounreay frowned. "Lecherous?"

"The beast had his hands all over her."

A frustrated sigh left the duke's lips. "That damn reprobate." He brought the interview to an abrupt end. "We'll leave ye to rest. It's late, and we've nae more questions at present."

Looking somewhat relieved the interrogation was over, Madame Delafont escorted them to the door and dropped into a deep curtsey. "Your Grace." She faced Lillian, her rouged lips curling into a coy smile. "If you're to gallivant about town with an unmarried gentleman, Miss Ware, you really do need a better disguise."

Lillian's heart missed a beat, but she had chosen her fate and had to deal with the consequences. "I risk nothing in coming here, madame. Should you spread gossip, few would trust your word. I bid you good night." She cast a confident smile before joining Dounreay in the corridor.

"Damn the devil to Hades," Dounreay cursed, taking hold of Lillian's elbow and escorting her along the dim passage.

"What? Are you annoyed she recognised me?" They could not hide forever. Soon, MacTavish's poisoning would become common knowledge, and most people would know they were working on a case for Mr Daventry.

"Now I'll have to interview the major, and I'll likely throttle the scoundrel this time."

"You despise men who abuse their position?"

"I despise men who remind me of my father," he snapped.

Like her, he rarely spoke about personal matters. That said, she had never dared to delve deeper. Family secrets were best left buried.

"I'd always assumed you were close." She presumed to know the duke's motivations when she did not really know him at all.

Was he a sad child? A sick child? A lonely child?

It suddenly seemed important.

"Let's just say Satan granted me a boon when he took the rogue. I imagine my father is warming himself in the fiery pits of hell."

They burst out of the exit and into the rancid alley. Still, the duke sucked in a deep breath like he would rather suffer anything than his suffocating memories.

Lamplight—a distant glow in the darkness—drew her gaze to the street and her brother's waiting carriage. Heaven knows when she would find herself alone with Dounreay again.

"Before we part this evening, there is something we should discuss." She shivered at the memory of his hot mouth and wicked fingers bringing her to completion.

Dounreay faced her, the shadows making his expression unreadable. "Does it relate to our experiment?" His voice turned low and husky. "Do ye want to talk about how I made ye come, Lillian?"

They should discuss the fact Madame Delafont had no cuts or bruises, nothing that would tie her to the bloodstained handkerchief. Yet there was only one topic on Lillian's mind.

"You play the seducer extremely well."

"Ye play the beguiling temptress with equal skill."

"And in doing so, I fear we are making a mistake."

He stepped closer, wrapping his arm around her waist, crushing her against his hard chest. "It didnae look like a mistake when yer eyes glazed with desire. It didnae sound like a mistake when ye panted my name and moaned in pleasure. It didnae feel like a mistake when ye hugged my thrusting fingers and came apart."

Her pulse raced.

Her blood burned so hot she should send for a doctor.

"Do ye want to end our arrangement, Lillian? If ye want me to return to the Highlands, just say the word. I shall take MacTavish home and let Daventry deal with the crime."

A hollowness opened in her chest.

An emptiness she felt whenever he departed.

She should tell him to leave. She should stop leading him along a merry path to Nowhere. But lust was the devil's daughter, a selfish, greedy minx determined to have her own way.

"I don't want you to go," she admitted, hoping the truth would somehow draw her back to the light. Did she not owe him that much? "Though I think we should stop the pretence. We should attempt to know each other properly. To determine what exists between us."

Fear closed around her heart like a dark storm cloud.

Such a venture would lead to an ultimatum.

In all likelihood, she would have to let him go.

But what if—

Either way, an unbearable pain hovered on the horizon.

"Madame Delafont thought she knew Lord Sheridan," Lillian said, attempting to sound less desperate. "Getting to know you would be an educational experience that would help with my book."

Dounreay captured her chin gently between his long fingers. "If ye want to know me better, Lillian, visit me at home tomorrow night. I'll send the servants away. We'll dine together, discuss personal matters. But be warned. Ye'll spend the evening with a Highlander, nae a duke."

She pictured them sitting before a blazing fire, sipping brandy, talking until the early hours. "My brother will never allow it."

"I'll speak to him, make him understand this is our last chance to explore our connection." He released her, his tone taking a determined lilt. "When I leave for Scotland this time, I'll nae return to London for a few years."

"A few years?" It sounded like a lifetime.

A prolonged agony.

Sadness hung in the air between them.

A sadness she could not bear to contemplate.

"If I'm to dine with a Highlander, I shall have to wear my warm velvet dress," she teased.

Dounreay chuckled, his accent turning as thick as his thighs. "Dinnae worry yer pretty head. I'll have the fires blazing so hot we'll have nae need for clothes."

Chapter Ten

Hart Street, Covent Garden
Office of the Order

The request to attend the Order's office read like a summons. Being a man of high rank, Callan might have sent a curt reply with the penny boy, but Lucius Daventry would be a duke if his parents had married. And the man's tireless work helping the poor and needy made him someone to be admired, not belittled.

Therefore, Callan arrived in Hart Street promptly at ten, the friendly housekeeper showing him into the elegant drawing room.

He was glad of the distraction. Whenever his mind stilled, he recalled being on his knees, gripping Miss Ware's creamy white thighs, sucking her sex, pleasuring her senseless.

He moistened his lips at the memory.

Hell, he was desperate to taste her again.

Every muscle in his abdomen hardened in response. Like

a feral horse, his body's needs trampled over his logic. A man might sacrifice his sanity just to have her once, yet Callan feared he had already gone too far.

Yet it wasn't far enough.

He wouldn't stop until he was buried deep inside her. Until she was his. Or until he was left alone and broken. Lost in the depths of despair.

As if his mind had the power to conjure the woman who dominated his thoughts, Miss Ware entered the drawing room, stopping abruptly upon seeing him sitting on the sofa.

"Your Grace. I thought we had agreed to meet at noon."

He stood and bowed, grateful he'd worn trousers as it was easier to disguise a cockstand. "Daventry requested an update on our progress. Had I known we'd both been summoned, we might have made the journey together."

"I came with Mr Sloane. He had matters to attend to in the study." She struggled to hold his gaze and kept straightening her blue pelisse when it needed no adjustments.

Was it embarrassment or nerves?

He could not tell.

After surrendering to her desires, did she have regrets? Would she offer an excuse to cancel their dinner arrangements tonight? "Is Sloane to accompany us when we question Mrs Gregory and Lord Sheridan?"

Did she want a chaperone?

Worry lines appeared on her brow. "No. He has an appointment at the British Museum. Something about a fake artefact."

Callan might have probed her about the artefact, but he cared to know what troubled her this morning.

He moved closer, giving her every opportunity to retreat, but she remained rooted to the spot. Reaching for her, he cupped her elbow when he wanted to claim her mouth in a searing kiss.

"Then tell me what has ye so vexed." He spoke softly, keen to tease a confession. "Does it have anything to do with what occurred between us last night? Do ye have regrets?"

Had she suffered a sleepless night too?

Had she touched herself, tortured herself, wondering where this would all end?

The brief flash of tenderness in her eyes held him entranced. "Your Grace, I regret nothing that happened between us."

He did not sag in relief. Though they'd shared a passionate kiss in the alley last night, today, she seemed less receptive. "But ye dinnae wish to pursue the matter any further? If ye would prefer to maintain a professional relationship, be honest."

"Quite the contrary. I'm keen to dine with you tonight." She glanced back at the door before lowering her voice. "It's just that I received a parcel from Mr Valmary this morning, though I did not give him my name or my address."

"A parcel? Nae perfume?" A wave of panic swept through him, almost knocking him off his feet. "Good God! Ye didnae inhale the scent?"

She shook her head. "It was a delicate porcelain bottle of May Bell, with a card inviting me to a select gathering at the shop to celebrate the new blend of lily of the valley."

Callan's fears subsided. "Doubtless he invited Lady MacTavish. And based on our connection, thought to include ye." Yet Valmary had scanned Miss Ware's figure as one did a tray of treats in a confectioner's window.

The licentious toad!

"Yes, I would have thought it a gesture to gain more custom had it not been for Madame Delafont's revelation."

Callan firmed his jaw. "Then I'll visit him today and ensure he has a genuine reason for issuing the invitation." Mr Valmary would learn not to lay claim on a Highlander's woman.

Miss Ware shook her head. "I'm sure it's nothing, and I feel more at ease having voiced my concerns to you. Besides, we have a lot to do today if we're to *dine* together later."

She said *dine* like it was a euphemism for something sinful.

He raised her hand to his lips and pressed a lingering kiss on her knuckles. "Based on recent events, we might do more than dine."

A blush stained her cheeks. "I find it impossible to control myself when I'm with you, Dounreay."

"And until recently, I've had a monk's restraint."

Daventry chose that ill-timed moment to march into the room, forcing Callan to drop Miss Ware's hand quickly.

"Ah, good! You're both here." Daventry gestured to the plush sofas. "Sorry I'm late. I had pressing business at the museum and promised to ride with my wife in the park this morning."

"A man must keep his vow," Miss Ware said, flashing Callan a teasing grin.

"Indeed, Miss Ware." Daventry glanced at Callan's trousers. "After the mystic's prediction, you must be glad Dounreay is not wearing a kilt."

Miss Ware coughed, spluttered, plagued by a sudden fit. Her cheeks turned raspberry red as she fought to catch her breath.

"Cough it up, Miss Ware." Daventry patted her gently on the back. "Shock often causes a tickle in one's throat."

Feeling like an imbecile who'd missed the joke, Callan

asked, "Why, what did the mystic predict? And what has it to do with my kilt?"

"N-nothing!" Miss Ware croaked, waving frantically in a fight to regain her composure. "Everyone knows fortune tellers spout nonsense."

"According to the seer, Miss Ware is to marry a man who bears his knees in public," Daventry blurted. "Now, unless she has designs on the chimney sweep touting his business on Long Acre, the most obvious guess is she will marry a Scotsman."

Miss Ware glared at Daventry as if wanting to stuff her reticule into his traitorous mouth. "It's all poppycock."

"Aye. Miss Ware has nae intention of ever marrying," Callan said. Though if he believed that, he would be six hundred miles away by now, meeting with his steward. He bit back a grin. "She hates the Highlands and admits to having a weak constitution."

Miss Ware jerked in response, rebellion gathering in her eyes. "I have a hardy constitution. I just don't like the cold or the bitter winds. And I refuse to eat food fit for dogs."

"Dogs! The blind cheek," he jested. "Anyone who understands the difficulties of life in remote regions, understands the need to utilise every available commodity. Ye're used to the finer things in life and would invariably struggle."

Her cheeks ballooned at his effrontery. "I assure you, I could adapt easily if I so desired. Oftentimes, I dislike the weather in London, yet brave it without thought or complaint."

Callan laughed. "Maybe I should put ye to the test, Miss Ware. See how easily ye adapt in cold climates. How well ye cope in trying times."

Her eyes gleamed with self-assurance. "Given every incentive, I'm confident I would pass the test, Your Grace."

"We shall see." The lady craved adventure. He had the perfect place in mind, though it would be better if they could remain in the woods overnight, frolic beneath the stars.

The mantel clock chimed the half-hour, reminding Daventry time was of the essence. He gestured for them to sit. "How did you fare with Madame Delafont last night?"

Callan explained all they had learnt from the opera singer. "The perfumers compete for lovers and sales."

"That explains the use of poison in the perfume. It is often the weapon of a spurned lover." Daventry flicked through the papers in his leather portfolio and studied one briefly. "They found a small amount of *Strychnos nux-vomica* in the Queen of the Orient sample bottle. Not enough to kill a man but enough to bring on a seizure if sniffed excessively."

"It can be deadly, then?" Callan dreaded telling Ailsa. She had forced MacTavish to sniff the fragrances, shoving the bottles beneath his nose. The news would leave her distraught.

"In the right quantities and with frequent exposure. I had London's best chemists inspect the bottles."

"So we need to prove someone added the poison to the bottle, find out who and why," Miss Ware said, as if the tasks were as simple as choosing ribbons from a box.

Daventry nodded. "The person would need to know how to mix the solution. It might be the proprietor or an assistant."

"Or a spurned lover who has done her research and had access to the perfumes in Monsieur Baudelaire's shop."

"Precisely, Miss Ware. Visit the premises in Bermondsey, the place Valmary uses as a distillery to manufacture his perfumes, and question the manager. And find out where Baudelaire produces his products."

"We mean to visit Monsieur Baudelaire this afternoon." Miss Ware removed the notebook from her reticule and scanned the first page. "Lord Sheridan could be involved. He considers himself quite the Casanova."

"Question him. Show him the letter from Melbourne and explain you're investigating the poisoning of your friend MacTavish."

"We planned to do that today," Callan said, yet his upcoming dinner with Miss Ware would be his main focus.

"I had a man investigate all dockworkers named O'Malley. None are capable of masterminding an abduction in Mayfair. We need to identify the woman in the garden and learn what was in the letter she gave to her attacker."

"We'll speak to Mrs Gregory, but the initials on the handkerchief might prove misleading." Callan doubted the accuracy of the stable boy's account. He might have found the handkerchief elsewhere and saw an opportunity to gain a sovereign.

"Agreed."

Miss Ware spoke up. "What about Anne Grimes, sir?"

"There's no record of her returning to the registry in Goswell Street. With hundreds of such establishments across town, it will be impossible to find her. Apparently, she has a sister in Cheapside. I'll post a boy outside the house."

"I suppose I could question the major again." Callan silently groaned. The last thing he wanted to do was to speak to that reprobate.

"See what information you uncover today. As soon as I have an agent free, I'll have them take charge of the case. I'm sure you're desperate to return to Scotland, Your Grace."

He was desperate to return home, but not alone.

"I'll nae leave until I've discovered who hurt MacTavish." It wasn't like Angus had foolishly picked the wrong berries. That said, an argument with Callan's father had led to his mother's mental lapse in the woods.

"Angus and Lorna MacTavish are like family," Miss Ware said, the warmth in her tone touching. "Like His Grace, I wish to see the person punished and mean to work until we catch the culprit."

Yes, because she had a duchess' determination.

"Very well. Keep me abreast of all new developments."

"With the Masters away, am I to have another chaperone, sir?"

Daventry glanced at Callan. "That depends, Miss Ware. Do you care about your reputation? Do you speak from the heart when you say you will never marry? Are you able to ride the storm if your name appears in the *Scandal Sheet*? You're a grown woman and can decide yourself."

"I don't care about myself," she said stoically. "But I don't want my actions to reflect badly on the duke or my brother's family."

Callan was touched.

No woman had ever cared about his reputation.

Daventry was quick to offer a solution. "I understand your concerns, but a man with Dounreay's looks and standing won't have a problem attracting the belle of the Season. Besides, you'll be fine visiting Bermondsey. When dealing with the *ton*, you will take Denton and Miss MacTavish. The lady could do with the company, and both can be trusted."

Denton? Bloody Denton!

Callan silently seethed.

The viscount's angelic good looks would make any woman swoon. And his sister was good friends with Miss Ware.

Before Callan could protest, Lucius Daventry stood. "Visit Bermondsey first. I will arrange for Denton and Miss MacTavish to meet you at Baudelaire's perfumery at two o'clock this afternoon. The magistrate closed the shop, but you'll find the Frenchman there, attempting to salvage his stock."

Then he bid them good day and left the room.

Miss Ware released a weary sigh. "I'm beginning to wonder if the pressure of managing so many agents is affecting Mr Daventry's logic. Yes, Lord Denton and Ailsa are friends, but he hates that she speaks her mind. They're often at loggerheads over their conflicting opinions."

"She's a Scot. He should know a fire blazes just beneath the surface." Ailsa had Lorna's kind heart, but she would not tolerate fools.

"Still, I should not have mentioned chaperones."

"For Ailsa's sake or yer own?"

"Both. I would rather we spent time alone." Her eyes held his, the energy in the room sparking a twinge of lust in his loins.

In the brief silence, he imagined them kissing rampantly, touching each other until every part of their bodies tingled with pleasure. He was pushing inside her as she clung to him, as she let down her barriers and welcomed him home.

Callan gulped.

The need to make his desire a reality ended with a throbbing erection pressing hard against the placket of his trousers.

"We'll be alone tonight," he said, despite his discomfort. "I told Roxburgh we would dine at six, and ye'd be home by ten." Although the lord did not know they would be entirely alone. "I doubt we'll have time to accomplish all our tasks today."

Miss Ware jumped to her feet. "Then let us be away to Bermondsey. If we're quick, we might visit Mrs Gregory after our two o'clock appointment at Baudelaire's."

Callan stood, wishing he could say to hell with it all, and just ask Miss Ware how she felt about him. Lorna MacTavish described her as being deeply sad beneath the bravado. Miss Ware certainly kept her feelings buried, and so he would need to dig deeper to understand her reluctance to marry.

After witnessing his father's blatant disregard for his marriage vows, Callan should be the one avoiding wedlock. But he was a duke. A man with responsibilities. Marriage was inevitable.

He'd rather marry the woman consuming his thoughts.

The woman he wanted to kiss until breathless.

The woman he could not forget.

St Saviour's Docks
Bermondsey

They crossed the Thames via London Bridge, the river teaming with ships bringing grain, coal and other commodities to the capital, the skyline obscured with lofty masts and plumes of billowing black smoke. Schooners, wherries and barges navigated the crowded thoroughfare, the river meandering around them like a slippery serpent.

The scene made Callan long for the rugged Highland mountains, to breathe deeply and fill his lungs with clean air. A struggle made worse when they entered Mr Valmary's warehouse on Mill Street, and a host of pungent smells invaded his nostrils.

Miss Ware sneezed, the concoction of rose and jasmine, musk and ambergris irritating her airways, too. "Good heavens! I'm inclined to agree with Ailsa. What I wouldn't give for a sprig of fresh heather."

Then come home with me.

Let me lay ye down on a bed of fragrant flowers.

Make love to ye. Give ye no cause to leave.

"The men must be accustomed to the smell," he said. None wore masks as they stirred large vats of liquid and operated the vast copper vessels used to extract oils via distillation.

Miss Ware chuckled. "I imagine a philandering husband would enjoy working here. His wife could not accuse him of smelling of another woman's perfume."

An unwanted memory burst into Callan's mind.

Ye smell like a whore!

Who is she, Douglas?

Ye've had her in our bed!

As a young boy, he had not understood what it meant. It was his mother's tears and bloodshot eyes that had scarred his heart.

"What is it?" came Miss Ware's insightful response. "Did I say something out of turn? You look like you've seen a ghost."

"Nae," was the only word he could muster.

Thankfully, Mr Barbour appeared, the middle-aged fellow looking flustered and unsure of how he should deal with a duke.

"Sir! Your Grace! Welcome!" The man bowed numerous times. "Let me escort you to my office, and you may tell me how I might be of service."

Callan introduced Miss Ware, then placed his hand on her back and guided her through the warehouse to the sparsely furnished room.

Mr Barbour scooped the pile of paper on the desk into the

top drawer and offered them a seat and refreshment. "I'm afraid we've tea and little else, though I have a flask of brandy in the cupboard." He shivered. "It comes in handy on cold winter nights. When the brisk winds blow in from the river."

Not wanting to consume anything on the premises, Callan declined on their behalf. He went on to explain the nature of their visit.

"Mr Valmary said someone took ill after inhaling his perfume. He feels Monsieur Baudelaire may have deliberately sabotaged his own stock to shift the blame. How easy would it be to contaminate one batch, for example?"

The man brushed a wisp of hair over his shiny pate. "Nigh on impossible. You've seen how many men work here. They're supervised at all times. If someone added a contaminant during the process, we would all know. And it would affect more than one bottle. Besides, we've men employed just to smell the fragrances and assess the quality. That said, I cannot vouch for Baudelaire's operation."

"But you can confirm there was an incident in Mr Valmary's shop?" Miss Ware said. "A customer took ill and had a seizure."

The man was quick to shift the blame. "Yes, but I assure you, that bottle did not come from this warehouse."

"But you cannot be certain, sir."

"I would stake my life on it, Miss Ware."

"How do you explain the accident?" she said.

"Someone planted the contaminated bottle to hurt Mr Valmary's business. That person must work for Monsieur Baudelaire."

"Or a woman they'd squabbled over and seduced sought to exact her revenge." Callan fixed the manager with a hard stare. "Ye do know they compete for more than sales?"

Barbour's cheeks flamed. "I know the Frenchman likes to prove charisma is more important than handsome looks. Baudelaire treats it like a game."

"Do ye know of anyone who would seek to damage either gentleman's reputation? Anyone out for revenge?"

Barbour shrugged. "Doubtless, many women wish to hurt him. I'm told Baudelaire tires of his conquests quickly. After gifting a lady a bottle of perfume, he always sends a note to Mr Valmary by way of a challenge. Baudelaire uses his For Lily scent like a pawn in chess. It signals his first move on the board."

Miss Ware inhaled sharply, evidently thinking about the special gift she received from Valmary this morning.

"Where does Baudelaire manufacture his perfume?" With the men being bitter rivals, Callan guessed it wasn't far away.

"Follow the road past the tannery. He owns a distillery near the old Bermondsey Spa. Some say he steals into the spa at night and steals the wildflowers from the garden. Maybe he picked toxic plants and used them to poison one of Mr Valmary's bottles."

Coldness shivered through Callan like the chill of death.

Amongst nature, one could find the resources to heal and maim. He had watched someone he loved perish on a peaceful woodland walk. Their investigations served to bring every terrible memory bobbing to the surface.

He stood abruptly. "We'll trouble ye nae further. I shall leave my direction in case ye think of anything important." Callan removed a crisp card from his case and handed it to Barbour. "Before we go, do ye have anyone working here by the name of O'Malley?"

He wasn't sure why he'd asked. What did perfume on a handkerchief have to do with MacTavish sniffing a contaminated scent? Still, they needed to know if the woman abducted from the garden was alive. A few bloodstains were hardly proof of murder.

Mr Barbour scratched his head. "No. There's an O'Donnell."

"Never mind."

They bid the man good day and left the warehouse.

Callan escorted Miss Ware to his carriage and instructed Dewart to follow the road past the tannery. "We should inspect Baudelaire's premises while we're here. I'll meet ye there."

Miss Ware frowned. "You're walking?"

"I need air." It was a foolish thing to say amid the pungent smells wafting from the Thames and the tanneries. "I need a moment alone to gather my thoughts." He needed to walk until the memories waned.

"Does it have something to do with what Mr Barbour said?" Miss Ware touched his upper arm gently, empathy swimming in her vibrant blue eyes. "Did it remind you of how your mother died?"

His throat closed like he'd ingested poison. He coughed to loosen the muscles. "Bad memories are like an army of sleeping assassins. One prod and they wake to attack with lethal force."

From a woman who rarely showed emotion, he expected words of encouragement, for her to tease him and drag him from his stupor. He did not expect her to slip her arms around his waist, to lay her head against his chest and hug him tightly.

No words were needed.

He closed his eyes, drew comfort from the warmth of her body, and lost count of how long he stood there, holding her close, struggling in the shadows of his pain.

Chapter Eleven

Lillian sat in Dounreay's carriage as they journeyed to Ludgate Hill for their appointment with Monsieur Baudelaire.

The Frenchman's warehouse had resembled Mr Valmary's premises, the air plagued by similar smells, the staff equally diligent. The manager, Mr Gibbons, blamed Mr Valmary for almost killing Lord MacTavish, assuring them no one could tamper with the perfumes without his knowledge. He knew an O'Connor but not an O'Malley.

She had walked to the deserted Bermondsey Spa with Dounreay, suggested climbing over the gate and scouring the gardens for the source of the poison.

He'd refused, his face turning ghostly pale at the suggestion.

Gripping her arm, he had pulled her away from the iron railings, quick to remind her the poison was likely imported from the Far East, and they had no business trespassing.

And yet, amid the silence inside his conveyance, Lillian was not busy analysing the evidence. The odd sensations flowing through her body dominated her thoughts. More than an hour had passed since she'd held Dounreay and comforted him, but her heart still pounded. The fire in her chest still burned.

Lillian glanced at him covertly. He kept his gaze fixed on the window, those dark, hypnotic eyes staring at a place far beyond the horizon, and she had to fight the urge to hug him all over again.

Something had shifted between them as they embraced on the roadside. Lillian could not explain it in words, but feared it was more potent than Dounreay's passionate kisses.

Her lustful cravings always subsided.

This strange ache had not.

Perhaps it was pity.

Yes, it was pity, she quickly decided.

She lived with pain, with constant reminders of what she had lost, with questions and doubts. Wasn't it normal to feel an affinity with the duke?

"I think we should postpone our meal tonight," he said suddenly, his tone as distant as his gaze. "As soon as we've caught the poisoner, I plan to leave for Scotland."

The words hit like a hard blow to the stomach, winding her momentarily, almost bringing her to her knees. "All the more reason we should cherish every second. 'Tis only a meal, Your Grace." It was more than a meal. They could not sate their hunger with venison and sautéed potatoes. Without him, she doubted she would ever feel replenished again.

Panic had her blood surging through her veins.

Life was easier when she tried to ignore him.

"We're walking a dangerous line, Lillian."

Relief calmed her pulse. "Oh, you're worried we will succumb to our base desires. Is that not the point of the game?"

"This isnae a game," he snapped, his expression as cold

as a December frost. "Ye're fooling yerself. It was a mistake to encourage it."

A mistake?

She mentally shook herself.

What had brought about this sudden change?

"We made a blood oath. You agreed to help me. You pledged your fealty. You've made me feel things I never thought possible." He'd given her hope when the future had looked bleak, hopeless.

He scrubbed his face and sighed. "I made an oath to protect ye, and I mean to abide by my vow. Trust me, ye'll thank me in the end. 'Tis better for both of us if we remain friends."

Better for both of them? Then why had he kissed her with a lust he could barely contain?

"Friends? But what—"

"My decision is final." He spoke with a stranger's indifference, a duke's sternness. He looked anywhere but at her. "We can continue interviewing the suspects, but we should refrain from spending time alone together."

Don't do this!

Please don't do this!

She sat there in a cloud of confusion, blinking to stop the tears from forming. "You don't want me to visit you tonight? You don't want to sit with me before a roaring fire and indulge in every wicked pleasure?"

His groan revealed an inner battle, a secret torment.

Those hot, chestnut eyes said he wanted to strip her naked and devour her body inch by inch. "It's nae about what I want. It's about what's best."

The carriage stopped abruptly, and she realised they'd parked on Ludgate Hill. "What's best for whom?"

He made no reply. Keen to place some distance between

them, he opened the door and vaulted to the pavement. When he handed her down, he gripped her elbow rather than take her hand.

She was going to cry.

She never cried.

She tried to breathe against a tidal wave of emotion. Not since her mother's passing had she experienced such sadness, such indescribable grief. This was exactly what she fought to avoid. Yet it had crept up on her like a thief in the night, catching her unawares, stealing her sanity.

Why was she so upset about missing dinner?

So what if the duke didn't want to kiss her.

Was she not the one who always rallied the troops? Yet she could find nothing to celebrate in this, no glimmer of light on the horizon, no rousing words to help face her fears.

Lillian pasted a smile upon seeing Lord Denton and Ailsa standing together on the pavement outside Baudelaire's perfumery. They were arguing about something. Indeed, Ailsa's maid lingered in the background, trying not to grin as she witnessed the verbal sparring.

Lord Denton snorted. "Of course I've never gifted a lady perfume. It sends entirely the wrong message."

With sunlight catching the lord's golden hair, he looked almost angelic. Those of his acquaintance knew he had the tolerance and temper of the devil.

"And what message would that be, my lord?" Mockery clung to Ailsa's tone, which had undoubtedly helped to rile the peer.

"Use your brain, madam. Where does one put perfume?"

Ailsa shrugged. "I never wear perfume."

"Never?"

"Never. It interferes with the natural order of things."

"The natural order?" His mouth curled with obvious cynicism.

"The body's own chemistry. 'Tis an important factor in attracting a compatible mate. One shouldnae tamper with nature's plan."

"You've spent too much time at bluestocking school, Miss MacTavish." Lord Denton lowered his voice. "Besides, as a man unsuited to marriage, I wish to avoid meeting anyone deemed compatible."

Dounreay coughed into his fist to gain their attention. "Good afternoon. Are we interrupting something?"

The duke tried to sound amused, but Lillian heard echoes of sadness, the remnants of a decision she sensed he had not wanted to make.

So why had he put a sudden stop to their research?

Why did he not want her?

She was compelled to find out.

Lord Denton turned. "Perfect timing, Your Grace. Miss MacTavish is trying to convince me it's pointless to wash."

"I said nae such thing," Ailsa snapped. "I merely meant to highlight why ye always attract the same kind of woman."

"And what kind of woman is that?"

"Do I need to spell it out?"

Lord Denton huffed. "Is this what ladies do in the Highlands, Dounreay? Browbeat a man until he is forced to concede?" He glanced at Ailsa. "You should know Englishmen are stubborn, madam."

Ailsa laughed. "Yet I'll wager ye'll wear less cologne tomorrow."

Lord Denton gave an arrogant grin. "I plan to send my valet to Floris to collect three more bottles. Heaven forbid I attract someone who likes my natural aroma."

At this rate, it would be six o'clock before they finished

questioning Monsieur Baudelaire. Mr Daventry was not thinking clearly when he chose this unlikely pair to play chaperones.

"Time is of the essence," Lillian said, impatient to finish their business so she could talk to Dounreay. He stood so close their arms almost touched, though he seemed a thousand miles away. She needed to find a way to reach him, to discover why he was so eager to force a separation. "Wait inside the shop while we question Monsieur Baudelaire. And don't smell the perfumes."

Ailsa's maid returned to the carriage.

Dounreay checked the time before knocking on the shop door. Amid the flurry of activity inside, a smartly dressed gentleman approached, fiddling with the lock before welcoming them inside.

"Your Grace," he bowed to Dounreay, the silver streak in his black hair flopping over his brow. "I am Baudelaire and must offer my sincerest apology for the dreadful incident that occurred here. As you can see, we are taking the matter most seriously, taking every precaution."

Monsieur Baudelaire gestured to the empty shelves and scattering of wooden crates. For a man who might find himself ruined or imprisoned, he appeared calm and unruffled.

Dounreay introduced the viscount, and then Ailsa.

Monsieur Baudelaire bowed low over Ailsa's hand. "If there is anything I can do to ease your suffering, madame, please name it."

Sounding annoyed, Lord Denton leaned closer and whispered, "The Frenchman is so smooth, she's bound to put him in his place."

"Aye, find the devil who poisoned my father," Ailsa said

bluntly. "Words are all well and good, but I'll nae rest until the villain is punished."

"I'm glad to see I'm not the only one who riles her temper," Lord Denton muttered. "The woman has Lucifer's temperance."

Monsieur Baudelaire slapped his hand to his chest, the large ruby in his signet ring catching the light. "The injury caused is unforgivable. I shall hunt my competitor down until I prove he's the culprit."

Lillian stepped forward when prompted, but the Frenchman spoke her name before Dounreay made the introduction.

"Miss Ware." Monsieur Baudelaire gripped her hand with unnerving intensity. "*Enchantée*, madame. It is strange, *non*? A man might name his perfume after his muse only to stumble upon her years later. For Lily, it speaks of a determined yet graceful woman."

For goodness' sake!

She could see why ladies might find his compliments flattering, yet she wondered how he knew her name when she rarely visited his shop. Perhaps Mr Daventry mentioned it during the investigation.

"I am sure you had another woman in mind when you named your perfume, monsieur. And without meaning to sound rude, we have a pressing appointment this afternoon and have a long list of questions we hope you can address."

"Of course, madame."

Lord Denton took that as his cue to escort Ailsa to the blue velvet chairs near the gilt counter. She could hear the couple exchanging jibes. For some reason, they enjoyed antagonising each other.

Dounreay told Monsieur Baudelaire what they knew so far. "Valmary and his employees blame ye for the poisoning.

Yer men insist the opposite is true. We're told yer conquests are legendary. That ye and Valmary are love rivals."

The Frenchman glanced at Lillian, the glint in his grey eyes like that of a wolf sizing his supper. "We are not rivals. That would suggest we play the game on an equal footing when my success rate is legendary."

And yet Madame Delafont chose Lord Sheridan as her lover.

"That might have been the case," she said, keen to put him in his place, "before Mr Valmary let Lord Sheridan play the game. Despite your generous gifts, Madame Delafont preferred to bed a man with a title."

Monsieur Baudelaire's eyes widened. Not because he felt threatened or inferior to the peer. "You intrigue me, Miss Ware. Rarely does one meet a woman who speaks so freely. While some men might seek to trap you in a gilded cage, such a creature should be allowed the freedom to stretch her wings and soar."

Monsieur Baudelaire made her skin crawl.

He was as slimy and as slippery as an eel.

Dounreay stepped forward, his puffed chest broader than the Frenchman's, his height giving him full advantage. "Put the lady out of yer head. She's nae a pawn in a game. Rest assured, I would kill any man who sought to hurt her."

Lillian looked up at him, her heart aching with a tenderness she had never known, the sting of tears building behind her eyes.

The duke was confounding.

He would kill for her but not share a meal.

She might remind him he was leaving for Scotland, but the thought brought a profound sense of despair she refused to address.

Monsieur Baudelaire inclined his head respectfully, yet

the flicker of mischief in his eyes said Dounreay had as good as dropped the gauntlet.

"Then ask your questions, Your Grace. I shall tell you all I know." He noticed his men had stopped working and barked something to them in French.

Lillian caught the assistant's terrified gaze. Christian, the man who'd served them on the day MacTavish sniffed the contaminated perfume, looked away sharply and continued loading bottles into a crate.

She would mention it to Mr Daventry, have an agent follow the employee and see what he had to hide.

"Did ye tamper with Valmary's perfumes?" Dounreay said.

"I enjoy stealing his women, not his customers."

"But ye think he poisoned yer perfume?"

The Frenchman shrugged. "Who else had a motive?"

"Madame Delafont," Lillian said.

Monsieur Baudelaire laughed. "We let Lord Sheridan think he'd won. In truth, neither of us wanted her."

Like the sludge lining the gutter, this man turned Lillian's stomach. "More reason for the lady to plot your downfall."

"This is true, yet she has not visited the distillery. If she had visited the shop, I would know. So I do not see how she managed to poison my perfume."

"Perhaps your staff are disloyal." She didn't dare glance Christian's way. The assistant might lose more than his job if he'd betrayed Monsieur Baudelaire.

The Frenchman's cold eyes turned almost predatory. "A wise man rules with an iron fist, madame. No one other than Valmary would dare to cross me."

Dounreay folded his muscular arms across his chest. "If ye're considering making an enemy of me, know poison is nae my preferred weapon. I'll nae sneak about in the dark. I shall look deep into yer eyes when I press my blade to yer throat."

Baudelaire batted the comment away like a summer fly. "All is fair in love and war. Some of us prefer different tactics."

Lillian gripped the duke's arm and tugged gently. "I think we've learnt all we can today." She faced the profligate perfumer who possessed as much charisma as he did remorse. "Might you tell us the name of the last woman you stole from Mr Valmary?"

Monsieur Baudelaire leaned closer, the cloying scent of his cologne making her want to heave. "A gentleman would not be so impolite. I prefer to keep my conquests close to my heart, madame. A lady's secrets are safe in my hands."

His arrogance beggared belief. But she had two final questions in this hopeless battle to unnerve him. "Have you ever been in love, monsieur? Have you ever wanted a woman so badly you would forsake the game?"

The Frenchman jerked in response, a dark cloud banishing his pompous grin. Deep frown lines on his brow said he was struggling to keep a painful memory at bay.

"Once. A long time ago. Rejection, it can make a man cold and unfeeling. Distractions are like a tonic for a broken heart."

"One feels the ripples of life's traumas long after the event," she said. The same applied to everyone, regardless of why they suffered.

"Indeed." A sudden crash behind them had Monsieur Baudelaire marching over to the counter. "*Sacré bleu*, drop another bottle and I shall deduct the cost from your wages."

One could tell a lot from a man's reactions. Mr Valmary had feared poison when his assistant broke a bottle. Monsieur Baudelaire was concerned about the cost, the inconvenience.

Only the poisoner would know not to worry about contaminated perfume.

Lillian kept a firm grip on Dounreay's arm. He was in a devil of a mood and she didn't want him fighting with a suspect. And touching him brought comfort amid painful thoughts of him leaving.

"Come, let us go," she said. Ailsa and Lord Denton were arguing about an upcoming book auction. Collecting ancient tomes was the only thing the pair had in common. "Men like Monsieur Baudelaire thrive on competition. Let's hope he knows you have no romantic interest in me, else he might rise to the challenge."

Dounreay huffed in frustration. "Madam, at what point did ye decide I had nae interest? When I grasped yer bare buttocks in the maze? When ye wanted more than the stroke of my tongue in the theatre?" He lowered his voice another notch. "Or when ye came so hard, my name fell from yer lips?"

Heavens! Her temperature soared, forcing her to fan herself at the memories. Still, she was not the one who had put paid to their plans.

"Since you decided to focus on the case. Since you rejected my offer to visit you tonight. I'm not sure what made you drive a wedge between us, but I sense your anger stems from something I have said or done."

A muscle in his jaw twitched. "It isnae yer fault. 'Tis mine."

That made the matter more confusing.

Much harder to fix.

She wanted to press him for information, but he said, "What we want and what's best are two different things." He cleared his throat to get Lord Denton's attention and beckoned him over. "Take Denton and Ailsa and question Mrs

Gregory. I need to visit MacTavish and make arrangements to return home."

Then he turned on his heel and left.

Through the window, she watched him march along Ludgate Hill, his sad expression at odds with his purposeful strides. Not once did he look back. Not once did he falter.

Feelings congregated inside like a colony of penguins, all crowding together, filling every space, waiting for her to realise that every interaction with Dounreay had helped to melt the ice around her heart.

"Penguins?" Lillian glanced heavenward and sighed. "When I need the Divine's guidance, you make me think of penguins. What have penguins to do with the duke?"

"During courtship, male penguins search for the perfect pebble to give a mate," Ailsa said upon hearing Lillian's mutters. "If she accepts, he knows he has found her."

Lord Denton's snort rang with mockery. "You mean he couldn't find her just by sniffing her natural scent? You see, Miss MacTavish, it's not unknown for a species to use props to attract the opposite sex."

Ailsa batted the lord's arm. "Romantic gestures and masking one's identity are nae the same at all."

The lord grumbled under his breath. "Daventry asked us to accompany you during your visit to Mrs Gregory. I take it Dounreay is meeting us there."

Lillian's heart lurched. Tears gathered behind her eyes. "The duke won't be joining us. He has pressing business elsewhere. But we need to ensure Mrs Gregory is alive and ask her a few simple questions."

Impatient to leave, the lord consulted his pocket watch. "You've another hour of my time, Miss Ware. That's all I can spare."

Ailsa laughed. "He needs to send his valet to Floris to

purchase a crate of expensive cologne. Lord knows, he wouldnae risk a woman catching a whiff of the real man beneath that fine coat."

The lord sneered. "I can tell you what I won't be doing, *lassie.* Scouring the riverbank looking for the perfect pebble."

"I have a letter from Lord Melbourne. It should be enough for your mistress to grant me an audience." Lillian pulled the letter from her reticule and handed it to Mrs Gregory's butler. She had insisted her chaperones wait in their respective carriages, though she hadn't expected the servant to be quite so obstinate. "This is a police matter. Hopefully, I won't need to fetch a constable."

The dour-faced butler left her waiting on the doorstep, returning moments later to show her into the drawing room. He did not offer to take her outdoor apparel.

Mrs Gregory lounged on an elegant chaise, a blanket draped over her legs while she played the sick patient. At least the woman was alive, though the scratch on her neck suggested she may have been dragged from Lord Kinver's garden at knifepoint.

"What on earth is this about, Miss Ware?" The dark-haired beauty pressed a limp hand to her brow. "Can't you see I am unwell?"

The widow's coiffure resembled a bird's nest, wild strands sticking up here and there. Faint remnants of red rouge stained her lips. Lillian would wager the blanket disguised the fact she was without stockings. That the widow had company, male company.

"I am here on behalf of Lord Melbourne to discuss a

matter of the utmost importance. To save time, I suggest you invite Lord Sheridan to join us. Or shall I inform the Prime Minister you're hindering an investigation?"

Mrs Gregory gulped. After a silent debate, she called, "Smithers! Fetch his lordship!" The widow grumbled to herself. "Let me guess. That devil has fabricated a story and implicated us in a crime. I should have known she would do something wicked to get Sherry's attention."

Doubtless she referred to Madame Delafont. "Three witnesses claim Lord Sheridan is in league with his cousin Mr Valmary. They compete for lovers. An innocent man was poisoned in their attempt to beat the competition."

"Poisoned? Who?"

Lord Sheridan entered. He hadn't shaved. His crumpled evening clothes said he'd spent the night in the widow's bed. From the sudden whiff of brandy, one might think he'd bathed in a keg.

He addressed Lillian and inclined his head before dropping into the chair. "I heard the ridiculous claims and know nothing about any poisoning. Though I imagine that fop Baudelaire made the statement."

"Then you admit to knowing him?"

"I know of his feud with Thaddeus Valmary. The men have been rivals for years. I find Thaddeus' stories amusing, but that is the extent of my involvement."

"I'm told they were competing for Madame Delafont's affections. That you beat them in a game to claim her first."

"You see!" the widow blurted, distressed. "Did I not say she would cause trouble? She will stop at nothing to exact her revenge on you. Oh, Sherry. That woman has the devil's own stare, and I—"

"Amelia! Calm down. This has nothing to do with her."

The pair argued, though Lillian interrupted to ask, "Forgive me, Mrs Gregory, but have you lost a handkerchief embroidered with your initials? Did you leave via the mews on the night of Lord Kinver's ball?"

"What? Ageing spinsters carry monogrammed handkerchiefs. Do I look like I'm struggling for male company? And we both left via the mews to avoid …" She waved at her lover, expecting him to finish the sentence.

"To avoid my wife and Madame Delafont," he said shamelessly.

"Did you see anyone else there?"

They shook their heads.

"Might I ask how you got the mark on your neck?"

Mrs Gregory shrugged. "How is it relevant to the poisoning?"

"If you will just answer the question, I shall leave you in peace." Indeed, she was like an automaton, going through the motions when her heart and head were consumed with thoughts of Dounreay.

How could she fix this?

How might she change his mind?

The widow gave a discreet cough. "Some men are quite *physical* in the bedchamber. I shall say no more than that."

Lord Sheridan's lips curled into an arrogant grin. "I doubt an innocent could comprehend your meaning, my dear."

"Rest assured, my lord. I understand perfectly well." She had witnessed enough amorous interludes to grasp the situation.

"You do? How intriguing." His gaze slipped over her body, his interest piqued. "Ladies rarely take me by surprise, Miss Ware."

Heavens! The world was full of reprobates.

The mantel clock chimed four.

Would Dounreay be home?

Was he meeting Mr Daventry to withdraw his assistance?

Her vision blurred as tears gathered in her eyes.

Knowing not to trust a word from either suspect's lips, and not wishing to stay a second longer, she thanked them for their time and hurried to join Ailsa in the carriage.

As soon as her bottom hit the seat, Lord Denton, whose vehicle was parked across the street, took it as his cue to leave.

Ailsa watched the lord's elegant equipage lurch forward. "Och, that man is insufferable. He plans to steal my book. Told me so as plain as day."

"It's an auction, and he collects old books. He means to bid on the tome because he wants it for his collection."

Ailsa huffed. "Why would he want a Tudor woman's diary unless he means to torment me?"

"Because it's three hundred years old and extremely rare. He might wonder why you want another book written in Latin when you have many in your collection."

"He'll drive up the price," Ailsa said, fretting.

In the scheme of what might have happened to her father, losing a book one didn't own should hardly cause sleepless nights.

Losing a friend, losing a man that made one's toes curl, one's heart beat so fast it might burst from one's chest—that was a reason to lie awake, crying in the darkness.

Chapter Twelve

Despite returning home to a house full of people, Lillian felt cold, desolate, so dreadfully alone. She crossed the landing to her bedchamber, her limbs so heavy it was like trudging through gorse and bracken on a walk up a never-ending hill.

Noises permeated the air: the children's squeals, the creak of boards, the distant clang of pans in the kitchen, the chime of the long case clock echoing like a death knell.

One sound drowned out all others.

The whispers of her soul calling for Dounreay.

She needed to write a note to Mr Daventry—a perfect distraction from her troubles—yet she flopped onto the bed, battling her tears.

How could she find a way forward when she had spent her life avoiding intimacy? How could she trust these newfound feelings when she had been tricked before?

Eliza passed the open door before doubling back and coming to lean against the jamb. "Lillian. How was your day?"

"Exhausting."

Heartbreaking.

"Have you decided what you're wearing to dine with the duke? You've not much time to dither." Eliza scanned the corridor as if scouting for eavesdroppers. "Although Adam means to allow you the freedom to make your own decisions, he is not finding the task easy. So I'll ask you again, are you sure you want to visit Dounreay? You'll have to arrive incognito."

She would not be arriving at all.

"I'm not going. There's been a change of plan." Her blasé tone failed to reflect her inner turmoil. "I shall dine at home tonight."

"At home?" Sensing something was wrong, Eliza slipped into the room and closed the door. "But I've never seen you as excited as you were this morning. What made you change your mind?"

For once, her mind hadn't wavered.

For once, she wasn't battling uncertainty.

Lillian stood and moved to stare out of the window. Eliza could detect a lie from the mere blink of an eye. "The duke plans to return to Scotland within the week. And though I enjoy his company, it is best not to become too attached."

"I see."

Those two dreaded words hung heavily between them.

Eliza was not a fool and had worked as an enquiry agent before marrying Adam. Indeed, in the tense silence, Lillian felt the heat of Eliza's assessing gaze.

"It was the duke's decision, not mine," Lillian blurted.

"Dounreay cancelled your plans?" Shocked, Eliza appeared beside her, her hand resting on Lillian's upper arm. "Did he explain himself? Do you feel disappointed? Hurt? Relieved?"

Lillian's sigh did nothing to unravel the knot of emotions in her chest. "I'm not sure how to feel."

"You don't decide how to feel." Eliza drew her around so she might peer into her eyes. "It's a reaction you cannot control. Not until you've applied some form of logic. And you can only do that once you've identified the problem."

Lillian shrugged.

"You're hurt. I see the torment in your eyes."

There was little point denying it.

"It is always the same. I trust someone. I finally feel able to lower my guard, then I'm abandoned." She should have listened to her head, not her heart. She should have kept the duke at arm's length, not let him take liberties.

"You're still not telling me how you feel, Lillian."

She closed her eyes against the sudden ache, wishing it away. "It's like I'm suffocating. I can't breathe, Eliza. It's like being full, then so empty I could die." It was like strolling in a sunlit meadow only to plunge into a dark hole.

"Because Dounreay is leaving London?"

"Because the thought of never kissing him again robs my lungs of air. Because it's like I am six years old again, standing on the water's edge, unable to make sense of what's happened."

Tears filled Eliza's eyes. She had heard the harrowing family tale many times, but knew the tragedy had left indelible scars. "Even when we know the answers, they rarely make sense."

"The worst part is I don't know what I did wrong."

"I'm sure you did nothing wrong."

"I must have done something. One minute we're embracing, hugging each other so tightly I can feel his grief. The next, he's cold and dismissive."

Eliza looked just as confused. "What did he say?"

Oh, she couldn't bear to repeat the words, but they festered inside like a weeping wound.

"That we can be nothing but friends. That it's not about what he wants, but what's best." Like the fool at the fair, the man spoke in riddles.

A smile touched Eliza's lips, but she did not reveal what she found so pleasing. "And so you mean to take him at his word? To give up and spend the evening alone in your room?"

Lillian wondered if they were trick questions. "What else can I do? March over there and demand dinner? Tell him he is being ridiculous? Challenge him for breaking his oath? He was quite firm." Every bit the commanding duke.

Eliza's shoulders sagged. "Yes, I suppose you're right. Who would want to fight for a man who makes them breathless? Who wouldn't surrender at the first sign of rejection? Who wouldn't take Dounreay at his word, a man who's spent years craving one dance?" Eliza drew her into an embrace. "Never mind. I'm sure you'll decide on a solution. I shall leave you to think on the matter."

And then Eliza left.

Left without uttering another word.

Lillian stared out of the window, the bleak scene failing to lift her spirits. Sunset was less than an hour away, but a dense fog had settled, smothering the last remnants of daylight.

Somewhere a clock chimed the quarter hour, drawing Lillian's thoughts to Dounreay. Was he at MacTavish's bedside making plans? Were his servants packing trunks for the arduous journey northwards? Was he at home, getting ready to dine alone? Had his sadness consumed him?

She hugged herself, conjuring a mental image of his handsome countenance, of the brandy-coloured flecks that warmed his eyes whenever they kissed.

Dounreay!

God, she felt so heavy, like her limbs were made of lead.

And yet the constant tug in her gut urged her to move, to run downstairs, to race to Park Lane and hammer on the duke's door.

Would he welcome her inside?

Would he send her away, annoyed she'd defied him?

There was only one way to find out.

Raising the hood of her cloak, Lillian climbed down from the hackney cab. Adam sat quietly inside the vehicle, resolved on waiting until she entered Dounreay's house before heading home. He was tense. Warned her men often had other motives when asking a woman to dine. With obvious reluctance, he agreed to let her decide her own fate, said he trusted the duke to do the honourable thing.

Was that why the duke had rejected her?

Did he feel his honour had been compromised?

Lillian clutched her basket, a prop to make her look like a lowly maid, though she had something important folded neatly inside. She marched to Dounreay's door wearing sturdy boots, not her pretty shoes.

Her heart thumped a rapid beat in her chest as she raised the brass knocker and let it fall. The sound echoed through the hall, as bold as her determination, but was met with silence, not the clip of hurried footsteps.

She hammered twice.

No one came.

Fighting to suppress the rising bubble of panic, she thumped the wooden panel with her clenched fist.

Please be here!

Please let me in!

Surely he would not leave for Scotland without saying goodbye.

MacTavish wasn't well enough to travel, though the lord enjoyed life in the metropolis and often spent half the year in town.

The stillness and the dreary fog smothered her, diminishing all hope. He was gone. He had left her. Had sworn not to return for years. By then, he might be married, kissing a woman who wanted to be a duchess. Loving a woman who could love him back.

It was the least he deserved.

Her shoulders sagged—the fight leaving her just like everyone else.

Goodbye, Dounreay!

Pain lanced through her heart.

The muscles in her throat tightened.

Tears filled her eyes, the first drop landing on her cheek.

More would have followed, but she heard the slow thud of footsteps beyond the door and dashed the droplet away.

The lock clicked.

Dounreay opened the door, the sight of him almost sending her crashing to her knees. Her relief conveyed in every rapid pant.

He wore the same glum expression, the same blue coat stretched tight over muscular shoulders, the same magnetic aura that made him utterly irresistible.

There were a few differences.

His sumptuous lips were drawn into a thin line. He'd replaced the smart trousers with tight breeches that hugged his solid thighs. The shoes were now Hessian boots.

"You've been riding," was all she could think to say.

"I longed to feel the wind in my face, but the fog came down too quickly." He gripped the jamb as if speaking proved tiring. "Thankfully, I didnae give my groomsman the day off."

She sensed he was about to turn her away, and so did the unthinkable and scooted under his arm, forcing her way inside.

"It's too cold and damp to converse on the doorstep, and I have much to say." She followed the glow of lamplight to the drawing room, expecting to find tartan curtains and trophy heads lining the wall, not elegantly carved chairs and walnut side tables. "If I didn't know better, I would think this is an Englishman's home."

He lingered in the doorway, governed by the invisible barrier he had placed between them. "I must keep one room fit for entertaining English peers. The rest of the house is nae so agreeable."

"Good."

He stepped into the room, his gaze moving to the basket resting on the plush Persian rug. "Why are ye here, Lillian?"

"You made a blood oath. One you cannot break." Quickly removing her cloak, she draped it over the chair and brushed her hands over her favourite green dress. "Let me see if I can remember the words verbatim."

"I know what I said." He dropped onto the plush sofa, stretching out one leg to prevent her from sitting beside him.

"You took my blood and mingled it with your own." Should she be shocked she'd found it an erotic experience? "You sucked it into your mouth and swallowed it down, cementing our bond."

"Ye don't need to remind me."

Was the memory etched into his soul, too?

"*I swear by Almighty God, I will be faithful and firm,*" she said, repeating his promise. "You tricked me. You made me believe you never break a vow."

He watched her, his eyes never leaving hers, not to examine her trembling lips, not to admire her heaving bosom as she battled her nerves.

"How have I broken my vow?" he challenged.

She moved to sit on the sofa, wedging her bottom between his legs and relaxing against his broad chest. His body was hard yet warm and comforting, the merest touch lighting her inner flame.

"You chose to forget why you made the promise." When she captured his hand, he inhaled deeply but did not pull away. She examined his long fingers and gold seal ring, touched the intriguing callous that had no place on a duke's hand. "You agreed to help me find the answers I needed. You were firm. Resolute. Now you're faltering."

His breath came quicker. "Though yer an innocent, it's obvious where our research will lead."

She snuggled into him, splaying her hand on his chest. "I'm no innocent. You parted my legs, pushed your fingers inside me, and made me shatter into a thousand pieces."

A groan rumbled in his throat, but he said nothing.

"Do you know why I accepted your offer to tutor me?"

Because he had caught her unawares.

Because she'd been unable to deny her darkest desires.

"Aye, so ye would know what lust feels like. I agreed because I couldnae bear the thought of ye experiencing it with anyone else. 'Twas perhaps the most selfish thing I have ever done."

His confession gave her the confidence to press him harder. It helped that she wasn't gazing into those entrancing dark eyes. "You showed me lust could be beautiful, not vulgar. You made me feel things, wonderful things, and I've felt nothing for such a long time."

"We've dealt with the deaths of our mothers differently,"

he said, a sense of distance in his voice again. "I want to live. I want to feel everything. Whereas ye want to live half a life. Feel nothing. Feel empty."

But I feel something now.

I feel something for you.

A hard lump formed in her throat.

She couldn't swallow past the obstruction.

"The difference was apparent today," he continued, unaware she was fighting her own inner battle. "When we embraced, I know ye felt my pain, yet I felt nothing in return. I cannae abide secrets, yet ye're keeping something from me."

She remained silent.

"I cannae give everything and receive nothing, Lillian."

Dounreay had brought her to a crossroads. A dark fog obscured one path, making it impossible to see the future. The safe path had the same predictable view. A lonely, well-worn track she'd trodden for years.

This was her only chance to change course.

It was now or never. No other man held her so enthralled.

If she stepped into the darkness, she had to hope he would take her hand, help her if she stumbled.

The risk was great indeed.

Sitting up, she shuffled round to face him. "We all experience things differently. You're right. You're ignorant of the facts, so I cannot blame you for drawing that conclusion."

A look flashed in his eyes, something akin to hope. "If ye want to continue our research, ye'll need to stop pretending to trust me. Ye need to give me something, Lillian."

She wanted to give him everything.

Could she take this giant leap of faith?

Before she changed her mind, she inhaled a fortifying breath. "Forgive my brevity, but I need to say this quickly."

He blinked in obvious surprise.

"My mother didn't have an illness or suffer an accident. She encouraged my brother Sebastian to learn to swim, practically forced him, and he drowned." Nausea roiled in her stomach. "She blamed herself. One night, after kissing me on the forehead, she walked into the lake because she couldn't bear to leave Sebastian alone."

A heavy silence descended.

Yet she heard a distant voice warning of an approaching wave, one monstrous enough to swamp a young woman, to overturn her confident facade and drag her down into an abyss. Still, she held on to her resolve as if it were driftwood, the only means of reaching the shore.

"So I am sorry if I cannot bear to talk about it. I'm sorry if you think I'll always be nothing more than an empty shell. But that's not true. I feel something when I'm with you, Dounreay. I just need time to define what that is."

She waited while he gathered his thoughts.

"If you still want me to leave, I will."

The agony was like hoping for a reprieve on the march to the gallows.

Pressing her for information would be the worst thing he could do. She would tell him more at some point, but not now. Indeed, desperate to release the breath she'd been holding since knocking on his door, she was glad when he smiled and said, "What's in the basket?"

"Props for our research."

Curiosity burned in his beautiful brown eyes. "Props?"

"Yes, and your English drawing room offers the perfect setting." Her heart lurched when she considered what she was about to do. "We have unfinished business. Important research to conduct. So, we will begin with an experiment of my choosing."

One she had only thought of moments ago.

"Begin? There's to be more than one experiment tonight?"

She arched a coy brow and nodded. "Afterwards, we will change into Scottish attire, and you can show me what it's like to live north of the border. You promised I would dine with a Highlander tonight, and I've brought a dress fit for the occasion. Don't break your vow."

Molten heat flashed in his eyes. He reached out, cupping her cheek, drawing his thumb slowly over her lower lip, surrendering. "I'd need more than a few hours to give ye a full picture."

"Then we should not waste another second."

"Tell me about this experiment."

A fire crept up her neck, but she had to be bold. "As you know, I'm a lady who must satisfy her curiosities."

"Aye, but ye'll only satisfy them with me," he growled.

"I hoped you would say that."

Don't be afraid.

If he can pleasure you in the theatre, you can do this.

"You've shown me what it's like to be at a man's mercy."

"At *my* mercy," he corrected. "Don't think any other man could make ye feel the way I do."

She bit back a smile, loving these jealous outbursts.

"If I'm to understand life in the Highlands, you must understand the ways of an English woman with a daring spirit."

He frowned as she perused his muscular form, stretched on the sofa like a god of Olympus. "What do ye mean to do?"

"Pleasure you." The metal buttons on his breeches shone in the candlelight. She shuffled closer. Despite her trembling fingers and his sharp intake of breath, she undid the first button, eager to set him free.

Callan didn't stop her.

Though his mind said otherwise, his needy body refused to let him intervene. He watched her slip the last button, his chest heaving like he'd run three laps around Hyde Park.

"I've seen a sketch of how this works, but I'm unsure of the mechanics. A series of sketches would have given a much better picture. You must tell me if I do something wrong. If I fail to please you."

God, she stole his breath and drove him wild.

The last few hours had been pure torture.

The tender embrace they'd shared on the roadside in Bermondsey changed everything. This was not a game. It had moved beyond the need to test a theory. He wanted more than rampant kisses. He needed more than a few stolen minutes of pleasure.

He needed everything.

Her mind, her body, her soul.

Even now, even after her heartfelt confession, he wasn't sure she could satisfy him on an emotional level.

Maybe he expected too much.

Maybe the trauma of witnessing his parents' volatile marriage made him crave perfection.

Lillian Ware was not perfect.

She was intelligent and stubborn. Beautiful and damaged.

In a word, she was incredible.

"Every touch pleases me," he said, his voice low and throaty as she peeled back the placket of his breeches. "But this would have been easier had I worn a kilt."

"You're in England now," she teased, the nervous tremor

in her voice making her all the more irresistible. "We make problems to test our resolve." She pinned him to the sofa with her gaze, lust's fires licking him. "And I mean to pleasure you, Your Grace. Thoroughly."

She reached inside the fall, her dainty fingers settling around his hard cock. Her shocked gasp and wide eyes had him throbbing against her soft palm.

"Good heavens. You're much larger than I expected."

He clenched his jaw against a bolt of pure lust.

Hellfire! This woman would be the death of him.

"It's a testament to how much I want ye." He closed his eyes against the gentle glide of her hand. She was beyond magnificent. "I'm hard every time we kiss. The impudent devil almost tore my trousers when I pushed my fingers inside yer snug channel."

"Hmm." Her throaty hum carried the teasing notes of her own arousal. "That's a problem easily solved. You'll change into a kilt before you have me tonight."

"Have ye?" The words strained against his throat. His cock strained against the slide of her curious fingers. He covered her hand and showed her how to pump him from root to tip. "Ye hope for a repeat of what happened in the theatre?"

"Yes," she breathed, her eyes bright with wonder as she stroked him. "And I want you to take my virginity."

What the devil!

His cock swelled in celebration, his hot flesh pulsing, his hips jerking in a primal dance. Devil take it. He was going to come.

"Dinnae throw away something so precious."

Did she think he would make love to her and not marry her?

"I'm living, living for today, living for these newfound feelings." With her free hand, the minx tugged his shirt from the waistband, pushed her fingers beneath to caress his abdominal muscles. "I need you. I trust you to keep our liaison a secret. But I want you to seduce me. I want to watch you as you move inside me, pushing deep. I want to feel your weight crushing me. I want all of you, Callan Maclean."

Holy Mother Mary!

His orgasm burst through him with such force his hips bucked as he moaned her name and spurted his seed over her hand.

She watched, mesmerised, her rosebud lips grinning in satisfaction. "Goodness. There's something quite invigorating about having a virile man at my mercy."

He was struggling to master his wits and his breath. "Use me at yer will." He needed her with him in the Highlands. Still, whenever he thought of England, he would remember this moment.

Indeed, while he used the linen square from his coat pocket to wipe her hand clean, he thought about remodelling his castle. Amid chambers steeped in Maclean history, he would make space for an elegant English drawing room, and a delectable English wife.

Chapter Thirteen

Miss Ware watched Callan tuck himself away and button his breeches. If she continued wetting her lips like she might devour him, he'd be hard again in seconds.

"Of course, that doesn't make us even." The minx referred to their interlude at the theatre. "Though considering the size of you, I'd likely choke before you reached the pinnacle of your pleasure."

Callan coughed in response—almost choked on a mix of excitement and surprise. "Today, I detested England. Tonight, I cannae bear to leave. Still, I couldnae let anyone but my wife indulge in such a wanton pleasure."

"Good luck finding a duchess who's willing," she teased. "While spying, I've heard arguments to suggest many ladies find it a chore."

Callan considered her amusing response.

She had told him about the greatest tragedy of her life, and this game was a means of settling her emotions, numbing the pain. He would play for a while, but he wanted to know her deepest desires, her darkest secrets. He wanted to strip her bare and soothe all her woes.

"Some ladies will do anything for such a prestigious title." He was not short of offers. He could wed the daughter of a duke, could have any debutante of his choosing. "Still, I've decided to follow Denton's lead and nae marry until I'm fifty."

"Fifty? Is siring an heir not a pressing matter?"

He could not bed one woman while desperate for another. He could not beget a son who grew up knowing his father despised his mother. "There's always a distant cousin willing to take the helm."

She chuckled. "We'll make a libertarian of you yet, Your Grace."

There's nae chance of that.

I mean to marry ye long before I'm thirty.

"Based on the way we touch each other, I'd say I've already embraced the role." Aware time was precious, he looked at the basket. "Shall we change into our Highland attire and dine on braised offal?"

Her pretty nose wrinkled. "Offal?"

He couldn't contain his laughter. "I told Mrs McClintock to keep it a simple bill of fare. We've pea soup. A pot of venison. Poached pears and apple tart."

Her eyes flashed in delight. "And are you playing footman? I like the idea of having you at my beck and call."

"Mrs McClintock insists on bringing the dishes to the table." His cook had a firm sense of duty. "Then she plans to visit her sister in Southwark."

"Did you not tell her you'd cast me aside to dine alone tonight?"

Callan inwardly groaned. He would have seen sense eventually.

"I didnae have the heart after she spent most of the afternoon waiting." And since returning home, he had done nothing but wallow in misery. Misery of his own making. "Perhaps I always knew ye'd come."

She swallowed, drawing his gaze to the slender column of her throat. "I couldn't stay away."

The need to kiss her, to claim more than her mouth, was like a coil winding tightly in his loins. "Come," he said before he succumbed to temptation. "Let me escort ye upstairs to change clothes."

She snatched her basket and linked arms with him as they mounted the grand staircase. "The wooden panelling makes everywhere appear dark, though it gives the house a warm Elizabethan feel."

Cold marble floors and fancy architraves were fashionable in London. "A man needs things that remind him of home."

"I've never felt connected to a particular place."

"Ye've been running from the past for so long."

"Yes, and I've learnt you cannot escape it."

As she rarely gave anything away, Callan took that nugget of wisdom and stored it in his treasure box.

Once on the landing, he directed her to what would be the duchess' suite if they were married. "There's nae need to rush. I shall wait downstairs in the dining room."

"You will wear a kilt?"

"Aye. I'm told ye're desperate to see my knees."

"I've seen them countless times before."

And tonight, she'd seen a damn sight more.

She lingered on the landing. Watched him open the door to his bedchamber, craning her neck to peek inside. "It might be easier if we change together. I've no maid, and yours are away getting sotted at the Bullhead tavern."

He grinned though his resolve hung by the thinnest

thread. Once he laid his hands on her bare skin, he wouldn't stop until he'd indulged in every wicked pleasure.

The angel on his shoulder prodded him.

Taking her virginity would be a mistake. There would be no more games, no avoiding their future. He would hurl ultimatums, drive a wedge between them, drive her away. Indeed, the time for an honest conversation was nigh—though he'd wait until after they'd dined.

"Ye're nae wearing a corset." He'd watched those loose breasts bouncing as she pumped his cock. "I'm sure ye'll manage well enough. Now, behave and get changed before I throw ye over my shoulder and play the heathen."

Her gaze softened. "You give me every reason to disobey."

His imagination ran riot. He was chasing her around the house, throwing her down on the rug before the fire, pushing up her skirts and plunging home.

"Lillian," was all he said, his tone a mild reprimand.

She dropped into a graceful curtsey. "Forgive me, Your Grace. I cannot help but tease you." All traces of amusement fell away, and her sweet sigh spoke of gratitude. "With you, I can be myself. With you, I forget I'm carrying a heavy burden."

His heart clenched, as did his conscience. "I have yer undivided attention for a few precious hours. I mean to savour every second, that is all. Hurry. Meet me downstairs."

They entered their respective rooms to change clothes.

Callan stared at his huge four-poster bed, picturing a naked nymph wrapped around him, nothing but a sheen of sweat between their feverish bodies.

Despite a throbbing erection, he dressed quickly in the Maclean tartan and a white lawn shirt, not bothering with a sporran or coat.

The fire in the dining room burned brightly. After placing the silver soup tureen on the table, Mrs McClintock had stoked the flames before bidding him good night.

Callan's breath caught in his throat when Lillian padded softly down the stairs wearing the red dress she had borrowed from Ailsa. She was so bonny his heart nearly burst through his chest. She entered the dining room, her hair hanging in a cascade of auburn waves about her shoulders, her feet bare.

"It's silly, I know," she said, giving a sheepish grin. "You obviously wear shoes in the Highlands, but I wanted to feel the wood beneath my feet tonight. I wanted to feel free."

Daring to glance at her tiny toes was a mistake. The woman wiggled them, the movement as seductive as a lover's beckoning finger.

"Then I must do everything in my power to keep ye warm." He took the tiny sprig of dried white heather from the mantel, twirled it between his fingers. "Might I put this in yer hair?"

Her lips parted. "You got me a gift?"

"White heather is a symbol of protection." He tucked her hair behind her ear and pushed the sprig gently into place. How he loved touching her. "Legend says the flowers only grow where the fairies dance."

She looked up at him, a glint of wonder in her eyes. "You swore to protect me. Now this will remind me you always have my best interests at heart."

"Nae always," he teased. He was fighting against the ravaging needs of his body. This wasn't a David and Goliath story. From the moment she unbuttoned his breeches, he'd been destined to lose the battle.

"No, you hurt me deeply today."

He felt those words like a blade to the soul. "The execution left a lot to be desired, but it was said with good intention. I was trying to spare us both from suffering further pain."

Her gaze journeyed over his hair, his face, his kilt. "I've spent my life knowing my mother chose my brother over me. Any form of abandonment leaves lasting scars, but that's not what hurts the most. It's anticipating the moment my life might collapse around me. That's what you did today. You shattered my world."

The blade cut so deep his body ached.

But he understood the importance of this moment, what it had cost her to speak from the heart. "So why did ye come? Why do everything to build bridges when it's more than I deserved?"

She touched the delicate sprig in her hair. "Because I don't want you to leave. You make me feel things I shouldn't, want things I shouldn't. The path ahead is clouded with uncertainty, but for the first time in my life, I'm prepared to face my fears."

He'd spent many sleepless nights praying he'd hear those words.

"What do ye want from me?" He had to know.

She placed her palm on his chest, flexing her fingers over the hard muscles. "I want to know you in all the ways a woman might know a man. Let's not worry about tomorrow. Let's live for this perfect moment because it might be our last."

He should drop down on one knee, make a declaration.

But he would take anything she had to give.

That's what he'd realised while sitting alone in the dark.

"I can do that if ye promise to speak openly." He cupped her cheek, stroked her jaw with the pad of his thumb. "I cannae live with secrets, Lillian. My father lied to my mother, and it broke her."

"I've never lied to you."

"But ye've nae been honest, either."

"Because I've spent a lifetime living in fear."

Callan understood fear. Being around poisonous plants brought a sweat to his brow. Hearing a hacking cough made his heart race. He could never carry a woman in his arms without recalling the day he had staggered back to the castle, a twelve-year-old boy bearing the weight of the only woman he'd ever loved.

Perhaps not the only woman.

He'd felt the faint stirrings of something the first time he'd danced with Lillian Ware. When she held him captive while telling wild stories about Mr Sloane's hunt for pirate treasure. He'd danced with her a handful of times the year after, his affections deepening. Then he mentioned marriage, and she spent what felt like a lifetime avoiding him.

"Yet ye risked coming here tonight," he said, wanting to make the most of this moment, not dwell on the past.

"The fear of not seeing you was too much to bear." A rumbling gurgle in her stomach drew a chuckle from her lips, a sign they had done enough soul-searching tonight. "Forgive me. I've been so busy today, I've not eaten since breakfast."

"Then amongst my many roles, allow me to play footman." Escorting her to the dining table, he pulled out a chair. "Be assured, I'm yers to command."

Her smile was like bright morning sunshine. "As you're wearing nothing beneath that kilt, you may have to bend down to retrieve my napkin."

He laughed and bowed. "If that's yer desire."

"I'm jesting. Serve the soup and sit with me."

They ate in companionable silence, stopping halfway through the course to discuss the interview with Mrs Gregory.

Lillian chuckled. "You know she calls him Sherry. Which is rather ironic, as I find him so dreadfully unpalatable."

"Might they be the couple we saw arguing in the garden?" The attack had been more violent than erotic. The victim had fought to escape.

"Mrs Gregory seemed more threatened by Madame Delafont than her married lover. Still, perhaps they're extremely good liars."

"As Daventry said, if we keep asking questions, we're sure to find the right answers." While he longed to return home, he prayed the investigation lasted a lifetime.

"I do have an idea," she said as he cleared away the soup dishes. "It would be dangerous, and you'll likely insist I wait in the carriage."

"Ye mean to force the lock on Baudelaire's office and search through his private papers," he guessed.

She blinked in surprise. "Yes. How did you know?"

"Because there's something about him that incites distrust. And his need for secrecy roused my suspicions." Every muscle in his body tensed. What if she stumbled upon the poison? Accidentally ingested something toxic? "But I cannae risk ye getting hurt."

She fingered the sprig of heather in her hair. "I have the fairies' protection, and I'll be with you. The man who would die to save me."

"If ye accidentally consumed poison, it would be the death of me." Was life not a series of repeating patterns? A way of testing a man to make sure he'd learned his lesson? "I cannae lose ye, Lillian."

Those arresting eyes narrowed. "You almost did today."

"After a sleepless night, I would have called on ye tomorrow." She was his only weakness. The one woman he could not forget. "I would have tried to explain myself."

Her lips curled into a playful grin. "You mean I seduced you, touched you so intimately, when I could have been at home reading and eating cake?"

Blood pooled in his loins as he recalled spilling his seed over her dainty hand. "Ye didn't seduce me. I've been a willing participant for five long years."

"Most men would have grown tired of waiting."

"I'm nae most men."

"No, you're superior on every level." Her gaze dropped to his mouth, her sweet sigh an obvious prelude to seduction. "You've never disappointed me, Callan, and I doubt you will tonight."

Hearing his name on her lips stirred a carnal hunger, a desperation to possess her and sheath himself deep in her heat. To live for this one perfect moment.

"Before we venture upstairs," he said, surrendering to his fate, "I need to explain why Roxburgh permitted ye to come here."

Her head snapped in his direction. "Did you speak to him?"

"Aye, when he joined me in the garden and prised his sleeping son from my arms. I always planned to tell ye what was said." He just didn't know how. Doubtless that made him a hypocrite.

She pushed out of the seat. "Did you change your mind? Did you tell him you'd marry me if I found myself ruined?" Her inscrutable expression had his pulse beating hard in his throat.

"Ye must understand. 'Twas the only way to pacify him."

"You'd cast aside your principles just to spend a few hours with me?" She stepped away from the table, edging closer to the door—the distance between them growing. A few more steps, and he feared she would be out of his life for good. "You said you'd only marry a woman who wants you."

"Did ye nae just confess to wanting me?" He stood, ready to follow her to the ends of the earth if necessary. "Tell me ye're nae leaving."

Time stopped for a few seconds.

Then the minx grinned. "Why would I leave? You promised me an evening of Scottish revelry." Desire glowed in her eyes, as hot as the fire's embers. "You said I would feast on a Highlander tonight."

Relief left him weak at the knees, almost giddy.

"Feast *on* a Highlander? Nae with a Highlander?"

"That's up to you, Callan Maclean. But if you want me, you'll have to catch me." Lifting her skirts to her knees, she darted out of the room and bolted towards the stairs.

Callan chased her, the sight of her bare calves turning his blood to liquid fire. "Madam, ye're about to be so full with this Scot, ye'll have nae need to dine for a week."

A squeal escaped her when she glanced over her shoulder and noticed he'd gained some ground. "It's about time you delivered on your promises."

Callan followed her into his bedchamber, but she came to a crashing halt before the fire, her breathless pants like a potent aphrodisiac.

"There's nowhere to go, love."

"I'm exactly where I want to be." With a trembling hand, she gestured to the dying embers. "You said it was always hot in a Highlander's castle. You vowed I would never suffer the cold."

"Ye'll be hot when writhing beneath me." Hungry for this woman, he dragged the back of his hand across his mouth, took a tentative step forward. "I plan to satisfy ye in more ways than one."

A whimper of excitement escaped her.

Now he had battled his conscience, he planned to drive into her so damn hard it would be worth the five-year wait.

Once would not be enough.

The need to make love to her, to pleasure her senseless, to slake every insatiable need had his cock rising to the challenge.

"I am a woman who craves adventure."

"And the best adventures happen when there's nae need to step beyond the front door. Let me touch ye, Lillian. I'll transport ye to a place ye could never reach on foot."

"Are you not going to feign a gruff voice and call me lass?"

"I'll play any damn game ye like." He dragged his shirt over his head and cast it aside.

She stared at his bare chest, gawping at every firm muscle. "I've heard the mountains north of the border are spectacular, but I'd rather gaze upon your fine physique, Dounreay."

And he'd likely spill himself the moment he saw her luscious curves. "Before I remove my kilt, tell me what ye want."

"I want an unforgettable memory, and I want it with you."

"Only one?"

She shrugged. "I know a lady shouldn't say such things. But if your kisses are any indication, I imagine I'll ache for you at night. Suspect I'll want you with shocking frequency."

He did not respond with words. He kept his gaze locked with hers while he undid the first buckle on his kilt. Then he moved to tackle the second fastening before letting the garment fall to the floor.

Lillian gasped.

He was thick and hard, solid as a butcher's block.

His cock jerked, desperate for her attention, eager to play.

Despite taking him in hand earlier, her mouth fell open, and she clasped her heaving breast. "You're like a warrior. All sinew and corded muscle. If I lived in a castle, I would keep the fires blazing. If only to encourage you to strut around naked."

He laughed, palming his erection just to tease her. "Well, lass, do ye want to feast on a Highlander, or do ye nae have an appetite?"

Her tongue slid over her bottom lip, sending his pulse skittering. "When I look at you, I realise I've been starved for a lifetime."

"Then show me what an English rose has to offer."

With a coy smile playing on her lips, she undid the side buttons on her dress and the few at her nape. Rather than let the gown slide seductively over her hips, she drew it over her head.

Callan had no complaint.

In the process, she dragged her chemise with it, tossing both garments aside, standing there like a nymph in all her naked glory.

Callan drank her in, all creamy skin and round breasts and rosebud nipples. He remembered parting those slender thighs, inhaling the sweet scent of her arousal, sucking that little bud.

"Come here," he growled, lust drumming in his veins.

She padded towards him, comfortable in her nakedness, and he wondered when she would feel as confident baring her heart.

"Touch me, Lillian."

Tentatively, she placed her hand on his chest, stroking his pectoral muscle as if it were marble sculpted by a master craftsman. She pressed her mouth to the same spot, his heart thudding wildly beneath her lips.

"I'm nae wearing cologne," he said when she inhaled the scent of his skin.

"No, you smell wild and untamed, so dangerous it would lead any woman to sin." Her hand drifted down his chest, down his abdomen, her fingers stroking his engorged cock.

Not wanting to miss a second, he didn't close his eyes against the rush of pure pleasure.

I'm in love with ye.

I'm so in love with ye, I might break ye tonight.

The thoughts mingled with the potent thrum of his arousal. He had heard them before, faint whisperings from his soul. Now, they rang with a constant beat he could not ignore.

"Tell me how this works," she breathed, her fingers encircling his shaft. "Tell me how we move from this to you being inside me."

"We kiss, love."

He should have known what would happen when he held her naked body and claimed her mouth. Five years of restraint made for a passionate explosion. The kiss was deep, all thrusting tongues and clashing teeth, their moans almost heart-wrenching in the depths of their desperation.

In a mad frenzy, they ended up on the bed.

Kissing, kissing, kissing until they couldn't breathe.

Touching each other with raw, carnal hunger.

His mouth was on her sex, his hand on her breast, rolling her nipple between his fingers, relishing her sweet cries. The thought of plunging into her wetness made his cock weep.

"Dounreay! Oh, Dounreay!" His name left her lips in rapid pants, over and over. She gripped his arm, dug her nails into his flesh, begged him to continue. "Yes! Don't stop! Never stop!"

She came hard. Her cry echoed through the room, her body trembling to his tune.

For a few seconds she went limp, and then she was dragging him up her body, spreading her legs wide, pulling him down. "Take me now. I want to give myself to you, to no one but you."

Callan held himself, stroking the broad head of his cock over her swollen bud, moving closer to the warm, wet depths he longed to explore.

"Do ye know how long I've waited for this?" he said, his voice fierce with the need to possess her. "Do ye know how long I've wanted ye?"

"Yes." Her blue eyes blazed with something other than lust. "For five years, two months and ten days."

Her answer knocked the wind from his sails.

Did she know how many nights he'd lay awake, trying to convince himself she felt something? Her confession might have dampened his ardour, but he'd waited a lifetime to have her. And by God, he would die if he didn't claim her now.

"Ye've been counting, love?" Callan pushed into her heat, branding this moment into his memory.

"Since the day you first held me in your arms."

Chapter Fourteen

In terms of her scientific studies, Lillian had made many miscalculations. Women did feel desire as powerfully as men. With the right partner, one had little control over one's mind and body. Lust was like a drug, a desperate addiction. Hence why it made sane people reckless.

Dounreay drove her wild.

He satisfied every craving.

The ripples of her release still coursed through her.

Yet, as she stared into his dark, compelling eyes, as he pressed her into the mattress with his impressive physique, and his manhood breached her entrance, she realised she had made another error.

Something else flowed between them.

Something so beautiful it left her breathless.

"Kiss me," she uttered, wrapping her thighs tightly around him, so there was no hope of him ever leaving. No prospect of him changing his mind.

He captured her mouth, the kiss so slow and deep it stroked the soul. Despite her body aching for him, their connection was based on more than physical need. She understood that now.

"Ye're the last person I'd want to hurt, but I need to drive deeper." He nudged inside her another inch, her sensitive flesh stretching to accommodate him. "We'll go slow until ye can take all of me. It's nae too late to change yer mind. To save yerself for another."

Another?

She had planted these doubts in his mind.

And she must do everything to restore his faith.

"I want you, Callan."

A profound tenderness filled her chest.

I've always wanted you.

But I've been so scared.

"Once I move, I swear ye'll feel nothing but pleasure."

"Don't wait." When he bent his head to kiss her, she said, "I want to look at you when you take me. Do it now." It was her turn to express doubt. "You do want me?"

"Love, I've never wanted anything more."

He pinned her to the bed with his gaze, the amber flecks in his eyes blazing so hot she would never feel cold again. Then he flexed his hips and, in one long thrust, buried himself deep inside her.

Dounreay!

They both inhaled sharply.

She at the sudden intrusion, the shock.

The slight sting lasted seconds. The memory of his expression—a look of raw, unadulterated bliss—would last a lifetime.

Sharing this moment with him was precious. Lillian had not realised how precious until Dounreay withdrew and drove forward again.

The feel of his hot flesh filling her was beyond exquisite.

They moved together, each slow stroke teasing a moan from her lips, reminding her what a fool she had been to deny him.

He moved in and out of her body, his intense gaze penetrating her with equal skill, both reaching places no other man could.

Their passion claimed them.

His thrusts came quicker and harder.

Her heart raced.

Their desperate pants echoed through the room.

The need to find release, to feed the addiction, took over. Callan's pumps grew rapid, his breathing ragged. Then he was on his knees between her thighs, gripping her legs, driving so hard and deep their bodies slapped together.

"God, Lillian." One hand clasped her hip, holding her tight against his thrusting manhood, the other massaging her aching sex. "I shall need ye again tonight. I shall need ye every night."

"Yes," she breathed.

Yes, to making love again. Yes, to being owned by this Highlander. Yes, because she could feel the tension tightening in every muscle, knew she was seconds away from experiencing a moment of utter bliss.

The bed creaked as he rammed into her. "When I withdraw, touch me like you did earlier. Make me come with yer hand."

Anticipating her release, he slowed as her body clenched and pulsed around his thick length. He watched as her orgasm ripped through her in powerful waves.

A few more thrusts and he withdrew quickly, moaning as she pumped his manhood until his seed came in hot spurts over her abdomen and breasts.

They stared at each other, gasping in wonder.

"Ye're incredible." The corners of his mouth curled into a slow, sinful smile. "That was our first time together. It willnae be our last."

"No." Some things one knew with absolute certainty: that the sun would rise and set, that she would crave this man's touch until her dying day. "I doubt we'll be able to keep our hands off each other."

"Stay the night." It was a plea, not a command.

"You know I can't."

"Stay with me tomorrow night. Find a way to pacify Roxburgh. There's somewhere I want ye to see. A magical place that will satisfy the need for a daring adventure."

Her curiosity piqued, she said, "You've just given me the best experience of my life. How do you propose to beat that?"

He gave an arrogant grin. "Find an excuse to stay away tomorrow night, and ye'll see." A sensual hum rumbled in his throat as he gazed upon her breasts.

She lay bare, exposed, stretched out before him as naked as the day she was born. He could see everything except for the chaos of emotion buried beneath her cool facade.

"Let me wash you." He climbed out of bed.

She studied his firm buttocks as he walked to the washstand. She wanted to keep him locked in this room, lodged between her thighs forever. Not because she craved his prowess in the bedchamber. Intimacy flowed between them like an ancient underground river. Something sacred that could withstand the test of time.

Mingled with lust was a more terrifying feeling.

One she suspected just might be love.

A distant sound dragged Lillian from her slumber. She was curled around Dounreay's naked body, clinging to him, taking comfort in the heat radiating from his bronzed skin.

The room was dark, the fire nought but dying embers, the hum of the city but faint echoes.

Memories stirred. The feel of cold water on her chest, the tingling, the tenderness in every stroke as Dounreay wiped her clean. The instant spark of arousal. The rain of hot kisses over her breasts. Pleasuring each other before tiredness claimed them.

The loud hammering on the front door jolted her to her senses. "Good Lord! Dounreay! There's someone at the door." She sat up, trying to rouse a coherent thought.

She'd not meant to fall asleep.

Had the midnight hour passed?

Had Adam come to threaten Dounreay, to berate her and drag her home?

"Callan! Wake up." She whipped the bedsheets back, the cold dragging a gasp from her lips and raising goose pimples on her skin. "I need to find my chemise."

"Come back to bed," her Highlander groaned, half asleep.

The caller took to hitting the wood with his fist, the dull thud almost murderous in intent. Adam wouldn't stop at taking an axe to the door.

Like a wolf sensing danger, Dounreay sat bolt upright.

"Adam won't be as forgiving if he finds me in a state of undress." She found her chemise and tugged it over her head, though it did nothing to chase away the cold or her fears. "Get dressed. Hurry."

He shot out of bed, the sight of his erect manhood distracting her mind and playing havoc with her body. "What time is it?"

"I have no notion." She watched him dress, wishing time

would still and she could indulge her desires. Sleeping in his arms was as satisfying as making love. "It must be late."

He threw on his shirt and tucked it into his kilt, his gaze darting to the door when the caller banged again. "How do I look?"

Like the love of my life.

Like heartbreak waiting to happen.

"A bit rumpled." Crossing the room, she combed her fingers through his hair, then attempted to brush the creases out of his shirt. "Know I don't regret what happened between us. Know I'm warming to Highland life. If you're still will-ing, I'll do everything I can to join you tomorrow night."

"Ye speak like ye're about to be dragged away to a nunnery."

"I fear something will spoil this dream."

Dounreay cupped her cheek and stroked his thumb over her lip.

A look passed between them, but the mystery caller persisted in trying to capture their attention.

"Stay here until I return." Dounreay kissed her forehead like he might never see her again, then charged downstairs, taking her heart with him.

Impatient, she tiptoed onto the landing, crouched in the darkness, gripping the baluster for support. Ears pricked, she waited for an unholy argument to erupt.

Tense seconds ticked by as she braced herself. Regardless of her reputation, she would race downstairs and defend the duke if necessary.

"Wait there, lad," Dounreay said, his tone mellow. The pad of footsteps preceded a door opening and closing. "There's enough for a hackney home, though I'm sure Daventry paid ye well."

Daventry?

Once alone, she descended the stairs to find Dounreay reading a letter. He looked up, his gaze roving over her mussed hair and thin chemise, the ravenous glint in his eyes warming her. "'Twas a penny boy with a note from Lucius Daventry. He was paid to ensure I received it within the hour. My groom told him I was home."

"What does it say?" She reached his side, catching her breath when he slipped his arm around her waist and pulled her close.

"He needs us at the Hart Street office tonight. One of his agents found Anne Grimes. Daventry wants us there when he questions her about the incident with Major Rowlands."

"Anne Grimes? I don't know why, but I thought she'd be on the next boat to Boston." Or worse still. Lillian feared the poor woman was dead. "We should get dressed. He will have sent a letter to Hanover Square, not knowing I'm here."

"This is addressed to both of us."

"It is?" She shouldn't be surprised. Mr Daventry knew everything about everyone. "The man is like the mystic at the fair. Heaven knows how he finds his information."

"He pays well and punishes liars severely."

"He leaves nothing to chance," she agreed. But a sudden thought hit her, making her gasp. "Along with my brother, Mr Daventry escorted my friends and me to the Bartholomew Fair last September. He spoke to the mystic before we entered the tent."

"What are ye suggesting?"

"Perhaps Mr Daventry told the mystic what to say because he knew something of our history." He knew she lacked the courage to follow her heart. Did he know she secretly longed for a duke who bared his knees in public?

Dounreay chuckled. "I think Daventry has better things to do than make predictions about a lady's marriage prospects."

"I'm not so sure. The mystic told Ailsa her husband would cast an ancient spell over her, a spell found in an old tome. Mr Daventry is one of the few people who know of her hobby."

"Daventry is many things, but he's nae a matchmaker."

"What if he is? What if it's not a force of fate guiding us?" What if Adam and Mr Daventry had conspired to force her to marry the duke?

Being intelligent and intuitive, Dounreay grasped the train of her thoughts.

"Dinnae fret." He pulled her against his hard chest and claimed her mouth in a searing kiss. "We've wanted each other for five years. You went to the fair months ago. Whatever we feel has nothing to do with Daventry or a seer's prediction."

It was there again—the swell of raw emotion, the potent energy vibrating between them, the pulsing of something primal.

Something perfect.

Something precious.

"You're right." She held him, pressed her cheek to his chest, the rapid beat of his heart mirroring her own. "No one has the power to predict the future."

He stroked her hair. "A seer didnae make ye moan my name. A mystic didnae make ye come so hard ye couldnae breathe."

She looked up into eyes that made her melt. "No, that was you and your wicked Highland tongue."

"And ye'll be dining on a Highlander tomorrow if ye can slip away." His fingers trailed slowly down her spine. "If not, I can always steal into yer chamber like a true heathen and carry ye off into the night."

"Should I be ashamed to say I find that appealing?"

Dounreay laughed—a beautiful sound she'd not thought to hear again. He smacked her lightly on the bottom. "Come, love. Let's dress and meet Daventry before I throw ye over my shoulder and have my wicked way."

Her body reacted instantly. The memory of them joined together ignited a fire in her blood. "Is this what it would be like in the Highlands?" Would he be wild and carefree? Or when playing the duke, would duty dampen his ardour?

He winked and chucked her beneath her chin. "Ye'll have to come home with me to find out."

They arrived in Hart Street to find Mr Daventry seated behind his imposing desk, his chin resting on his clasped hands as he stared into the darkness.

The housekeeper, Mrs Gunning, gave a discreet cough, stepping forward while they lingered in the doorway. "His Grace, the Duke of Dounreay has arrived with Miss Ware, sir."

"Thank you, Mrs Gunning." He stood, fastening the top button on his waistcoat. "You may retire for the evening. I shall lock the doors on my way out."

They all moved into the hall.

Mr Daventry waited until Mrs Gunning mounted the stairs before giving them his undivided attention. "Miss Grimes is waiting in the drawing room. When left alone to contemplate their future, suspects are more inclined to confess."

The comment prompted Lillian to broach the subject burning hot on her tongue. "Perhaps I might employ your tactics and force you to confess, sir."

"Me?" Mr Daventry's gaze flicked to her simple chignon, his brow quirking in mild amusement. "Yet it appears you're the one with something to hide, Miss Ware."

Heat rose to her cheeks, but she pressed on. "It was you who made the predictions at the fair, was it not? You who fed the mystic the information?"

Mr Daventry held a somewhat bored expression. "Do I strike you as a man who plays games with mystics?"

No, he carried himself with complete sangfroid. Yet Lillian had seen his playful interactions with his wife. Then, one glimpsed a different man. One much less restrained.

Is that what marriage to Dounreay would be like?

By night would she have the wild Highlander in her bed? By day would he appear aloof while dealing with ducal business?

"You have more important things to do than play match-maker," she agreed. "Hence why I'm so intrigued."

A slow smile formed on his lips. "I spend my life finding solutions to problems, giving people the answers they deserve. Bringing peace."

"Your work is commendable, sir."

"Still, there is nothing more important than love, Miss Ware. Like you, I once thought love a painful concept," Mr Daventry admitted, though now she wished she had not asked. "It's one of the few times I have been wrong."

He did not elaborate further, but strode into the drawing room, forcing them to follow.

The young woman on the sofa jumped to her feet, shaking as if she'd been imprisoned in a murky gaol on some forgotten island. "You're back! What's this about? You can't hold a woman hostage. You've kept me here half the day."

"Don't exaggerate, Miss Grimes. You've been here for two hours. You came of your own free will and were paid."

Mr Daventry gestured for them to take a seat. Despite numerous chairs, Lillian sat next to Dounreay. Anne remained standing.

"I didn't know you'd lock me in here."

"The door was open."

"Oh!"

Based on Anne's penchant for dramatics, Lillian doubted she would be a credible witness. "Someone mentioned your name in relation to the theft of a figurine from Lord Kinver's home, and we need to establish a few facts."

The maid blanched. "You're accusing me of theft?"

"We're not accusing you, but Major Rowlands said you took something from his home before you left and—"

"I knew it! I knew that murdering devil was involved." She snatched her tatty reticule from the seat as if preparing to bolt. "He means to see me hang. He'll not rest until I'm six feet under."

"Sit down, Miss Grimes," Mr Daventry said, his tone as icy as his expression. "We were told Major Rowlands assaulted you. As for the figurine, we want to know if you saw it in the study?"

Anne pursed her lips as if fighting to stop the words bursting out. She shook her head and made an odd squeaking sound.

"Very well." Mr Daventry slapped his thigh. "I'm placing you under arrest. You'll remain here until the magistrate arrives."

"Under arrest?" Anne blurted. "What for?"

"For the theft of a priceless figurine."

"But I didn't steal it! *He* broke it and made me clear up the mess." Tears formed in the maid's eyes, banishing her bravado.

Lillian crossed the room. "We mean to help you, but you

must tell us what happened." She held Anne's arm, encouraging her to sit. "We have your bloodstained handkerchief. We know the major pressed a knife to your throat and forced you from the garden."

It was mere speculation.

Anne's brow furrowed, her gaze darting between them all. "It weren't my handkerchief. I cut my finger on the broken ornament, got blood over his lordship's fancy floor."

Lillian's heart skipped a beat. They were getting close to the truth. But her elation faded as quick as misty breath on a mirror.

Once they'd solved the case, Dounreay would have no cause to stay.

"Perhaps we should begin with why ye left Major Rowlands' employ," Dounreay said, keen to know if the major abused his position and mistreated his staff.

Anne dashed her tears away and wiped her runny nose with the back of her hand. "I ain't staying in a house with a ... a ..."

"Philanderer?" Dounreay offered.

"With a murderer, sir. He killed the mistress good and proper."

Mr Daventry sat forward. "Do you have any evidence to support your claim?"

"The major knew them men were sending her perfume. Fancy stuff that cost more than some women earn in a year. But he's only got himself to blame, carrying on the way he does." Anne paused for breath. "Then the mistress packed a valise and said she was leaving. Next thing she's on the floor, her heart giving out."

A hundred questions raced through Lillian's mind. There had been no evidence to link the incident in the garden to the poisoning, not until now.

"Mr Valmary and Monsieur Baudelaire sent Mrs Rowlands perfume?" she asked.

Anne nodded. "Not just perfume. Tickets for the theatre. A fur stole. Silk stockings from Paris. A pretty ruby brooch from Woodcroft's on Bond Street. But I saw Mrs Jarvis wearing that at Lord Kinver's ball."

"Is that why you argued with the major?"

Anne's nose wrinkled in disgust. "That devil broke Mrs Rowlands' heart long ago. It wasn't enough that his threats killed her. No. He gave Mrs Jarvis that brooch before my mistress was cold in the grave."

"And when you confronted him, the major broke the figurine?" Lillian attempted to clarify. "The one given by Madame Delafont as a wedding gift?"

The blood drained from Anne's face, her eyes growing wide. "The major grabbed me so hard I've still got the bruises. He said if I told anyone he'd killed his wife, he would throw me in the Thames."

Lillian considered what they had learned at the theatre. Madame Delafont claimed to have witnessed the argument but made no mention of the broken figurine or seeing the major.

"Did Mrs Jarvis nae intervene?" Dounreay said calmly, much to Lillian's relief because he had sat there, practically seething, while the maid spoke of the adulterous major.

"Mrs Jarvis fled the study when the argument started."

"Is that when Madame Delafont arrived?" Lillian wondered what business the opera singer had in the study. Unless she had been looking for Lord Sheridan.

Anne fell silent.

Having rambled off her story as keenly as a fishwife on market day, the maid's sudden reticence raised suspicions.

"Madame Delafont gave you the handkerchief to clean up

the blood," Mr Daventry said, attempting to confirm whether the initials bore any real relevance. "She helped you clear away the broken fragments. That's why you left the Kinver residence. You knew the major would blame you and ruin your prospects of further employment."

A sob burst from the maid's lips. "The major said he'd tell his lordship I stole the figurine. That I'd better stop spreading gossip, or he would make sure I swung from the gallows."

While the maid had been quite forthcoming with information, a nagging doubt, an element of distrust, knotted in Lillian's stomach.

She stood, looming over the servant girl, hoping it might intimidate her slightly. "Did you steal anything from the Kinver residence? This is your one and only chance to confess."

Anne met Lillian's gaze. "No. I swear it."

"Did you steal anything from Mrs Rowlands?"

"No." Anne stared blankly, the single word lacking conviction.

It was most certainly a lie.

"Then we will visit Major Rowlands and take a statement." What could the maid have stolen? Was it the letter given to a villain in the dark? "We'll ask him to confirm you stole a letter from his deceased wife."

Mr Daventry stood. "I shall summon the magistrate. We know you stole a letter. We're not interested in the theft, Miss Grimes. We care about the truth."

He made for the door, but Anne cried, "Wait! I'll tell you. But I can't hang, sir. My sister is ill and needs me to work, else she'll not afford the medicine."

Being as compassionate as he was dangerous, Mr Daventry faced the maid. "Then I suggest you stop playing games, Miss Grimes. We don't care what you took. We care that it might have something to do with attempted murder."

Anne thought he was referring to Mrs Rowlands. "You believe the major killed my mistress? Sir, she'd been feeling ill all morning, was frothing at the mouth before she died, jerking in my arms like them devils in Bedlam. But the major wouldn't let me fetch a doctor."

Dounreay's sharp intake of breath said he had witnessed someone he loved perish in much the same manner.

Oh, Lillian wanted to race across the room and hug him tightly.

"We'll deal with that once you tell us what you stole," Mr Daventry snapped. "It's important, madam."

Anne gulped. "It was the gift Mr Valmary gave to Mrs Rowlands."

"The gift?"

"A recipe, sir. A list of ingredients he uses in his May Bell perfume. He said it was the most precious thing he owned, and trusting her with it was a sign of true love."

"Why the devil did you steal it?"

Despite a trembling lip, Anne said, "Because *she* offered me a hundred pounds. I swear I don't know how she knew about the letter. But my poor Mary is sick, and there's nothing I won't do to help her."

Silence ensued—a moment to process the facts.

She? Lillian pictured the tussle in the garden. The attacker was most definitely male. "Anne, who offered you money for the letter?"

"You can't say it was me what told you. She's been kind and gave me the money in good faith."

"We want a name," Mr Daventry barked.

Anne whimpered before crying, "Madame Delafont!"

Chapter Fifteen

Covent Garden Theatre
Bow Street

Reminiscent of the night they first questioned the opera singer, Callan stood in the alley with Lillian, hammering on the shabby theatre door. The same stench filled his nostrils. The same need to drag the truth from Madame Delafont's lying lips drummed in his veins.

Some things were different.

Though Callan had not spoken the words aloud, he had acknowledged his love for the woman beside him. In her arms, he'd experienced the most satisfying night of his life. Once they had finished with the deceitful singer, he planned to take Lillian to his cabin in the woods and let her feast all night on a Highlander.

Avoiding the puddle on the ground, Lillian stepped forward. She gave a huff of impatience and banged on the door. "There's only an hour until they raise the curtain. We must question Madame Delafont before she goes on stage, or we might not get the chance."

Lucius Daventry received word this would be the Frenchwoman's last performance. After the upset with Lord Sheridan, she had decided to return to Reims and abandon England for good.

Or was that merely a story to escape her attacker?

According to Anne Grimes, Madame Delafont had agreed to meet someone in the garden at the Kinver residence. Hence why she needed the letter Anne had stolen from Mrs Rowlands' secret box.

"It wouldnae surprise me if she's fled." This afternoon, they had visited the lady's rented property in Long Acre. The flustered maid confirmed her mistress had not been home for three days.

"Maybe she feels safer at the theatre."

The sudden scraping of the rusty bolt said someone was about to open the grubby door.

Pike appeared, grimacing as their gazes collided. "You can't come in tonight, Your Grace. Mr Warren is pacing the corridors like a guard at the Fleet. He'll not have Madame Delafont late to the stage again."

Callan grabbed Lillian's hand and pushed past the man.

"We'll need five minutes of her time. We answer to the King, nae Mr Warren." He pulled Lillian along with him. The sooner they took the singer's statement, the sooner they could head out on the road to Epping Forest. "Besides, we didnae question her until after the performance."

"Yes, but Lord Sheridan came barging in last night, so sotted he could hardly stand. Mr Warren had to throw him out. It took Madame Delafont half an hour to stop sobbing."

"Sheridan? What did the feckless fool want?" Callan

turned the corner, almost crashing into a scrawny grey-haired man and knocking him on his arse.

"Pike! What's going on here?" The fellow gathered himself and straightened his coat. "Who is this? I said no visitors tonight."

"But Mr Warren, His Grace is here on behalf of the King."

Callan didn't wait to explain himself or watch Warren bow and scrape to a man with a title. He made for Madame Delafont's door while the men argued behind him.

Lillian knocked but received no response. She opened the door, gasping when she peered around the jamb. "Quick, Callan. Hurry."

They burst into the room to find Madame Delafont sprawled across the floor, eyes closed, as still as the grave.

Mr Warren appeared and was as useless as a watch to a corpse. "Heavens! The show is about to start. Wake her up, damn it! Wake her up."

Lillian shot him an irate look. "Checking for injuries is the priority, sir." She crouched over the body, pressing her fingers to Madame Delafont's wrist, searching for signs of life. "She has a pulse."

"Thank the Lord!" Mr Warren jumped into action, firing orders at Pike. "Fetch her a glass of brandy. That should bring her round. We've got less than an hour to chivvy her along and make sure she's ready."

"I'll fetch her smelling salts from the drawer, sir." Pike hurried to a tall mahogany chest. "She uses them when she's got an attack of nerves."

Pike found the crystal vinaigrette and handed it to Callan.

He removed the stopper and waved the bottle beneath the opera singer's nose. It took a few seconds to rouse a reaction.

Then she jerked her head violently and winced against the pungent whiff of hartshorn.

"What? No!" Madame Delafont blinked rapidly, groaning as she moved her limbs. Recognition dawned. "Your Grace? What are you doing here?"

"Have ye broken anything? Are ye in pain?"

A little confused, the lady clutched her abdomen. "I—I'm fine. I often swoon before I'm due on stage. Will you help me up?"

"Praise be." Mr Warren gripped the lady's arm and helped Callan ease her into a chair. "Tell me you'll be ready for the performance."

Her smile failed to reach her eyes. "I shall be fine once I've eaten. Perhaps you might send Pike for tea and cake. And ensure there's a chair for me backstage."

After minimal fussing, both men left the room.

"Mr Warren can be quite demanding, but he means well." Madame Delafont pressed her fingers to her temple and winced. "I assume you've not come to bring flowers and wish me farewell."

"We heard you're leaving London." Lillian sat in the velvet chair, her cheeks turning pink as she met Callan's gaze.

The memory of him pleasuring her flooded his mind. He moistened his lips and stared into her eyes, wondering if she'd realise he was a man in lust and in love.

"I'm escaping London," the opera singer admitted. "I've grown tired of the games men play. And there's no one here worthy of my esteem."

Callan forced himself to concentrate. "Pike said Sheridan made a scene here last night. Did he come to accuse ye of slandering his good name?"

Again, the woman touched her abdomen. "Sheridan enjoys the chase. He always wants what he cannot have. He tried to persuade me to stay. But like the most deadly of snakes, he spits nothing but venom."

"Forgive me," Lillian began, "but we must ask you a few questions before you leave. With the magistrate involved, and you being named as an accomplice to theft, we would hate for the authorities to detain you."

The lady's face turned as white as fresh snowfall. "An accomplice to theft?" In a failed bid to sound shocked, she sounded guilty.

"We know about the letter Anne stole from Major Rowlands." Lillian's voice carried a hint of pity. "We know about the broken figurine. Know the handkerchief is yours."

"We need to know who ye met in the garden," Callan said, "and what it has to do with a man named O'Malley."

Shoulders hunched, the lady seemed to shrink into herself. "Please. Don't make me tell you. Let me sing tonight and leave this godforsaken place before it's too late."

Callan thought of MacTavish writhing in the carriage seat like an injured animal. He'd almost lost the only man who'd ever treated him like a son. One of the few men he respected.

"My friend almost died sniffing that damn perfume. Ye'll tell us what ye know. The cells in Newgate are nae pleasant, especially for a woman expecting a child."

Madame Delafont almost swooned again. She pressed her hand to her forehead. "Sheridan told you about my condition?"

It was a calculated guess. Whenever Callan's father complained about begetting only one heir, his mother touched her abdomen.

If ye came to my bed, it wouldnae be a problem.

"Who did ye meet in the garden?" With his patience stretched as tight as a bow, he'd have no more distractions tonight. "Was it Rowlands or Baudelaire?"

Who else would want Valmary's recipe for May Bell?

Tension hung in the air, thick, palpable.

As the lady contemplated her future, she started mumbling about surviving long enough to board the boat. "Mrs Rowlands made a dreadful mistake. She told Baudelaire about the gift from Mr Valmary. When the poor woman died suddenly, Monsieur Baudelaire had me bribe the maid to steal the letter."

"Why risk yer neck for Baudelaire?" Callan asked, but then recalled the violent tussle in the garden.

"He terrifies me. It's why I must leave tonight."

"Who's O'Malley?"

She gulped. "A chemist who used to work for Monsieur Baudelaire. He has a house near St Saviour's Docks, but he met us outside the old Bermondsey Spa. Monsieur Baudelaire, he wishes to create the perfect scent. He means to win the game at all costs."

Someone needed to teach the Frenchman a lesson.

Threatening women was no game.

"But Mrs Rowlands died weeks ago," Lillian said, quite certain of the facts. "Why did Anne wait to give you the letter? Why visit the Kinver residence and risk being seen?"

Madame Delafont's weary sigh said she found the questions draining. "Because she changed her mind. She didn't want to betray her mistress and said she would return the letter to Mr Valmary."

"But her sister is sick, and ye offered her a hundred pounds," Callan surmised, "a sum she couldnae refuse."

The lady had the decency to look ashamed. "You must understand, I had no choice. Anne was just as terrified. When I sang for Lord and Lady Kinver on their wedding day, she suggested I come to the house to make the exchange."

Pike entered, carrying a tea tray, the china cup clattering

on the saucer. "We've pound cake and cheese. Mr Warren said that should see you right. He wants you on stage in fifteen minutes to warm up your vocals."

"What will happen to me now?" the lady muttered when Pike turned his back to set down the tray.

Lillian stood, as eager as Callan to leave this place and partake in a late-night adventure. "We will speak to Mr Daventry. But you know how these things are. It may be as late as tomorrow afternoon before he has time to act on the matter."

Callan smiled to himself. He'd wager Madame Delafont would be in Dover come dawn and across the Channel come nightfall.

The depth of Lillian's compassion touched him deeply. She was a champion for the downtrodden, a defender of mistreated women. If she would just believe in herself, she would make an excellent duchess.

Understanding they'd granted her a reprieve, Madame Delafont reached out to clasp Lillian's hand. "I shall not forget this kindness. And if you ever find yourself in an unfortunate position, Pike knows my direction."

"She'll never find herself abandoned," Callan said, wanting the singer to know he was not like the randy lords of the *ton*. "I would protect her with my life. Some men know a woman's worth."

Madame Delafont smiled. "I hope Miss Ware sees yours, Your Grace. Few men accept their responsibilities."

Lillian's eyes brightened. "I assure you, I do."

They wished the lady farewell and left the theatre.

Once in the alley, Callan pulled Lillian into an embrace. The need to touch her, to hold her, proved as compelling as the need to breathe.

"She'll flee the second the curtain falls," Callan said,

hoping Daventry didn't want them to detain the opera singer. "Though I cannae blame her. I'd nae put it past Baudelaire to make her the scapegoat."

"And it seems unfair to punish Anne and Madame Delafont when they're merely pawns in Monsieur Baudelaire's game," Lillian agreed.

"I should have throttled the devil when I had a chance."

"Mr Daventry will make sure he gets his comeuppance. We'll visit the Hart Street office and leave him a note. We can explain everything in detail tomorrow."

Callan's thoughts turned to their plans for the evening. "Do ye still want to accompany me on a wild adventure? I plan to do more than test yer mettle."

"More than anything." A flash of tenderness in her eyes held him transfixed. "Do you mean to test how well I cope in the cold, Callan?"

"On my oath, ye'll nae be cold." He captured her chin and kissed her slowly. Let her feel the depth of his affection with every gentle stroke of his tongue.

She breathed a happy sigh when they parted. "I never knew there were so many ways to kiss."

"Aye, and we've all night to invent more."

"Then let us not delay."

He stole another quick kiss. "What did ye tell Roxburgh?"

"The only thing that would pacify him." Mischief danced in her inviting eyes. "I told him I would marry you if you found yourself ruined."

Chapter Sixteen

Edmonton Manor
South of Epping Forest, Essex

Dewart brought the carriage to a stop at the entrance to the Edmonton Manor estate and climbed down from his box to unlock the rusty iron gates.

Needing a haven away from the hustle and bustle of city life, Callan had bought the land at auction four years ago. The house was a pile of charred timber and crumbling walls. A place nature had slowly reclaimed once the last of the fire's embers had died.

Callan handed Lillian down to the weed-infested drive.

Looking confused as to why they had alighted at the gate-house, she peered into the never-ending gloom. "You never mentioned owning a home in the country." She sounded deflated. Doubtless, playing lord of the manor did not consti-tute an adventure.

"The house perished long ago. The drive leads to an old ruin."

"Oh!" Her gaze darted to the thatched cottage, her blue eyes shining like polished sapphires. "We're staying in the gatehouse?"

Callan grinned. "Dewart is staying in the gatehouse. When here, I sleep beneath the stars." He dropped into a thick Scottish burr. "Do ye think ye've the courage to brave the wild weather, Miss Ware?"

She lifted her proud chin. "I'm sure I'll adapt, Your Grace."

"There ye have it, Dewart. We'll stay in the woods and use the gamekeeper's cabin for supplies."

"Aye, Yer Grace." Dewart closed the gates then busied himself lighting two lanterns, giving both to Callan. "Mr Jenkins checked the paths last week."

"Did he clear the area near the pool?"

Dewart nodded. "He scouted the woods for half a mile or more, though little grows at this time of year." He handed Lillian a wicker basket. "Mrs McClintock prepared a supper for two like ye asked. There's wine but nae glasses. I trust it will be to yer satisfaction."

"Aye, I'm sure it will." Callan thanked his man. "We'll leave ye to see to the horses and will return at dawn. Dinnae enter the woods." He'd not have the man stumbling upon an amorous scene. "Ring the handbell if ye need to raise an alarm."

Holding one lantern aloft, Callan told Lillian to follow him along the dirt track running parallel to the boundary wall. "It's a ten-minute walk, but stay beside me. Ye'll nae stray from the path."

She must have heard the thread of panic he could not suppress. "Are you afraid I'll pick something I shouldn't,

Callan?" Her reassuring hand came to rest on his back. "You've not told me what happened the day your mother died, the day of the accident."

A fire ignited in his chest—flames capable of razing a man to the ground if he didn't keep his wits.

He glanced at Lillian. While they had dealt with death differently, neither wished to revisit the haunting memories. And though they had made love and taken pleasure in each other's bodies, barriers still existed between them.

"One mistake in the woods changed everything," he said solemnly. Life was cruel. Fate dealt cards like a drunken croupier, casting them here and there with nary a thought to the consequences. "I've nae come this far to lose ye now."

An uncomfortable silence moved between them.

Unspoken words neither had the courage to say.

He trudged through the darkness, emotions gathering in his throat. Chilling images forced their way into his mind. This was not what he'd planned. He needed her warm body crushed against his, needed to lose himself in the woman he loved, not feel the cold echoes of the past.

"It's difficult to speak about painful memories," she said, clutching his coat sleeve for balance as she stepped over exposed tree roots. "But you know you can tell me anything."

I'm in love with you.

He could not tell her that.

A heavy sigh left his lips. "I want nothing to spoil our time together." He wanted to kiss her when his heart was full. Make love to her beneath a star-spangled sky, not a thunderous storm cloud.

She gripped his arm, bringing him to an abrupt halt, making him face her. "Callan, I allowed my past experiences to affect my future prospects. You helped me realise that I don't want to live like that anymore."

Her gaze caressed his face. Coming up on her toes, she pressed a chaste kiss to his lips, the soft stroke warming every cold extremity.

A guttural groan escaped him. He deepened the kiss, sliding his tongue over hers, drinking from her like a man at a desert oasis.

Lillian broke contact, her hand slipping from his shoulder to cover his heart. "Why come to the woods if it rouses so many painful memories?"

He shrugged as he inhaled the damp, earthy aroma, let the stillness soothe every tense muscle. "Because I feel at home here. Because I mean to conquer my fears, nae let them beat me."

He'd not meant it as a personal attack but he watched her eyes dull, heard the hitch in her breath.

"Everyone has a battle plan. Doubtless they all have flaws." She glanced at the darkness ahead. "But I'm quite proud of my progress. For the first time in my life, I believe I can win the war."

God, she was so incredible he could hardly breathe.

"Ye've held me spellbound since the day we waltzed at MacTavish's ball. Happen yer plan was to keep suitors at bay so one day I might claim the prize."

Her lips curled into a smile. "You see, I'm a great strategist."

"What if I'd grown tired of waiting?" Those months away were long and lonely. A woodcutter might fell a thousand trees to pass the time. Callan had only one focus. Being a better man than his father. "What if I'd believed ye were indifferent to my Scottish charm?"

She swallowed deeply. "Then I would have felt the loss keenly. Pretended I was protecting myself from heartbreak when I had been heading towards it all along."

Weeks ago, he could not have imagined having this conversation. He had only dreamed of kissing her, let alone what they would invariably do tonight.

"Come. We need to reach the gamekeeper's cabin and collect provisions." He paused, attempting to gauge her mood. "If ye prefer somewhere warmer, the gatehouse is comfortable and we can always venture back to London."

He never quite knew where he stood with her.

Couldn't shake a deep sense of foreboding.

Perhaps neither of them were destined to experience lasting happiness.

She straightened, repositioning the basket on her arm. "Callan, there's no place I'd rather be than here with you. Besides, my brother thinks I'm with the Sloanes in Little Chelsea. Best not disappoint him."

They discussed the case as they walked to the cabin.

"You know what we forgot to do at the theatre," she said.

"Aye, ask Madame Delafont about the initials on the handkerchief."

"I doubt Mr Daventry will offer either of us employment."

Callan chuckled. "Good. I'll nae miss the late nights." But he would miss spending time alone with her. At some point, he needed to confess his feelings, perhaps risk proposing marriage before heading back to the Highlands. But he'd say nothing that might distract him from his mission tonight.

"We've another late night tomorrow."

"Aye," was all he said. Forcing their way into Baudelaire's office was not what bothered him. The thought of inhaling something toxic chilled his blood. He had to hope fate had a new croupier.

The small stone cabin sat nestled amid the ancient oaks. There was but one sparsely furnished room with a fire, a table and a narrow bed. Outside there was stabling for a horse, kennels for a pack of dogs, a cold room for hanging game, and a wood store.

Callan placed the lanterns on the crude table. "There's nae chance of rain, but we'll make camp near the house."

"Have you ever slept in this bed?" Jealousy marred her tone. She inspected the mattress as if imagining an erotic scene, him wrapped around a lover.

"I've nae slept in it or brought anyone else here." She had been the only woman in his life for the last five years. "If ye want to remain inside we can."

"Do you always come here alone?"

"Aye. I like peace and quiet. Few people understand."

Her sudden huff conveyed her frustration. "I'm just so annoyed with myself. If I were a skilled pugilist, I'd punch myself on the nose."

He smiled. "For what?"

"For not dancing with you three years ago."

"Ye had yer reasons."

"They seem silly now. Fear can be quite debilitating."

"They were nae silly at the time."

Her gaze roamed over his face and body, the need to sate this soul-deep hunger evident in her pretty eyes. "I could never quite understand why women risked everything for their lustful urges. Yet I would risk everything to spend one night with you."

One night?

Not a lifetime?

An inner voice rushed to caution him, urging him to be wary. The pain of losing her would do more than break his heart. It would break his spirit. There'd be no heir to his bloodline. He'd be forever known as the Scot slain by an English maiden.

"Lillian."

"Yes?"

"I need more than one night."

"Yes, I'm certain one more night will not suffice." She quickly distracted herself by peering inside the basket. "Oh, we've shortbread and fudge."

"It's nae fudge but tablet. A Scottish confectionary. Mrs McClintock knows I've a fondness for all things sweet."

"So, we're to have a picnic beneath the stars." A giggle of excitement burst from her lips. The sound was so contagious it forced him to cast aside all doubts. "Will you make a fire outside?"

He laughed. "Aye, else we'll freeze to death."

She glanced at him through lowered lids. "We can keep each other warm. What do we sleep on?"

"I had Mr Jenkins erect a Round Tent. He stored blankets and furs inside. If we were staying for more than one night, I'd hunt and cook, but we've Mrs McClintock's basket." And he wanted to spend every minute worshiping her, not stirring the pot.

Intrigue flickered in her eyes. "Do you ever sleep in the woods when at home in the Highlands?"

"I'm the Duke of Dounreay." Though she knew what that entailed, he sought to remind her of his responsibilities. "By day, I've an estate to run. As Laird, I've a duty to my clansmen. But at night, and every spare moment I have, I live like a free man."

She fell silent, but he could almost hear the cogs turning in her mind. "I've never considered fitting freedom into a schedule."

"I'm a free man by choice, a duke by birth. There's nae difference between us, Lillian. We both use our free time to do what we love."

She raised a brow. "You mean me being a woman of noble birth, I have more time to indulge my whims."

"I mean life's better when there's a balance."

She exhaled, long and deep, like she had been holding her breath for years. "Come. Show me how to brave the elements. Show me what you're like when you roam free."

"Ye'll have to carry wood."

"I'll do whatever ye ask," she teased.

"We've nae far to walk. We're sleeping ten feet from the house."

He'd not wanted to venture too far. A lady might wake at night and wander into the woods. Besides, the next time they shared a moment like this he prayed they'd be camping on the banks near Balliemore.

They made a camp beneath the ancient oak trees.

Using the blankets and furs, Lillian created a makeshift bed inside the Round Tent. After stripping off his cravat and coat, Callan built a fire and piled enough wood beside it to last the night.

She came to join him by the fire, though kept her hands hidden behind her back rather than warm them against the flames.

"I have a confession." A chuckle escaped from her pursed lips. "You'll think me terribly selfish."

"Ye've eaten something from the basket," he said, noting the glimmer of mischief in her eyes. "Judging by the way yer licking yer lips, I'd say it's the tablet."

Laughing, she showed him the piece in her hand. "You're wasted as a duke. Mr Daventry would have you working as an agent if he could persuade you to spend more time in London."

And yet he couldn't determine how she felt about *him*.

He stood, closing the gap between them, slipping his arm

around her waist, keen to feel the heat of her body. "Feed me. It's the least ye can do after stealing the provisions."

"Open your mouth." She held the small confectionary square between her finger and thumb, teasing him to taste it. "And close your eyes. It's so much sweeter when you focus your senses."

Curbing a smile, he did as she asked.

The minx drew the sweet treat slowly over his bottom lip, snatching it back whenever he tried to claim a bite. Just when he thought he'd caught the edge with his teeth, she denied him the pleasure.

He was about to protest, when she kissed him, kissed him slowly, deeply, pouring everything of herself into his mouth along with the sumptuous taste of tablet.

She linked her hands behind his neck, pressing her body to his, squashing her breasts to his chest, desperate for physical contact.

Her urgency roused a primitive hunger in him. A fierce need to strip off their clothes and claim her amid the firelight.

On a ragged breath, she pulled away, clasping a hand to her heaving chest. "Make love to me, Callan."

The plea was enough to send him into a lustful frenzy.

Capturing her face between his hands, he kissed her, plunging wildly into her wet depths, his tongue mimicking what he'd do with his throbbing cock once they were wed.

A rational part of his brain urged him to slow down. A quick tupping wasn't on his agenda. They had the whole night to enjoy each other. He wanted to rain kisses over every inch of her body, to worship her as he would if she were his duchess.

"Ye're in a Highlander's territory now, lass." He kissed her jaw and nuzzled her neck. "We play the game by my rules. And I need to test yer mettle."

She gripped his shirtsleeves, moaning into the chill night air as he sucked at the sensitive skin on her neck. "What would you have this Sassenach do?"

Everything!

He released her. "Strip down to yer chemise while I stoke the fire."

She blinked in surprise. "Are you undressing?"

"Aye. I'm going to bathe in the pool." The cold water would cool his heated blood. She could sit on the water's edge, paddling her feet while he pleasured her beneath the heavens. "Jenkins built it a few years ago."

She scrunched her nose and pointed to the oval stone structure sunken into the ground behind them. "You're bathing in that dirty pond?"

"It's nae a pond." He laughed. "It's a natural pool."

"But there's netting covering it." She seemed to find some relief in that.

"To stop animals drinking and contaminating the water. It's easy to remove. The plants help keep the water clean."

"It must be freezing. Don't go in!"

"It's warmer than ye think."

She stood watching him, an incredulous look on her face as he stripped off his clothes and draped them over a low-hanging branch. Her gaze dropped to his flaccid manhood, her licentious hum audible in the cool night air.

He rolled back the netting and dipped his toe in the water.

Hell, it was cold.

A hiss escaped him, every part of his body tensing. "If I dinnae surface in a few seconds, ye'll have to jump in after me."

"What? Wait! No!"

But he stepped off the edge where the pool was at it's deepest.

The cold swamped him, seizing command of every muscle. Biting into his skin, sinking into his bones. He rose quickly, moving to float on his back and gaze at the night sky while he calmed his breathing.

Lillian stood statue-still.

"Do ye want to come in?"

She didn't answer.

He swam to the edge and looked up at her. Only then did he realise his mistake. He knew the pool was shallow, that he'd been teasing her about jumping in to save him. Still, in his excitement, he'd not considered she'd have a fear of water.

Ye're a damn clodhead, Callan!

"The water is shallow here," he reassured her, desperate to make amends. "There's nae danger."

There was no danger of eating poisonous berries in the woods, yet he paid Jenkins to clear the paths every few months.

He climbed out, shivering against the cool breeze, and hauled her against his wet body. "Can ye forgive a pea-brained idiot?"

She sagged against him, hugging him around the waist.

"In my eagerness to make love to ye in the pool, I'd nae considered asking if ye were afraid of the water."

"I—I can swim," she muttered into his damp chest. "Adam insisted I learn for he wished to avoid another tragedy."

Callan cradled her face between his palms and forced her to look at him, his heart nearly breaking for making such stupid assumptions. "But ye hate the water?"

"No, but I've not been in a pool for years."

"Then what left ye so shaken?"

She gulped. "When you jumped in, I suddenly realised I

could lose you, too. That what exists between us is as fragile as the threads of a spider's web."

He brushed his lips over hers, caressing more than kissing, relishing their softness. "I'll never make ye worry like that again. Let me get dressed and we'll—"

"No. I'm tired of living in fear." She ran her hand over his wet arm as if loving the feel of the firm muscles. "I want to enter the water, Callan. I want to enter the water with you."

He doubted he'd ever meet a braver woman in all his life.

Love filled his heart.

Love brighter than any star shining tonight.

"Then undress while I stoke the fire."

Despite throwing on more logs and poking the embers, he didn't linger near the flames. Entering the water at the shallowest point, he waited for her to strip down to her chemise.

Lillian padded towards the pool, her auburn hair draped around one shoulder, every curve visible through the sheer undergarment.

Callan straightened, the water lapping at his waist, so she might gauge the depth. "Sit on the edge, take my hands and slide in. 'Tis shallow here."

Like a woodland nymph intent on seduction, she drew her chemise over her head and dropped the garment on the ground. "I've no wish to be encumbered."

Callan's mouth was dry.

Lillian stood before him, a wondrous vision in her nakedness. In the moonlight, her skin had an ethereal sheen. Her blue eyes looked fairy-like, fragile yet so arousingly inquisitive.

Never had he seen anything more beautiful. The need to bury himself deep inside her body hardened his cock.

Coming to sit on the stone edge, she squealed as she dangled her legs in the water. "Good Lord. It's freezing."

"I know of a way to warm ye."

He pushed between her soft thighs, snaked his arms around her waist and drew her slowly down into the water. Settling his hands on her bottom, he encouraged her to wrap her legs around his hips.

"Callan, no!" She shivered against him.

"Hold on to me, lass." He was trembling, too, from lust and love and the need to sate this clawing hunger.

"Callan, do something." Her teeth chattered, and she clutched him tightly. "Kiss me before my blood freezes in my veins."

He crushed her to his chest, thrusting his tongue deep into her mouth in a kiss that tugged at his ballocks and drove him near insane.

"God, I'm desperate to be inside ye, love."

"Then take me now," she panted. "Hurry."

"Do ye nae want to find yer release first?"

"Later. Make me yours."

The primal need to claim her proved powerful. "Then ye're about to get the full measure of this Highlander."

Holding her tight to his body, he pushed into her sex, meeting a little resistance. He worked himself in and out slowly before burying himself to the hilt.

"Heavens!"

"Ride me," he growled.

"Is that how a Highlander claims his woman?"

"Aye, when he's about to spill his seed in a bathing pool."

They soon found a rhythm. He devoured her mouth, his tongue sliding over hers, mimicking the frenzied thrusts of his cock.

Lillian tugged his hair as he sucked her nipples. "Oh, it feels so good, Callan. Don't stop."

So good he'd need her every hour until dawn.

And yet as water lapped at their bodies and their moans penetrated the stillness, he wasn't thinking about taking her on a bed of furs.

He was thinking how he could persuade her to move to the Highlands.

How he might convince this woman to be his wife.

Chapter Seventeen

Hanover Square
London

Shivering against the chill air, Lillian fastened her boots, pulled her cloak tightly around her shoulders and crept downstairs. All was dark and deathly quiet now the long case clock had finished chiming ten. By some miraculous feat, Alexander slept soundly. And so everyone in the house—except for her—had decided to get a good night's rest.

She was waiting for Dounreay to ferry them to Ludgate Hill, so they might force the lock on the office door and rifle through Monsieur Baudelaire's private papers.

With carefully placed steps, she reached the hall without the stairs creaking and moved to the console table. Easing the drawer open, she reached inside and took the front door key. There was no reason for anyone to know she'd gone out for a few hours.

A few hours?

She scoffed silently at that.

After spending a magical night in Dounreay's arms, she'd travel the world with him if he asked.

The murmur of voices in the study stole her attention.

Eliza appeared, backing out of the room and giving a playful giggle. "Come and find me, my love. I shall hide in the garden." She spoke so seductively Lillian thought to cover her ears. "Don't be long." Eliza turned abruptly, almost jumping out of her skin. "Lillian! I thought you were in bed."

Lillian wasn't sure who was more embarrassed about being caught in the act. "I—I am just waiting for the duke. We're to visit Monsieur Baudelaire's establishment on Ludgate Hill. Did I not mention it during dinner?"

Heavens! Only guilty people rambled like a Bedlamite.

"No, I don't think you did." Eliza sighed. "Now, I owe your brother a boon. I wagered you were staying home tonight, yet he was convinced you would be sneaking away somewhere."

"Lillian!" Adam called from the depths of the dimly lit study. "Might I speak to you for a moment?" He sounded most displeased.

"Coming," she replied, cursing her misfortune.

Eliza smiled and rubbed Lillian's arm affectionately. "Try to leave him in a good mood. Do you have a weapon?"

"A weapon?" Even when in a foul temper, Adam was always reasonable.

"When you're out, you might encounter footpads."

"Dounreay has a *sgian dubh*."

"You should take a pocket pistol. I'm surprised Mr Daventry didn't ensure you were equipped. I'll fetch mine. It's simple to use."

As Eliza climbed the stairs, Lillian took a moment to calm her breathing. She entered the study to find Adam seated behind his imposing desk, his hair a little mussed, his cravat missing.

"You wished to speak to me."

Adam relaxed back in his seat, observing her over steepled fingers. "Do you want to tell me where you were last night?"

"With Dounreay." There was no point lying.

"You said you were staying with the Sloanes."

"It was late when we left Madame Delafont. Dounreay invited me to—" She stopped abruptly. The woods were his secret place, known to a handful of trusted people. A special place where she had spent the most thrilling night of her life.

"Dounreay invited you to do what, Lillian? I think I've been more than tolerant in allowing you to explore your feelings for the duke, but I cannot—"

"I'm in love with him."

Good heavens!

She gasped as the words tumbled from her mouth. She had been so close to telling Dounreay last night. Fear still held her back, a nail snagging her cloak, making her falter.

Adam blinked in surprise. "If you're trying to placate me by—"

"No. I suspect I've always loved him." A chuckle escaped her lips as she let love flood every chamber of her heart. The rush of euphoria was so intense, tears filled her eyes. "I love him deeply, Adam."

So deeply it hurt.

"Are you sure that's what you feel?"

She shrugged, trying to find the right words to convey her emotions. "I cannot bear it when we part. When I think about him, I get so giddy I crash into the furniture. His happiness is more important than my own. And I could listen to him talk all night." The sound of that soft Scottish burr did strange things to her insides.

And when Dounreay made love to her, the whole world tilted on its axis. She didn't want to avoid the future. She wanted to live with him and sleep beside him in bed. Wake to feel his strong arms wrapped around her. Laugh with him every day of her life.

Adam released the breath he'd probably been holding since she was six years old. "Thank the Lord! I thought you'd never let yourself love him. I thought you'd be forever alone, pushing everyone away."

Tears slipped down her cheeks—tears of joy, relief.

The wonder of it all tightened her throat.

"I'm sorry if I've made you worry." He was the last person she wanted to hurt. "I'm sorry if I've ever disappointed you. But I love you and don't want you to worry about me anymore."

Upon hearing her endearment, his mouth fell open in disbelief. He pushed out of the seat, rounded the desk, and hugged her. "All I've ever wanted is for you to be happy. Promise me you'll tell Dounreay how you feel."

"I will." She would tell him when they were alone together in the carriage. Before they forced their way into Monsieur Baudelaire's shop to search for evidence. Hopefully, they'd find the letter, find proof he was the poisoner, and be done with the business of murder.

"Be prepared. Dounreay will ask you to marry him."

She cupped his cheek. "I know." The thought of being a duchess proved terrifying and exciting in equal measure. Being Dounreay's wife was all that mattered. "I'm prepared to do whatever it takes to have him. I cannot lose him, Adam."

Adam smiled as he wiped away her tears.

Eliza knocked lightly on the open door. "There's a carriage waiting outside. And it occurred to me you wouldn't have time to load a pistol. You can have my blade instead."

Love filled Adam's eyes as he gazed upon his wife. Lillian had seen a similar look in Dounreay's dark brown pools when he'd buried himself inside her body last night.

"I'm not taking a reticule, so it must be small enough to fit in my pocket." Her heart raced, her gaze moving to the window as she pictured Dounreay waiting in the carriage.

"I can see you're impatient to leave." Eliza gave her the small weapon encased in a brown leather sheath. "If you're detained this evening, promise to send a penny boy with a note."

"Don't expect me home tonight. Dounreay has a property out of town." She was talking quickly, edging towards the door, too excited to stand still. "Adam will explain. I shall see you both tomorrow."

Before they kept her a moment longer, she unlocked the front door, closed it behind her, and hurried to the carriage.

Her heart sank.

It was not Dounreay's elegant vehicle.

The black unmarked equipage belonged to Mr Daventry. The man himself opened the door from the inside, but it was Dounreay who held out his hand and helped her to mount the steps.

Heat flooded her palm, spreading quickly up her arm.

Their gazes locked, her heart skipping to his tune.

I love you!

Forgive me for being so foolish, so blind.

Searching his eyes, she tried to convey the words by thought alone, hoping to see the same abiding affection shimmering there.

Concern marred his brow. "Are ye unwell? Do ye have a fever?"

Memories of sliding into the cold water assailed her. The shock had left her gasping for breath. The chill had penetrated her bones, but Dounreay had warmed every numb extremity.

"I'm perfectly well."

I'm lovesick and desperate to tell you.

Dounreay guided her into the seat beside him, his thigh covertly stroking hers. "Ye've been crying," he whispered as Mr Daventry closed the door. "Yer eyes are all puffy and swollen."

"Yes, but only happy tears." She reached between them and secretly clasped his hand, squeezing it tightly. "I assure you. I am perfectly well, Your Grace."

He nodded, though seemed unsure whether to believe her. "Daventry wished to accompany us to Baudelaire's perfumery."

Mr Daventry rapped on the roof, and the vehicle lurched forward. "If the Frenchman is capable of using poison, I'll not risk you going there alone." In the gloomy confines of his carriage, she noted his expression turn grave. "Sadly, they found his assistant dead this morning. The coroner thinks the fellow suffered a seizure and hit his head."

"Dead?" Dazed, she struggled to speak. "The assistant?"

Dounreay heaved a sigh. "It's Christian."

"Christian!" Lillian pictured the man's last moments, as gruesome a story as any heard at a public execution. She stared at Mr Daventry. "A seizure brought on by a poison? Do you think Monsieur Baudelaire is responsible?"

"That's what we must establish. Christian was dead in his rented room when his colleague called. The fellow is being questioned at the Hatton Garden police office while they wait for the coroner to confirm the precise cause of death."

Lillian recalled the assistant's nervous manner. "Evidently, he knew something and paid with his life." Like everyone else, was Christian terrified of Monsieur Baudelaire?

"I had an agent interview the young groom from the mews."

"To see if he could remember Madame Delafont?" She thought it odd the boy hadn't mentioned French accents. But he had probably been hard at work since dawn.

Mr Daventry nodded. "The scamp said he thought they spoke like other nabobs but couldn't quite remember. Even after pocketing three sovereigns, his mind was a blur."

"Madame Delafont has nae reason to lie about bribing the maid." Dounreay absently stroked his thumb over hers. "And why would she lie about being in the mews?"

"Who can say?" Mr Daventry mused, his gaze dropping to their clasped hands. "Mrs Gunning said you were in a hurry when you dropped the note at the Hart Street office last night."

Lillian's heart fluttered. "It had been a long day."

"You didn't think to wait outside the theatre to spy on Madame Delafont?" Suspicion clouded his tone. But he probably knew why they'd not lingered in Covent Garden. "Had you not been in such a rush to return *home*, you'd know the opera singer did not make a mad dash to Dover."

"She didn't? But she was desperate to leave." Lillian could scarce believe it. Madame Delafont gave the impression she would skip the encore and board the next boat to France.

"We had nae reason to doubt her word." Dounreay firmed his tone, giving her a glimpse of the powerful duke she hoped to marry—unless fate had other plans. "We're nae employed to do yer bidding. We offered our help. It wouldnae hurt if ye showed some gratitude."

Mr Daventry smiled. "Forgive me. I expect too much. My wife says it's my greatest flaw. And clearly you have other matters on your mind."

"Is Madame Delafont still at the theatre?" Lillian said to defuse the tension. Then a thought struck her. Mr Daventry must have paid someone to keep watch outside the theatre. Had this person seen her kissing Dounreay in the alley and reported back?

"No. She's staying under an alias at the Musgrove Hotel."

"The Musgrove? How odd." Doubts crept into Lillian's mind. Had she been wrong to trust the opera singer? "Perhaps Lord Sheridan persuaded her to stay. She used the alias because she's afraid of Monsieur Baudelaire."

"Perhaps. We'll keep pressing for answers until we uncover the truth." Mr Daventry glanced out of the window as they passed the obelisk. "We're almost at Ludgate Hill."

The coachman steered the carriage through the narrow archway into the courtyard of the Belle Sauvage. The old inn faced Monsieur Baudelaire's establishment.

Mr Daventry alighted first, conversing with a shifty-looking fellow who'd slipped out from the shadows wearing a dusty coat and weather-beaten hat.

Lillian shuffled around to face Dounreay. "When we've finished here, might I return with you to Park Lane? I have something to tell you, and it cannot wait until tomorrow."

A shadow of unease passed over his features. "Aye, but can ye nae tell me now? I'm nae sure I can wait."

She glanced over her shoulder, saw Mr Daventry was occupied and quickly kissed Dounreay on the lips. "We need to concentrate on finding evidence if we mean to put this sorry business behind us." And she'd not declare her love in the yard of a grotty inn.

"Well? Are you coming?" Mr Daventry appeared at the open carriage door. "We'll access the perfumery via the rear entrance in Dolphin Court. Swithin will pick the lock."

Swithin stepped forward and offered a toothy grin. The man's neck was wider than the average person's waist. "We'll need to be quick. Old Baudelaire often returns to his office late at night."

Dounreay turned to her, raising the hood of her cloak, tucking a loose strand of hair behind her ear. "Ye'll nae leave my side tonight. Ye'll nae touch anything without me examining it first."

When Dounreay swore to protect a woman, she could be sure he would die for the cause. "You cannot put yourself at risk. You're a duke without an heir."

"I'm nothing without ye, Lillian. Agree, else we're nae leaving this carriage." He looked set to show her he was every bit a Highland lord.

With some reluctance—and because she wanted this matter over with so they might spend a few hours alone—Lillian agreed.

They followed Mr Daventry across the street, the majestic spire of St Paul's looming large above the cramped buildings. Dounreay kept his arm around her waist as they navigated the dingy alley, and did not release her until Swithin had forced the lock on the perfumer's door.

"I'll wait 'ere." Swithin scoured the darkness like a hawk looking for the first flicker of movement. "Be quick now. This place ain't safe at night."

With Mr Daventry leading the way, they crept through the storeroom and along the narrow corridor. The sickening stench of perfume hung in the air, drawing her mind to those early conversations with Dounreay.

There's nothing more alluring than a woman's natural aroma.

He'd sought to prove his point in the last few days. Kissing every inch of her bare skin, pressing his mouth to her neck, her sex, breathing her in like an addict did smoke in an opium den.

Mr Daventry stopped at a door. "I'm told this is the office." He reached into the leather satchel draped across his muscular body and removed various metal implements. "I need Swithin to keep guard," he said, answering a question she had not thought to ask.

He tripped the lock with ease.

Then he removed a candle and a tiny metal box. "Walker's new invention saves time as long as one keeps the tapers dry." He drew a wooden splint, striking the sulphur tip against the folded sandpaper to generate a flame.

Dounreay took the lit candle, and they crept into the dark room.

"What are we looking for?" she whispered.

"Something to link Baudelaire to O'Malley." Mr Daventry rounded the cluttered desk to inspect the ledgers lining the bookshelf. "Documents confirming he imported the poison. Most likely seeds from India or Ceylon. Letters to suggest Baudelaire has threatened Valmary. Anything to confirm our suspicions."

"We'll search the desk." Dounreay ran his hand beneath the locked drawers and rummaged inside empty ink pots before finding a small brass key. "A man doesnae need four pots on his desk."

Wax dripped down the candle. Mr Daventry suggested wrapping a handkerchief around the base rather than using the empty brass holder on the desk. "We don't want Baudelaire to know we've been here."

Dounreay did as suggested, handing her the candle while he rifled through the first drawer. "There's nothing here but legal documents, gaming debts and loose coins."

Mr Daventry squinted as he read the entries in a ledger. "There's nothing unusual here, either. Though I suspect only a fool would record purchasing poison."

"Perhaps it's listed in his household accounts." Such things were often used to kill rats and other vermin, and would not draw suspicion. "We could question his housekeeper or maid."

Mr Daventry returned the ledger to the shelf and took another. "We'll keep looking. Arrogant men often leave a clue to their nefarious deeds." He turned to Dounreay. "Have you found anything?"

Dounreay snorted. "Aye. A paper on how to use bear grease to preserve a head of hair. And a diary listing all the ingredients used in his perfumes. But nae the letter we need."

Lillian raised the candle aloft and scanned the contents in the next drawer Dounreay opened. "What's in that metal box?" She moved to take it, but Dounreay snatched it first, removing the lid as if it were home to a deadly spider.

"It's powder."

"Don't breathe it in." Mr Daventry moved to examine the finding. "It could be anything, though it looks like snuff. We need to take a sample." He removed a handkerchief from his pocket and used a quill to scrape a small amount of powder onto the linen. Then he folded it carefully and slipped it inside his satchel.

Dounreay replaced the lid and returned the tin to the drawer, wiping his hands vigorously on his trousers lest a speck had touched his skin.

"There's another notebook." Lillian pointed to the small leather item hidden amongst more papers. It looked old, the brown leather worn, the pages tatty around the edges.

Dounreay opened it, skipping to the last entry. He frowned, jerking his head before paying closer attention and cursing in Gaelic. "Why, I'll strap that devil to the obelisk and whip him with a birch."

"What is it?" Judging by his reaction, it was something shocking.

"'Tis a record of Baudelaire's games with Valmary. The man lists each conquest as if it were a game of piquet. Yer name is the last one entered."

"Mine?" She put her hand to her throat like she had already inhaled the toxin. Had already been violated by two deranged men. "What did he write? Has he mentioned Mr Valmary's gift?"

"Aye."

"What gift?" Mr Daventry snapped.

"He sent me perfume, sir."

"Why the hell didn't you mention it before?"

"Because we've not had a moment to catch our breaths." And she had been so obsessed with Dounreay, she had not considered the threat. "Surely only an imbecile would target the person hired to find the poisoner."

"Based on recent events, Baudelaire may be capable of murder."

"They score points," Dounreay said with a measure of disgust, flipping to the previous pages. "They take it in turns to play a hand. Valmary was the first to give Madame Delafont perfume, but both men threw down their cards and folded in the second round."

Keen to think of something other than being a pawn in Mr

Valmary's game, Lillian focused on gathering evidence. "How strange. Has that ever happened before?"

Dounreay quickly glanced at the other pages. "Nae that I can tell."

"Is there any mention of Mrs Rowlands?" Mr Daventry asked.

"Aye. She has a page between Lillian and Madame Delafont. Mr Valmary was declared the winner."

"Damnation." Mr Daventry groaned. "We need time to study the book, but the villain will know if we take it. I need to speak to the coroner about Mrs Rowlands' death. Based on Anne's description, there's every chance the woman was poisoned."

Lillian's mind was all a jumble. "You think Monsieur Baudelaire killed her because she chose Mr Valmary?"

"The Frenchman has delusions of grandeur. I'd not put anything past him. We need to find Baudelaire and detain him."

Lillian considered the tatty notebook. "How long have the men been competing for lovers? How old are they?"

"They're in their forties," Mr Daventry said before continuing like he had a thick dossier on both men. "They spent time in India before inheriting the businesses. Their fathers were perfumers who trained together in Paris."

Dounreay opened the notebook at the first page and gasped. "Ye'll nae believe it, but Baudelaire stole Valmary's lover twenty years ago. All the details are listed."

Twenty years ago!

"So they've been competing since they were young men." Lillian was both astounded and confused. Why play the game for so long? What had made them so wicked and bitter?

Dounreay shook his head. "Ye'll need to investigate the deaths of all the women mentioned in this book. From the dates recorded, the men end the relationships once they've been declared the victor."

There could be twenty women nursing broken hearts? Women used in such a cruel manner. Hence why Lillian had decided to write a book. So ladies might recognise scoundrels.

Dounreay started reading aloud. "Miss Swanson was the first, though she was only nineteen." With his nose wrinkled in disdain, he continued naming the victims as if they were casualties of war. "Lady Beaumont. She was ten years their senior. They had nae scruples—"

He stopped abruptly, stood rigid.

"No! It cannae be." Callan's eyes grew wide, his face deathly pale.

"Callan, what is it?" she said, not caring that she had used his given name. By now, Mr Daventry knew they were lovers. "What's wrong?"

He did not reply.

His eyes glazed.

The muscles in his shoulders tensed.

His breath came in shallow pants.

Without warning, he thrust the book at Mr Daventry. "Will ye see Miss Ware safely home? I must go." He didn't wait for a reply but raced out of the room like footpads were hot on his heels.

"Callan!" Candle in hand, she made to give chase.

But Mr Daventry clasped her elbow, his grip firm. "You'll not catch him. He seems determined in his course, and I'll not have you wandering these streets alone."

Tears stung her eyes. "I have to go. He needs me."

"Wait! You might be of better use to him if we can establish what caused such a volatile reaction." Mr Daventry opened the notebook at the first page. He worked his way slowly through before jerking his head and sighing. "Curse the saints. It makes sense now."

"What does? Tell me."

His mouth took a downward turn. "Dounreay's mother is listed in the book. It seems Mr Valmary won her heart, too."

Chapter Eighteen

Callan ran as if the *cù-sìth* bounded behind him. The mythical hound hunting him over the Highland moors, waiting for him to drop dead in terror.

If he stopped, his mind might explode from confusion. If he stopped, he would have to acknowledge what he'd read. Still, Satan meant to torment him tonight with wicked lies and dark secrets.

Words and visions crept into his mind.

His mother's name scrawled in that filthy book. Bets placed. Scores kept. Details of her womanly attributes recorded as if she were a mare for sale at Tattersall's.

Old memories took on new meanings.

She'd worn perfume on their walk in the woods. The smell was so potent it smothered the refreshing scent of pine. So potent, Callan had covered his nose when she hugged him, had almost choked, too. So potent, his father had emptied the rest into the chamber pot and tossed it out of the window.

Recognition dawned. Her last words were not a means of explaining the tragedy. They were a plea to a distraught son.

Tell yer father I picked the wrong berries.

I love ye, Callan, but ye'll nae save me.

Tears trickled down his cheeks. Tears he'd not shed since he was twelve years old. Tears unbecoming a duke or a man of his brawn.

Pain tore through him anew.

Slashing at the heart that had brimmed with love an hour ago.

Yet his hands throbbed with the need to murder someone tonight. He had to pray he'd find Valmary at the perfumery. Didn't care if he hanged from the gallows. It would be worth it just to make the bastard pay.

He had a duty to punish the men who'd murdered his mother. In his eyes, Baudelaire and Valmary both bore the guilt. He didn't care who poisoned her perfume. On his oath, no other woman would suffer at their hands again.

His lungs burned.

His muscles ached.

But he pushed on, sprinting along Fleet Street and onto the Strand, knocking into drunkards and vagabonds—cursing every villainous bastard to Hades.

A shady fellow slithered out of the darkness, the glint of a blade catching Callan's eye. The footpad moved to block his path. "I'll 'ave yer blunt, guv'nor."

"Ye picked the wrong man to cross tonight." Callan launched his fist into the miscreant's face, knocking the fool on his arse.

Like his kin of old, he would wield a claymore and slice through anyone who dared to stand in his way.

With anger surging through his veins, he reached Pall Mall. Seeing MacTavish's house roused another crippling emotion.

Betrayal.

Did MacTavish know why the Duchess of Dounreay

loved visiting the metropolis? Had he lied to Callan all these years? Conspired with Lorna to hide the truth? Was that why he never condemned Callan's father when he should have cursed him to the devil?

He hammered on MacTavish's door, loud enough to wake the dead. Except Angus wasn't dead. He had sniffed the damn perfume and survived.

No one answered.

Callan stepped back and stared at the upper windows. Much like his heart, the house was shrouded in darkness.

"MacTavish! Open this door! Do ye hear me?" Lucifer's temper consumed him, a fire hot enough to singe all the liars in hell.

He banged until the blurry-eyed butler opened the door. "Your Grace?" Monroe had thrown his coat over his crumpled nightshirt and stood blinking at Callan like he was dreaming.

This isnae a dream.

'Tis a bloody nightmare.

"I must speak to MacTavish." Callan barged past him, mounting the stairs two at a time.

Lorna appeared from the spare room, tying the belt on her wrapper, her long braid hanging over her shoulder. "Callan? What brings ye here at this late hour? Is it Miss Ware? Dinnae say something terrible has happened."

"Aye, something terrible has happened. But it's MacTavish who will hear my gripe. I dinnae care if he's ill. He'll speak to me now before I head out on a murderous rampage."

Lorna stumbled back in shock.

She knew the sweet boy who hated his father.

She knew the honourable man, the respectable duke.

She did not know the vicious Highlander. The beast who'd not rest until blood coated his hands.

"Angus lied to me," he cried, hurling daggers of disdain at Angus' door. "Ye lied to me all these years. Let me think an accident in the woods claimed my mother when ye knew her secret."

He saw it the second Lorna's lips trembled.

The truth they'd never dared speak.

"Callan, ye need to calm down and tell me what's happened."

"I want to speak to MacTavish."

"Angus needs his rest and—"

"Lorna!" Angus' weary voice echoed from the depths of the master chamber. "I'll see him. Send him in."

Lorna muttered under her breath. "Be mindful of his condition. He's been a dear friend to ye all these years. Remember that."

"Aye, a friend who's lied through his rotten teeth." They knew he valued honesty. They were the closest thing he had to kin. Now he had no one. "Happen my forebears were right."

Trust no one but yer clansmen.

A MacTavish will stab ye in the back.

Hearing the commotion, Ailsa appeared on the landing. "Tell me something hasnae happened to Lillian."

Lillian!

He'd left her in that bastard's office with no explanation.

Daventry would take care of her.

Callan was incapable.

Nothing but hatred flowed in his veins.

Vengeance had encased his heart in stone.

Lorna ushered Ailsa back to bed, reassuring her Miss Ware was safe and well and there was nothing to fear. "This is a private matter between Dounreay and yer father. It will all be fine come the morning."

It would not be fine.

Not unless Lorna could bring his mother back from the grave. Or knew a spell to make him forget the depth of everyone's betrayal.

Inhaling deeply, he opened the door to MacTavish's bedchamber and marched across the room to glare at the pale man in the bed.

Angus raised a shaky hand and pointed to the chair near the washstand. "Bring the seat closer and sit down. I'll nae have a crick in my neck."

"I'll stand." Nervous energy meant he could not keep still.

"Ye'll sit. I may be in this bed, but I can still put my boot up yer arse."

"Ye're in nae position to make threats. Tell me the truth about my mother." He had a date with the devil and didn't have time to linger.

"Sit down, lad, or I shall leave ye to wallow in self-pity."

"Self-pity!" Callan growled as he snatched the chair, brought it closer to the bed and sat down. "I watched her take her last breath. She died in my arms, fighting the poison writhing in her veins. I carried her a mile or more, fell to the ground too many times to count. So dinnae pretend I've got nae reason to be angry."

"Aye, 'twas a tragedy." Shadows moved like ghosts over the wall behind Angus' head, dancing with every flicker of the firelight.

"'Twas murder."

Angus jerked, and not from the effects of the poison. "Murder? Come now, yer father was nae kind but—"

"For once, my father is innocent." Frustration tightened every muscle. For years, he'd been blaming the wrong man.

"Do ye mean to play dumb? Am I to act the governess and spell it out for ye?"

"What is it ye think I'm hiding?" Angus wiped the beads of sweat off his brow. "If I've kept something from ye, it will have been for yer own good."

"My own good?" Callan firmed his jaw. He told him about Baudelaire's notebook and why the perfumer kept a tally. "My mother's name was in that damn book. They fought for her affections in the months before she died. Valmary won. Baudelaire poisoned her. And ye kept the truth from me."

Silence swung between them like the executioner's axe.

"We knew Moira had a lover," Lorna said, entering the room. "And who could blame her? Nae one wants to spend their life in a loveless marriage."

Callan sat back in the seat, the truth like an elixir for his troubled soul. "I wouldnae have blamed her, either. That's nae the issue here."

"We didnae know who it was." Lorna came to sit on the bed. "But I found a letter amongst her personal papers. A letter from a man named Thaddeus. I didnae want yer father to find it, didnae want anything to tarnish her memory. And so I threw it on the fire and watched it burn till it was nought but ash amid the embers."

Callan's sigh came from the heart, not the lungs. "Thaddeus Valmary used her in a game with Baudelaire." That made three men who had taken Moira Maclean for a fool.

Three men who'd pretended to love her.

Three men who'd ruined her life.

The thought tore him to shreds.

"Why keep it a secret all these years?"

Angus reached out and gripped Callan's coat sleeve. "We had nae proof other than the letter. And when she died, we thought only of protecting ye, Callan. Why in blazes would we think she'd been murdered?"

Lorna placed her hand on his shoulder. "Moira wouldnae want ye getting embroiled in this mess. She wouldnae want ye chasing about London threatening men. Getting into bother."

"I'll nae rest until they're dead."

"Ye're a duke with a long life ahead of ye," Angus pleaded. "Dinnae do anything rash. Punish the men if ye've evidence, but nae at the cost of yer own future."

Callan hung his head, his roiling anger turning to despair.

"Daventry will see justice served," Angus added.

And yet the need to kill the men with his own hands compelled him to stand. "Ye're like kin to me. Ye should have told me the truth when my father died. But I understand why ye kept the secret."

Lorna rubbed his upper arm in soothing strokes. "I'll fetch some tea. Happen we'll think of the best way forward once we've taken some time to reflect."

"I cannae stay, and I'm sorry for charging in here, causing distress." Perhaps he would let fate decide the outcome. Perhaps he would visit the shop in Old Bond Street. Scout Baudelaire's known haunts. "Rest now. I shall see ye soon."

Angus must have sensed Callan's restlessness. "What's going on in that thick head? Tell me what ye have planned."

In truth, he didn't know.

But one thing was certain.

"I cannae stay here. I'm leaving town tonight."

Lillian kept her nose pressed to the window, scouring the dark streets for Dounreay. He could have been attacked by footpads. Could have fallen into the river and drowned. Could be anywhere by now.

"Where is he?" The desperation in her voice must have tugged on Mr Daventry's heartstrings.

"Dounreay will run until the shock wears off," he said, his tone reassuring. "That, or he won't stop until he has answers. We should visit Valmary's shop in Old Bond Street. He may want to confirm the perfumer was his mother's lover."

He would want answers. He would want to kill the man. Only a fool would mistake Dounreay's calm persona for weakness.

Pain lanced through her.

She'd wanted to wrap him in a warm embrace, soothe him, ease his woes, but he'd not given her a chance.

"I think you underestimate what he might do. He'll seek revenge for his mother's death. He'll be out searching for Monsieur Baudelaire."

"Dounreay is an intelligent man. If he wants Baudelaire dead, he knows there's an honourable way to achieve his goal."

"Sir, I don't know your family history, but—"

"It's tragic, Miss Ware. I understand suffering. But when a man waits years to dance with one woman, he's not about to throw his life away on a whim."

Oh, it hurt to think of how she'd pushed Dounreay away.

Of how many lonely nights he'd spent in the Highlands.

Hot tears gathered behind her eyes. "I was to tell him I love him tonight. I was going to prick his finger with a blade and pledge my troth." She would have sucked his finger and swallowed his blood.

"It may have to wait until tomorrow."

"There may not be a tomorrow if I don't find him."

She would die if she lost him now.

"The mystic had an eye for detail. You're marrying a man who bares his knees in public. I doubt she was wrong."

"You're the mystic," she said, managing a smile for the first time in an hour. "Though why you concern yourself with affairs of the heart is anyone's guess." She considered Ailsa's prediction. "Indeed, you have made a mistake if you think Miss MacTavish will marry. She's resigned to spinsterhood."

Mr Daventry shrugged. "Then it's fortunate I'm not the mystic. Though, if I recall rightly, someone means to cast a spell over her. Is that not merely another term for falling in love?"

Lillian turned back to the window, peering into the darkness as she considered Mr Daventry's words. Perhaps the predictions weren't silly. Dounreay had bared more than his knees in public. In marking her dance card year after year, he'd been baring his heart too.

"Do you know how long it's been since I first danced with Dounreay?" she said, though it was a rhetorical question.

Still, Mr Daventry said, "Five years."

"Five years, two months and twelve days."

"That's quite precise."

"A lady does not forget dancing with a man like Dounreay." Her soul sighed at the beautiful memory. "I should have been stronger. I should have known you cannot escape heartbreak and should have stolen every happy moment instead."

Mr Daventry was quick to offer sensible advice. "The pain of regret lasts long after the heart has healed. Be assured. Everything happens as it should. You took the path that led to the treasure. Who's saying the others were the same?"

Lillian cast him a sidelong glance and gave a curious frown. "Are you sure you're not the mystic?"

"I haven't the patience nor the time."

"No, I think we can both agree on that."

They reached Old Bond Street minutes later to find a scene of utter chaos. Two constables stood outside Mr Valmary's shop, wielding wooden batons and shouting for the gathering crowd to disperse.

The carriage stopped. Mr Daventry assisted her descent before presenting his card to a constable and explaining his interest in the premises.

"Looks like someone kicked the door off its hinges, sir." The constable raised his lantern aloft so they might assess the damage. "By all accounts, the same person entered the premises and toppled all the shelves. There's barely a bottle left intact. I wouldn't go in there, sir. The pong will likely kill you."

"It was a growling beast," called one old woman. "I saw him with my own eyes."

Dounreay was all muscle and brawn but was by no means a beast.

"It was Lucifer himself," said the drunken man staggering near the back of the group. "Eyes as red as hot coals."

Mr Daventry lowered his voice and addressed the constable. "I had an agent break into the premises on a matter approved by the Home Secretary. We were to apprehend Mr Valmary, which may account for any damage inside."

"It *was* the devil," someone cried. "His feet never touched the ground as he flew towards Piccadilly."

"Then he must have seen the suspect approaching." Mr Daventry drew her aside. "We should visit Dounreay's house on Park Lane. Wait in the carriage while I defuse the situation."

It took Mr Daventry less than a minute to clear the crowd and placate the constables. When they arrived in Park Lane, Dounreay's English butler confirmed his master had not been home.

Lillian barged inside, only satisfied once she had checked every room. She met Mr Daventry in the hall. "We should visit Lord MacTavish. Dounreay may be searching for answers, and Lorna MacTavish was friends with his mother."

The butler returned, his discreet cough gaining their attention. "According to Dewart, His Grace entered the mews twenty minutes ago and had him saddle Rebus, his Arabian stallion."

"His stallion?" Her heart thumped against her ribs. "Did he say where he was going?" Had he gone in search of Baudelaire? Did he need to gallop along the Row and feel the wind in his hair?

"No. Just that he had to leave town tonight."

"Leave town?"

Leave without saying goodbye.

Leave without giving an explanation.

Leave without her.

Painful memories surfaced. A mother's tender kiss good night. A broken soul who perished in the lake, leaving her daughter floundering, struggling to remain afloat.

"Dewart said he took the keys to the manor, miss."

The news was like a branch she could cling to, a means to help her scramble back to the riverbank. A chance to live.

"Have Dewart ready the carriage."

The butler inclined his head respectfully. "I take orders from no one but His Grace, miss."

"And I mean to bring His Grace home and marry him." She clutched the man's arm. "Dewart knows I'll be welcome at the manor. Mr Daventry can ferry me there, but I doubt the duke would want others knowing about his country *estate*."

The butler hesitated.

"I love him, and he needs me. Please." She was not averse to begging.

The man nodded. "If Dewart agrees, I shall have him bring the carriage around. Please remain in the drawing room, and I'll have a maid fetch tea."

Mr Daventry waited for the butler to leave before speaking. "If Baudelaire discovers I've taken his notebook, he may flee. When you find Dounreay, bring him to the Hart Street office. We must deal with this matter swiftly, before the men murder each other."

"I shall be four or five hours, six at most."

"Very well. I'll do what I can until then." He left her waiting for Dewart.

The Scot drove like the devil chased his heels.

The gates to the manor were closed, but not locked.

There was no sign of Rebus.

"Dounreay must be here. Why else would he ask for the key?" Where else would he go? She searched the gatehouse, finding the rooms cold and empty. "Wait here. I'll head to the gamekeeper's cabin."

"I'll walk with ye, miss. His Grace would whip me silly if anything happened to ye en route."

She agreed and followed the burly coachman along the dark woodland path, stopping to pick up a pebble and slip it into her pocket.

They heard the horse snicker before they spotted the beast in the rickety stable. The faint flicker of candlelight in the cabin confirmed Dounreay was inside.

A sense of urgency drove her to clasp Dewart's hand,

whisper her thanks and tell him to rest in the gatehouse until they were ready to return home.

No longer trapped in a mind of indecision, she took a fortifying breath and stepped up to the cabin.

The wood creaked as she pushed open the door. Her heart wept as her gaze fell upon the man sitting on the bed, his head clasped in his hands, every breath full of despair.

Perhaps she was always meant to suffer a childhood tragedy.

She understood shock, disbelief, anger and blind confusion. No one was better equipped to deal with the range of distressing emotions.

She didn't speak. No words were needed.

With slow steps, she closed the gap between them.

He didn't look up until she touched his shoulder. He didn't seem surprised to see her. In the fathomless depths of his beautiful eyes, she read his silent plea.

She hiked up her skirts and came to sit astride his thighs, cradled his head to her breast. Hugged him the way someone should have hugged her all those years ago.

These woods held a special place in his heart. They kept him sane when he missed his homeland. She had joked about never feeling connected to a place. Now anywhere felt like home as long as she was with Dounreay.

She brushed her mouth across his hair, breathing him in. She couldn't tear her lips away, and kissed him thrice on the temple.

He wrapped her in an embrace, his large hands stroking her back as she rained soft kisses in every place she could reach. Sensing her need to taste him, his mouth found hers, his tongue sliding across the seam before plunging into the moist depths.

She poured everything of herself into that kiss.

Her abiding love. Her deepest respect. The sincere apology she should have made for denying him every dance.

As was the way with them, the kiss left them rampant. Within minutes, they would be making love in bed or on the floor, writhing in each other's arms.

She pulled away, stroking the lock of hair from his brow, almost crying from the power of her contained emotions.

"Who brought ye here?" he said.

"Dewart. I barged into your home and barked commands." Cupping his cheek, she dared to broach the subject she'd rather avoid. "When I saw your mother's name in that book, I feared you meant to kill someone tonight."

"Aye. I'd have blood on my hands if I'd nae stopped to visit MacTavish."

"Was he surprised? Did Lorna know about Mr Valmary?" Had he argued with his friends? Did he feel a deep sense of betrayal?

"They knew my mother had a mystery lover, but didnae want to soil her memory by telling me." He spoke quickly. She knew why. He would tell her everything in his own time, but she would not press him now.

Smoothing her hair with his hand, he stared into her eyes like a man in love. "I'm sorry for leaving, for nae staying to explain. But realising everything I'd believed was a lie ... well, it stole my breath and squeezed my lungs until I couldnae think straight."

"I know that feeling well."

Tears built behind her eyes, a few falling.

Dounreay dashed them away. "Forgive me. I didnae mean to make ye think of yer own terrible memories."

Clasping his face in her hands, she pressed a gentle kiss to his lips, though the rush of love made her giddy. "I'm not grieving for my mother, Callan. I'm grieving for all the years I could have spent loving you."

His eyes narrowed as he tried to grasp her meaning.

"Remember when you gave me a sprig of heather?"

"Aye."

"Now let me give you a gift." Reaching into her pocket, she withdrew the pebble she had collected on the path. It was rough around the edges, not quite white. "When penguins find their perfect mate, they give them a perfect pebble." Ailsa had mentioned male penguins, but it didn't matter.

Amusement and confusion flashed in his eyes.

She took his hand and placed it in his palm. "It's a little like me. I'm far from perfect and not at all chaste, not since you ruined me quite thoroughly. But I am yours if you want me."

He swallowed hard as he gazed at the pebble, then at her. "Lillian, ye're the only woman I've ever wanted. The only woman I'll want till my dying day."

She took a second to breathe, to let his words infuse her. "Good. Because it's my turn to make an oath." Taking Eliza's weapon from her pocket, she whipped the blade from its sheath. "Give me your hand, Callan Maclean."

"If this is some strange form of handfasting, prick away."

Capturing his finger, she stabbed the tip, drawing a drop of crimson blood. She did the same to her finger, rubbing it with his, their life forces mating.

"On my oath, I pledge my undying loyalty." She didn't look at his mouth but gazed beyond the duke and the Highlander to stare into the soul of the man. "I vow to love you until the end of my days. I promise, wherever you go, I shall follow."

She took his finger into her mouth and sucked it clean.

A growl vibrated in his throat. "Ye'll marry me. That's nae a question. Ye'll be my duchess."

"Yes. I'm in love with you. I never want to be without you again."

He claimed her mouth in a fierce kiss. "I've loved ye for so long. It's taken every ounce of strength to keep the words at bay."

"You don't need to keep it a secret anymore. And when we've punished those devils for hurting your mother, we'll tell everyone that the mystic was right. I *am* marrying a man who bares his knees in public."

He kissed her again with a feverish intensity, his hands scooting under her skirts to grab her bare buttocks. "I need to be inside ye, love. 'Tis the only place I feel at home now."

The need to take him deep consumed her, too.

"Yes. Hurry."

They didn't undress.

There was no need.

She had exposed her whole self to him tonight.

Soon, they were gasping and panting as he freed his thick shaft. Moaning in the chill air as he pushed inside her, stretching her until she was so full with this Scot she would never feel starved again.

Chapter Nineteen

They reached London at eight o'clock the next morning, and Dewart drove them to the Hart Street office as instructed. Their clothes were crumpled, their lips swollen and bruised because Callan hadn't stopped kissing Lillian since she'd agreed to be his wife.

They'd made love in the cabin and again in the carriage.

Determined not to spend another day without her, they'd agreed to marry as soon as he could procure a licence.

Daventry was about to climb into his vehicle when he saw them alight. Though dressed in a fine black coat and trousers, his bloodshot eyes said he'd not slept a wink.

Daventry scanned their less-than-pristine attire and grinned. "I mean to surprise O'Malley and force him to make a statement. I have his address in Bermondsey. It's probably best if we take one vehicle."

"Do ye have Baudelaire and Valmary in custody?" Punishing the men was Callan's priority. He'd not return to the Highlands until they were ruined, imprisoned, or dead. "Lillian said ye have the notebook. It shouldnae be difficult to make a case against Baudelaire."

"

"No. Neither man went home last night." In a rare display of frustration, Daventry shoved his hand through his black hair. "I'm hoping O'Malley might know where we can find the Frenchman."

The desire for vengeance stirred like a beast in Callan's belly. "Then we'll come with ye, for I want this matter settled today."

The four-mile journey through town and across the Thames took an hour. Daventry spent the time explaining what he'd been doing while they'd been indulging in every lustful pleasure.

"The coroner is examining the report on Mrs Rowlands. He's meeting with Anne Grimes this morning to question her about her mistress' symptoms. And Lady MacTavish said your mother owned numerous bottles of perfume, though couldn't recall which ones."

Callan reached for Lillian's hand. "One was lily of the valley." No wonder the scent made his stomach roil. "In a temper, my father threatened to empty the bottle. My mother smothered herself in it the morning she died, and he threw the rest away."

The missing parts of the story were easy to piece together.

"Afterwards, he took to his bed for a few days. Part guilt. Part grief. Perhaps part poison. Though the devil soon regained his vigour."

A rare glimpse of compassion passed across Daventry's features. By all accounts, his father had been a blackguard, too. "I shall do everything in my power to punish those responsible. I know you're keen to return to the Highlands, and so we'll work night and day to get the desired result."

"*We're* keen to return," Callan corrected, glancing fondly at Lillian. "We've decided to marry here and have another ceremony north of the border."

Daventry nodded, unsurprised at the news. "Then let me be the first to express my felicitations on your good fortune. Indeed, based on Miss Ware's reluctance to wed, one might think the mystic is a magician."

"Or a matchmaking enquiry agent," Lillian said, grinning. "I should tell Ailsa to refrain from attending auctions in case she encounters a man with a book of spells."

The slightest smile touched Daventry's lips. "If the mystic is a magician, it won't matter. She'll not be able to avoid her fate."

"Then who could the mystery man be?"

Daventry arched a brow. "Perhaps it's not such a mystery. It's likely someone who shares her passion for old books."

The carriage stopped outside a terraced house on Printer Lane, south of the docks and yards from the old Bermondsey Spa. Despite the early hour, the chemist was working in his basement laboratory when they called.

His maid-of-all-work opened the door.

Daventry gave his usual speech about it being a police matter and did not give the confused lass time to refuse them entrance.

"Mr O'Malley, sir." The woman stood at the top of the basement stairs, wringing her hands, terrified out of her wits. "You'd better come up here and speak to this gentleman."

"Glenda, I'm busy," the man cried, his accent bearing no trace of Irish roots. "Close the door. You know how the light affects the chemical reactions."

Callan stepped forward. "Do ye want me to drag ye up the stairs? Be warned. I'm of a mind to break something, and it might be yer rotten neck."

They heard sighs, the clinking of glass, the sound of footfall on the wooden steps. A studious-looking man appeared, wearing spectacles and a black apron, his wiry grey hair sticking this way and that like he'd not combed it in weeks.

"Who are you?" he said nervously, removing his eyeglasses and polishing them on his apron. "What is this about?"

Daventry explained the reason for their call. "Madame Delafont confirmed you received the list the maid stole from Mrs Rowlands. Baudelaire asked you to make a new version of his For Lily perfume based on his rival's recipe."

The man blinked rapidly. "What? No. He said he'd invented a new blend because he was desperate to restock his shelves. I'd have refused if I'd known of his nefarious methods."

Callan introduced himself, and the fellow nearly toppled down the stairs in shock. "Your Grace. I assure you, I'm the innocent party in this mess. I merely work for Monsieur Baudelaire so I can afford to conduct other scientific research." He motioned to his maid. "Tell them, Glenda."

She blushed and bobbed a curtsey. "The master's right, sir. He does all sorts of experiments down in that basement."

Callan wondered if the couple researched the effects of lust in their spare time.

"Have you ever added toxins to the perfume?" Lillian reached for Callan's hand, clasping it tightly before continuing. "We have evidence to suggest Mr Baudelaire may be guilty of murder. That he used poisoned perfume in an act of vengeance."

Callan silently sighed. Whenever anyone mentioned poison, the last moments of his mother's life flooded his mind.

"Murder?" O'Malley clutched his chest. "Monsieur Baudelaire may be many things, arrogant and far too opinionated, but I doubt he'd risk his reputation." The man seemed dazed. "And no. Why would I do something so despicable?"

With his patience stretched so thin it might snap, Callan said, "Have ye seen Baudelaire recently? We need to talk to him before someone else dies."

O'Malley started shaking. "Y-yes. He purchased the old Bermondsey Spa. It's to be his new business venture. He wants to create perfumes from flowers grown locally."

"He's been at the Spa since yesterday afternoon," Glenda said in the tone of London's best gossiper. "I saw him wandering about making sketches. From the upstairs bedroom, you can get a good view of the gardens."

Daventry thanked the couple. He told them he would send an agent to take their statements and insisted on inspecting the basement laboratory while Callan and Lillian waited outside.

"I'd stake my reputation on their innocence," Daventry said when he joined them on the pavement. "Let's walk to the old Spa and see if we can gain entrance."

They followed Daventry to nearby Grange Road.

"I've heard many wonderful stories about the Spa," Lillian said, accepting Callan's arm. "They say the firework displays were as spectacular as any seen at Vauxhall."

"Dandies used to flock to the Spa to take the waters," Daventry said, striding ahead. "The buildings have since been demolished. Baudelaire's venture will come to nought. The railway company wants to buy the land, and will force him to sell. One cannot stand in the way of progress."

Callan gave a mocking snort. "I mean to ensure they lock the devil away in Newgate. We should have brought a constable. I'll nae rest until we have the Frenchman's confession."

The rusty iron gates were unlocked, and though they creaked when Callan pushed his way inside, no one came to chase them away or demand to know why they were trespassing.

With spring fast approaching, the beds were barren but for a scattering of snowdrops. The wide paths were littered with dead leaves and tufts of grass. Nothing remained of the grand house except for bits of rubble and the outline of the old foundations.

They walked for a few minutes, all hope of finding Baudelaire replaced by rising frustration.

"If the devil stayed here last night, there must be somewhere warm and dry to sleep." Callan doubted the pompous Frenchman had camped beneath the stars.

"The gate is unlocked, so someone must have used the key." Lillian pointed to a wooden structure in the distance. "Might that be an old potting shed or the gardener's house?"

Keen to investigate, they hurried along the path with a renewed spring in their steps, quickly reaching the round wooden hut.

Lillian considered the facade and conical roof. "It's in a good state of repair. Someone could have slept here."

"Aye." Callan's thoughts turned murderous when he heard the low rumble of a man's voice inside the building. "And I mean to make sure the blackguard dies here," he whispered.

Hearing it, too, Daventry urged them to remain quiet. He gestured for them to advance, and they crept along the grass verge to muffle their footsteps.

"I do not know why you're so irate," Baudelaire said, his voice tight with fear, not confusion. "If you would just lower your weapon, perhaps we might speak like civilised people."

The mention of a weapon had Daventry reaching into his coat pocket. He removed a sheathed knife and tucked it into the waistband of his trousers.

"Civilised people?" came a woman's mocking reply.

Lillian's eyes widened upon hearing the soft French accent. It explained why Madame Delafont had not fled on the first stage to Dover. "The last time we met, you pressed a blade to my throat."

She had not helped Monsieur Baudelaire because she'd been terrified; she had helped him to cause trouble between the men.

Baudelaire growled. "Yes, because I couldn't trust you not to tell Valmary. I may have been too forceful, yes, but was I not the one who warned you about that scoundrel Sheridan?"

"I've seen your notebook. The one containing the long list of conquests. It is pathetic. Men of your age, playing games like wicked children."

Baudelaire groaned. "So, you're angry because you saw your name scrawled in a little book. We did not pursue you because it was clear you wanted Lord Sheridan, and Valmary owed him a favour."

"I'm angry because Christian confirmed what I'd suspected. My mother's name was recorded in your stupid book."

Lillian shot Callan a surprised look.

He was not so alarmed.

Based on the men's disregard for their lovers' feelings, there must be many victims plotting revenge. And Christian must have played a role, else he'd not be dead.

A deathly silence ensued.

Daventry said he would give the signal when it was time to storm the building. That they should listen carefully so they could repeat the facts to the magistrate.

"Surely you remember her name." Madame Delafont sounded so cold, so calm, so confident. "Angelique Grellier. A woman with the voice of an angel. A woman who once sang for Queen Charlotte. A woman fed poison by you three years ago because she spurned your advances."

Moira Maclean, Callan silently cried.

You murdered her too!

"Fed Angelique poison?" Baudelaire gave an incredulous snort. "You have lost your mind. Why would I hurt her? I'm the one who gave her the funds to return to France."

"Liar! You were consumed with jealousy when she chose Mr Valmary. The truth is in your notebook."

"I did not kill Angelique," he insisted. "She came to me for help because she wanted to go home. I did not know you were her daughter until Lord Sheridan told me a few days ago, or that she had died aboard *The Sovereign.*"

A keen cry rent the air. "My mother didn't just die. She was murdered and you will pay the price for your treachery, monsieur."

"Wait! Don't shoot! I'll tell you what I know."

Daventry pointed to the door. "If she shoots him, she'll hang. We must prevent her from firing. He'll kill her if she misses."

Lillian stepped forward. "I shall go inside and—"

"For the love of God, I'll nae let ye enter alone."

"We'll all go," Daventry whispered. "But let Miss Ware enter first. We'll be right behind her."

"Perhaps ye didnae hear me the first time. Let the woman shoot the bastard, but I'll nae risk losing Lillian."

Daventry conceded, and they all crept up to the open door.

Baudelaire sat slumped in a chair in the middle of the large circular room. Blood trickled from the cut above his left eye. The truckle bed in the corner said the Frenchman had stayed the night. As did the whiff of beef stew coming from the black iron pot over the fire.

"You'll tell me the truth from the beginning." Madame Delafont wore men's clothes, her long black hair shorn to the shoulders. She shoved a glass bottle into Baudelaire's hand. "And then you will drench yourself in perfume and we shall see what fate has in store."

Callan prayed there was enough poison in the perfume to kill the Frenchman. But then he wondered how the woman had come by the toxin, and a hundred questions ran through his mind.

Madame Delafont backed away from Baudelaire, though she kept the pistol trained on the devil. "Why did you kill her?"

Daventry cleared his throat. "Lower your weapon, madame. I promise you there are better ways to deal with scoundrels."

The lady gasped and swung around, taking her eyes off Baudelaire.

"Watch out," Lillian cried when the Frenchman jumped off his seat and charged forward, grabbing Madame Delafont around the neck and stealing her pistol.

The perfume bottle hit the floor, shards of glass shattering, the noxious scent spilling out.

"Move aside else I will kill her." Baudelaire shuffled forward. "Let me leave and I'll release her at the gate."

"Ye killed my mother," Callan snarled. "Ye poisoned her with that bloody perfume because she chose Valmary. Dinnae think ye're leaving this place alive."

The devil frowned. "You've all lost your minds. Why does everyone think I committed these atrocities? Moira died from eating berries in the woods."

"Ye'll nae call her by her given name," Callan spat, bile bubbling in his throat. "And she died from inhaling a poison in her lily of the valley perfume." He met Madame Delafont's terrified gaze, then looked at the puddle on the floor. "Let her go. Take me instead. Let's fight like men."

"No!" Lillian tugged at his arm.

"Get out, love. Cover yer nose and mouth and leave this place."

"I'm not leaving without you."

Daventry moved farther into the room, his wary gaze darting to the spilled perfume. "Be assured. If the duke doesn't kill you, I will. If you didn't murder the women who spurned you, who did? And if you're innocent, why hide here?"

Baudelaire's hand shook as he held the pistol. "Because Christian was seen adding something to my perfume. When I went to confront him, I found him dead and feared Thaddeus had lost his mind. He blames me for everything. The man is deranged."

Based on their sick games, both men belonged in Bedlam.

"Valmary didn't poison your perfume." Daventry sounded so confident, Callan wondered how he'd come to that conclusion. "You've been playing the game for twenty years. Neither of you would have jeopardised your businesses. And the culprit hasn't the heart to kill, just to maim in order to ruin your reputations."

Lillian gasped and pointed at the opera singer. "It was you, madame. You wished to destroy the men who killed your mother."

A pained cry burst from Madame Delafont. "I did not mean for anyone to get hurt, but I wanted to turn their game against them. Have them hurt each other. Poor Christian. I can only assume he was careless and ingested the poison." Tears ran down her cheeks. "I am so sorry."

"And you'll answer to the magistrate for your crimes," Daventry said, determined to see justice served.

Much to Callan's horror, Lillian moved closer. "At the theatre, I believed your story and you've made me look like a fool. You are not with child, and merely used the matter to incite our pity."

The madame choked on her tears. "Forgive me. I needed to make them pay. Needed to teach them a lesson for playing games with people's lives."

Callan knew how quickly anger overcame logic.

"You're by no means a fool, Miss Ware," Daventry said sincerely. "You were the one who identified the perfume. Yes, you were in the wrong place at the wrong time. But together with Dounreay, your fight for justice has reaped results."

Daventry was rarely wrong.

But he was this time.

They'd been in the right place at the right time. Callan would never regret creeping up the stairs to confront Lillian. Witnessing the tragic scene in the garden had been the first step on the path to lasting happiness.

"Were ye my mother's lover?" Callan stabbed his finger at the Frenchman. He needed answers. And he needed them now.

A haunted look filled the man's eyes. "I loved Moira. She was beautiful, inside and out, a flower amongst thorns. But Valmary won her heart, and it almost killed me." He closed his eyes briefly as if battling pain. "She was—"

"Dinnae speak about her like ye cared."

"Neither of us would have hurt a hair on her head. You must believe me. Everything changed when she died."

Confusion rained like a torrent of biblical proportions.

If Madame Delafont paid Christian to tamper with Baudelaire's perfume, who added the toxin to Mr Valmary's scent?

And why did a twinge deep in Callan's gut make him

suspect Baudelaire was innocent? He was the only one with a motive.

"Madame, what have you done with Mr Valmary?" Daventry asked, his voice thick with suspicion. "You said you mean to make both men pay, yet only one stands accused."

The lady pursed her lips.

Baudelaire nudged her with the muzzle of the pistol, yanking her tighter to his chest. "Don't say you've killed him."

"No. He's to meet me here at eleven o'clock." The lady coughed and fought to catch her breath. "I told him I had proof you poisoned his perfume. That you're copying his May Bell scent."

Daventry drew his watch and checked the time. "We have less than ten minutes until he's due to arrive." He paced for a moment, lost in thought.

"Do ye have a plan?"

"Confronting Valmary is our only option," he said, fighting with an obvious dilemma. Daventry turned to Baudelaire. "If you're innocent, then Valmary might have poisoned the women."

"Valmary?" Baudelaire muttered something in French. "Why would the winner sabotage the game?"

"Why did Angelique Grellier leave England if Valmary won her heart? Why did Moira Maclean return to the Highlands if she planned on taking Valmary as her lover?"

Baudelaire and Madame Delafont frowned.

"You're right," Lillian said. "It makes no sense. What do the two women have in common?"

Baudelaire gasped. The arm holding the pistol fell to his side like a ton weight. He stumbled a little, releasing his hold on Madame Delafont.

She darted forwards, throwing herself into Lillian's arms, trembling and weeping and begging for mercy.

"I loved Moira," Baudelaire said, visibly shaking. "Valmary loved Angelique, but I didn't know that until after I'd given her the money to leave. But I cannot think he would hurt either woman."

There was no time to ask questions.

The clip of footsteps on the path outside had them all creeping back from the door. Callan silently cursed. Lillian and Madame Delafont stood huddled together to the left of the door. While he was stuck with Daventry on the right.

Baudelaire stood in the middle of the room, blood trailing down his cheek, the pistol dangling from his loose grip.

Valmary entered cautiously, jerking in shock when he saw Baudelaire swaying and mumbling like a ghost in a graveyard.

"Jaques?" he said with some surprise. Sensing a presence behind him, he turned abruptly, confusion marring his brow. "What's going on here? What have you done to him?"

"You killed them," Baudelaire cried before anyone could speak.

"What? Who? Why are you holding a pistol? And what happened to your head?" Valmary scanned their faces. "Forgive me but this feels rather like a trap."

"There'll be time for questions and answers at Bow Street." Daventry pushed away from the wall. "Thaddeus Valmary. I'm placing you under arrest for the murders of Moira Maclean, Angelique Grellier and Marjorie Rowlands."

"Under arrest?" Valmary shook his head, confused, and glared at Madame Delafont. "Madame, I thought you'd summoned me here to explain how Jaques stole my perfume. I thought you had evidence to prove he's been adding poison to the bottles to discredit my name."

Looking like an escapee from Bedlam, Baudelaire took aim, pointing the muzzle at his rival's chest. "Tell the damn truth or I will shoot."

Valmary raised his arms in surrender. "The truth about what?"

"You did not win Moira's hand. None of it made sense at the time but when a man nurses a broken heart, he cannot think clearly. Dounreay found her diary," the Frenchman lied.

If only it were true.

Callan might have punished this blackguard long ago.

"Moira returned to the Highlands because of her son," Baudelaire snarled. "You told me she chose you. That you rejected her because you knew I loved her."

Valmary stuttered, the first few words not making any sense. "Yes. Only because I knew you would chase after her and it was clear she didn't want you. I couldn't let you give up everything we've worked for."

Baudelaire shuffled closer. Like the best enquiry agent, he was determined to get to the truth. "She mentioned you gave her perfume as a parting gift. You gave Angelique perfume when she left. You said you hoped she would smell the scent and realise how much she missed you."

Valmary gulped. "We give lots of women perfume."

"Yes," Daventry mused. "Including Mrs Rowlands. How strange that those women should all die from poison added to your May Bell fragrance. The maid stole Mrs Rowlands' bottle, but luckily hadn't used more than a dab. We have a chemist analysing the contents."

Ironically, lying was the best way to get to the truth.

"Did you kill Moira?" Baudelaire cried, spittle dribbling down his chin. "Did you poison her perfume? Tell me, damn it!" He cocked the pistol, his hand trembling so violently the lead ball might miss the target.

"Yes!" Valmary clasped his hands together in prayer. "She would have come between us. You were not the same when she left."

The devil's own rage consumed Callan. He charged forward, his Gaelic battle cry filled with the pain he'd borne for fifteen years. With hatred flooding his heart, he lunged at Thaddeus Valmary.

The crack of pistol fire was but a distant echo.

Much like Lillian's scream.

A sudden jolt stole his thunder. The shock whipped him round, sending him crashing to the floor and to the sudden darkness that claimed him.

Chapter Twenty

Lillian curled her body around Callan's, hugging him as she had done since the surgeon left half an hour ago, relishing the heat of his body. He looked pale against the burgundy bed hangings. His eyes were closed, his breathing slow, but he was alive and would make a speedy recovery—as long as a fever didn't claim him.

The morning scene played out in her mind. The pistol shaking in Monsieur Baudelaire's hand. The lead ball missing the target and hitting Callan, sending him crashing to the floor.

Her heart had almost stopped beating.

Blood had pooled around his body, seeping from a wound she feared had killed him. While she dropped to her knees beside him, sheer terror holding her in a steely grip, chaos had erupted around her.

Monsieur Baudelaire had fainted from the shock.

Mr Daventry had hit Mr Valmary to prevent him from escaping, rendering the villain unconscious with a single blow to the temple.

Madame Delafont had slipped out of the room, only to be

apprehended by the two constables summoned by Mr O'Malley.

Lillian didn't care if they all hanged.

She cared about marrying Dounreay, loving him, living with him in the Highlands and bearing his children.

Adam tapped lightly on the open chamber door before entering the room. He made no comment about her being draped over a semi-naked man in bed.

"The surgeon said there will be no lasting damage. Dounreay should be on his feet in a few days." Adam spoke in the grave tone of someone who knew to expect the worst. "He'll need to rest for a week or two before making the arduous journey north."

"We'll remain here until he is fit enough to obtain a marriage licence. We'll marry in London before we head to Scotland."

She told herself there was no reason to alter the plans. And thoughts of their upcoming nuptials would help her through this trying time.

Adam managed a weak smile. "I'll send word to his steward."

"Have him reschedule all appointments, but assure him we'll be home within the month." Home. She had convinced herself she hated the blustery Highland weather but would brave Arctic conditions for Dounreay. "Tell him I'll sleep in the duke's chamber, but they should air the duchess' suite in case—"

"Lillian."

"Yes?"

"You're allowed to be afraid."

Oh, she was afraid.

She was scared to the marrow of her bones.

"I know."

His gaze dropped to Dounreay's bandaged arm. "Why don't you come home with me? You need rest, and—"

"I'm not leaving this room without him." She had made an oath, pledged her love and loyalty. "Let them write what they like in the *Scandal Sheet*, but I'll not abandon him in his hour of need." She offered Adam a reassuring grin. "Besides, you live amid utter chaos, though now I see why you wouldn't have it any other way."

"I love Eliza and the children. I love my life."

"Yes, there is nothing more important than love."

"Are you stealing my lines, Miss Ware?" Mr Daventry strode into the room, scanning Dounreay's form keenly. He looked tired and in need of a stiff drink.

"I'm learning from a master," she teased. "Forgive my rudeness, but I'm not moving from this bed."

Mr Daventry shrugged. "I come merely to update you on current events. I shall leave you to explain the details to Dounreay when he wakes."

She listened intently.

The case was over. The villains would be punished.

The only thing Lillian felt was relief.

It was almost midnight when Dounreay stirred. The maid had crept into the room to stoke the fire and leave a dose of laudanum on the side table. Lillian noticed the change in his breathing as soon as the maid closed the door.

"Now I know I've died and gone to heaven," he said weakly, brushing his lips against her hair. "Why else would the love of my life be lying in my bed?"

Lillian shot up, a burst of happiness filling her chest. "Thank heavens. You're awake! Do you feel hot? Do you have a fever? Are you in pain? The maid has left more laudanum."

"I'm fine, love." With his good arm, Dounreay reached up

to tuck her loose hair behind her ear. "Ye're marrying a Highlander nae a foppish English ninny."

She grinned. "Then you'd better hurry and get yourself well. We've a wedding to plan. Bairns to make."

Mischief sparkled in his eyes. "I'm well enough to work on the last task, though ye'll have to sit astride me and do most of the riding. Happen I might be ill for some time." He stretched, wincing when he moved his right arm.

"Does it hurt terribly?"

"Nae more than a thorn in the arse."

He sounded in such good spirits she gave her emotions free rein. The tears she'd kept at bay tumbled down her cheeks. "I thought I'd lost you. I thought my life was over. I never thought I'd hear that sensual Scottish burr again."

He wiped the tears from her cheeks. "When I die, it will be from exhaustion, after a lifetime spent chasing ye over brook and glen and tumbling ye in the heather."

It sounded idyllic. "When I die, I'll likely freeze to death while making love to my husband in a bathing pool."

Dounreay laughed and groaned in agony at the same time.

She might have told him that Mrs Rowlands had stolen the recipe from Mr Valmary after finding out about the game. That Anne had taken receipt of the poisoned perfume and thought her mistress had ordered another bottle.

She might have told him that Monsieur Baudelaire did not recover from the shock of shooting Moira's son, and his heart had given out.

Mr Valmary was charged with three counts of murder. Madame Delafont managed to escape from the constables and hadn't been seen since.

But she would tell him all that tomorrow.

Now she had a different agenda.

She scooted off the bed, padded towards the door and

turned the key in the lock. "Do you think it would hurt if we got your heart racing a little? Surely getting the blood flowing will aid your recovery."

He arched a brow. "Do ye mean to strip off those clothes and lie next to me in bed?"

"In the scheme of what I might do to you, Your Grace, is that not a little tame?" She hesitated, not wanting to hurt him. "You will tell me if it's too much. You won't have to move a muscle."

Curiosity burned in his eyes. "What will ye do, love?"

"Just a little research for my book." She prowled towards him, pulled back the sheets girding his waist and stared at his impressive manhood.

Dounreay grinned. "I recall yer last experiment did more than raise my temperature. But it wouldnae hurt to lie here and watch ye flex yer fingers."

Lillian moistened her lips. "It's not my fingers I'm hoping to flex."

Wester Ross, Scotland
Two months later

The west wind blew Lillian's hair across her face. It nipped her cheeks, cleansed her lungs, and sent shivers rippling to her toes. Staring out over the slate-blue waters of the Inner Sound, she could see the rolling hills of Raasay and Skye. Behind her, the Torridon Mountains acted as a breathtaking backdrop.

She loved everything about the Highlands.

The land was remote, rugged, and so beautiful she would never tire of walking the glens and absorbing the wondrous scenery. There was only one other place on earth she felt so alive, so free—when she wrapped her thighs around her husband's hips and clung to his sweat-soaked body.

Dounreay!

She hugged her abdomen, the rush of emotion stealing her breath, bringing tears to her eyes. Never a wife. Never a duchess. She had chanted the mantras many times. Hadn't thought to add never a mother.

Now, she was married to a duke and had missed her courses. Now, she was so blissfully happy she couldn't stop grinning.

They had married in London by special licence, Lord Melbourne insisting Dounreay be granted one without fuss. They had exchanged vows amid a throng of Highland lords in the castle's great hall.

The haunting notes of the piper had touched her deeply, more than any tune played on the pianoforte. Like her love for Dounreay, Scotland's soothing song had resonated deep in her soul.

"Are you waiting to catch something, Lillian?" Eliza appeared over the brow of the hill, her hair fastened in a pretty braid, her cheeks aglow. "You're holding out your arms like you're expecting the heavens to fall."

"I'm surrendering to the elements." She twirled around, a child of Mother Nature, wild energy pumping in her veins.

"I'll be sad to leave this place," Eliza panted, bracing her hands on her hips and taking in the view. "And we'll all be sad to leave you."

"You're welcome to stay." She wouldn't press the matter. Adam would never leave London permanently, and his sons would one day be the toast of English society.

"It's tempting. But we stand at the beginning of a new railway age. We'll soon be able to make more than half the journey by train."

Lillian reached for Eliza's hands. "You will write and visit often?"

Eliza hugged her. "Of course. And don't worry about Adam. I'm with child, and the chaos will keep him occupied."

"Again!" *I think I'm with child too*, she added silently.

Adam came charging up the hill, chasing his two eldest sons. The wind ruffled his dark hair, laughter danced in his brown eyes.

"Ye'll get back here, ye wee rascals," he said, feigning Dounreay's Scottish burr. "Else ye'll nae get yer supper."

Both boys squealed, but then Theodore took a tumble.

Adam snatched him up and held the child against his shoulder. "Look! I've found a wee lamb for the stew, Mama."

Theodore kicked his legs. "Don't eat me, Papa."

Eliza laughed. "Aye, there's plenty of meat on those bones." She turned to Lillian. "We're heading inside. Are you coming?"

"No. I think I'll stay here a while."

Eliza gave a coy smile. "Doubtless, Dounreay will come and find you when he's finished with his steward. It's odd that a man who's walked these hills for years would get lost for hours."

A flush of heat warmed Lillian's cheeks. She had spent most of yesterday afternoon frolicking with her husband in the heather.

"I think he pretends he's lost because he loves walking." Dounreay loved kissing, rolling around on the grass and touching her intimately.

"I think he pretends he's lost because he loves spending

time alone with you," Eliza corrected. She glanced at Adam and sighed. "There's nothing I love more than seeing my husband smile."

"Yes," she said, understanding perfectly.

They left her alone to wait for Dounreay.

He came striding towards her, so strong and handsome, the wind teasing the hem of his kilt. But Eliza was right. His smile held her spellbound. The glint of happiness in his eyes was perhaps the most mesmerising thing she had ever seen.

I've finally found my way home!

He snaked his arm around her waist and scooped her into his arms. "Sneaking off with nary a word. A man might think ye want a good tupping."

"Do you ever think of anything but bedding me?"

He pretended to ponder the question. "I think about kissing as much as I think about bedding ye. But nae as much as I think about loving ye."

"Well, as the months pass, we may do a little less bedding. You'll not want to make love to me when I'm fat."

"Have ye been stealing the tablet again?"

She cupped his cheek. "I've not had my courses for two months. We must be a little more careful when rolling around outdoors."

He stared at her, his Adam's apple bobbing. Then he buried his face in her neck and hugged her so tightly she could hardly breathe.

"Are you pleased?"

Callan looked at her, love filling his eyes. "Aye. I'm so happy, I cannae explain it in words."

"Then will you dance with me, Dounreay?"

He had never broken his vow.

She had been the one who'd asked him to dance at the

ball Adam had held in their honour. She had asked him to dance every day since.

"Aye. Seeing as ye asked so nicely."

He twirled her around while the wind whistled a tune.

They kissed and professed abiding love before laying on the grass.

"I had a letter from Ailsa this morning," she said, straddling his muscular thighs. "She cursed Lord Denton to the devil."

Dounreay gripped her hips. "I know the lass is five and twenty, but I still cannae believe Angus let her remain in London."

It was the mystic's fault.

Angus wanted his daughter to marry and hoped fate might intervene. It helped that she had been left in the charge of Helen St Clair, Lord Denton's married sister.

"Ever since Lord Denton won the Tudor lady's diary at auction last month, Ailsa is determined to punish him."

"What, by giving him a perfect pebble?" Callan snorted.

"Don't be ridiculous. She said he's pigheaded, stubborn, and too arrogant for his own good."

"The lass does provoke him." He took to sliding her back and forth over his growing erection. "She gets a thrill out of making him angry."

"He'll be furious if she wins the copy of Thomas More's *Utopia* at auction tomorrow. Lord Denton has been trying to source a first edition for years."

Perhaps Ailsa would meet a mysterious stranger at the auction.

Just because Lord Denton liked books didn't mean he was the man Ailsa was to marry. Indeed, they were not at all suited.

"'Tis unlikely the mystic meant she'd marry Denton,"

Callan said, echoing her thoughts. "Now, can we stop talking about Ailsa? Happen I've got some making up to do, and mean to ravish ye thoroughly."

Lillian narrowed her gaze. "Why? Did you really tell Cook to stop making tablet?"

He laughed. "I meant now ye're a duchess and a lady with responsibilities, ye'll never have time to visit Egypt."

Lillian bent her head and kissed him deeply, passionately. "There's nowhere I'd rather be than the Highlands. Besides, you're all the adventure I need for one lifetime."

Thank you!

I hope you enjoyed reading *Never a Duchess.*

Will Ailsa find the funds to outbid Lord Denton at the auction? Will she encounter a mysterious stranger who possesses a book of spells? Or has a matchmaking enquiry agent got something more thrilling in store?

Find out in …

No One's Bride
Scandal Sheet Survivors - Book 4

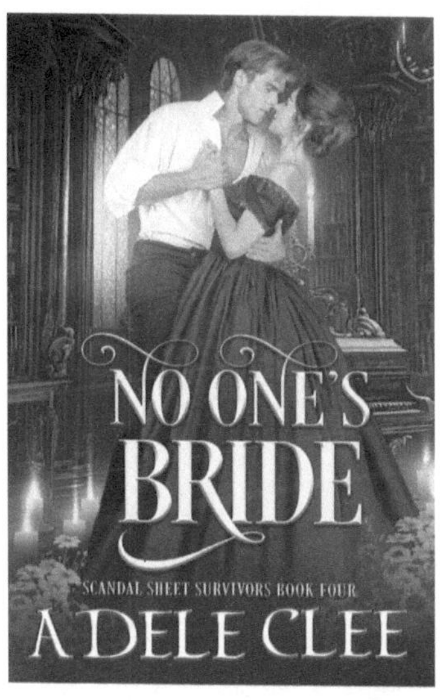

More titles by Adele Clee

Scandalous Sons

And the Widow Wore Scarlet

The Mark of a Rogue

When Scandal Came to Town

The Mystery of Mr Daventry

Gentlemen of the Order

Dauntless

Raven

Valiant

Dark Angel

Ladies of the Order

The Devereaux Affair

More than a Masquerade

Mine at Midnight

Your Scarred Heart

No Life for a Lady

Scandal Sheet Survivors

More than Tempted

Not so Wicked

Never a Duchess

No One's Bride